A LETHAL LAKE EFFECT

LORRAINE BARTLETT

Polaris Press

A Lethal Lake Effect (Victoria Square #9)

Cover by Wicked Smart Designs

eBook ISBN: 978-1-940801-73-5
Print ISBN: 978-1-940801-74-2

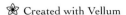 Created with Vellum

Description

Things go awry for Katie Bonner when her former mother-in-law, Margo, throws a housewarming party at her lakeside rental, and one of her guests ends up dead in the water. Maxwell Preston was a devoted husband—and a not-so-great dad. He was a beloved pharmacist who didn't take care of his ramshackle property, destined to be a hot commodity on Victoria Square when his heir puts it up for sale. But most of all, Preston was a stranger to the guests at the party.

Meanwhile, Nona Fiske takes charge of Victoria Square's big summer extravaganza—a disaster in the making as what little power she's seized has gone straight to her head. The Davenport sisters have their own agenda, and they've not only been poking around to find out more about the dead man, but what other mischief has been going on around the Square.

So, who killed Maxwell Preston and why? That's what Katie wants to know—and she's willing to risk everything to find out.

CAST OF CHARACTERS

Katie Bonner: owner-manager of Artisans Alley, the anchor on Victoria Square, and co-owner of the Tealicious tea shop

Margo Bonner: mother of Katie's deceased husband and Katie's Tealicious business partner

Ray Davenport: former homicide detective and owner of Wood U on Victoria Square

Nick Ferrell: co-owner of Sassy Sally's B&B on Victoria Square

Don Parsons: co-owner of Sassy Sally's B&B on Victoria Square

Brad Andrews: Noted chef, hired to manage Tealicious tea shop

Nona Fiske: owner of the Quiet Quilter on Victoria Square

Moonbeam Carruthers: owner of The Flower Child florist and gift shop

Carol Rigby: Monroe County Sheriff's Office detective

Sadie Davenport: Ray Davenport's middle daughter and a budding entrepreneur

Sasha Davenport: Ray Davenport's youngest daughter and a budding entrepreneur

Phoebe Preston: daughter of Maxwell Preston

Andy Rust: owner of Angelo's Pizzeria and Katie's former boyfriend

Vance Ingram: vendor at Artisans Alley and Katie's second-in-command at Artisans Alley

Rose Nash: jewelry vendor at Artisans Alley and Katie's friend

Ann Tanner: co-owner of Tanner's Bakery and Cafe on Victoria Square

Charlotte Booth: owner of Booth's Jellies and Jams on Victoria Square

Seth Landers: McKinlay Mill's only attorney and Katie's friend

Maxwell Preston: owned a decrepit building on Victoria Square

Acknowledgments

My thanks go to The Lorraine Train of beta readers who support me in all my efforts. They are: Amy Connolley, Pam Priest, and Debbie Lyon. Also thanks to my friend Mary Kennedy, who encourages me in everything I do.

Chapter One

Katie Bonner stood on the deck of her former mother-in-law's rental house and gazed at the horizon. The pinks and blues fading to purple gave her a sense of peace. Unfortunately, the vista was not improved by the odor of cigarette smoke that wafted from the other people who had come outside to enjoy the view—her Victoria Square neighbors: Charlotte Booth, owner of Booth's Jellies and Jams, and Gilda Ringwald-Stratton, of Gilda's Gourmet Baskets.

Heaving a shallow sigh—Katie didn't want to breathe in any more of the smoke than she had to—she opened the door to the brightly lit living room where the rest of Margo Bonner's guests mingled, closing the sliding glass door behind her.

Margo had gathered her friends and the other merchants around Victoria Square, a small business district in the village of McKinlay Mill, New York, for a housewarming party. Not that Margo intended to live in the furnished house for more than six months. She had plans—as did a number of the merchants—for a certain warehouse located behind Victoria Square.

Katie and Margo owned the Tealicious tea shop on the Square, while Katie also owned and managed the Square's anchor, Artisans Alley, an arts and crafts arcade. Katie also split her time acting as the head of Victoria Square's Merchants Association. Several members of the Association had gone in together to not only buy a building on the Square, but had recently taken on the warehouse behind it, as well. It was to be a mix of residential and retail spaces—and Margo had leased one of the lofts and space for an art gallery.

But all that was in the future. On that golden evening, Margo hosted a party to celebrate her short-term home.

Katie sauntered past the buffet spread that had been placed on the dining room table. Tealicious chef Brad Andrews had outdone himself. Katie had helped him prepare the feast, but Brad's superb recipes and attention to detail had given the food a starring place at the party.

Brad stood nearby as though ready to jump in and serve the guests if need be. Katie moved to stand beside him. "At ease, soldier," she said, and laughed.

Brad shrugged. "I want Margo's first party to go off without a hitch," the handsome chef said. He was a couple of years older than Katie and Victoria Square's most eligible bachelor. Sadly, Brad's heart had been broken a couple of years before and, instead of looking for love, he seemed content to hang out with friends on his off hours, playing poker and golf, but that didn't keep women from throwing themselves at him—women of varied ages, too.

As it happened, Katie was the most eligible woman on the Square, but her feelings for Brad were purely platonic. It was someone else she thought of when loneliness hit hard. But then, she was so busy with all her businesses and her volunteer position at the Merchants Association that she barely had time to think and often fell into bed at night in pure exhaustion. For now, snuggling with her cats Mason and Della was as much company as she was able to keep.

Katie snagged a shrimp puff and took a bite, looking around

the living room. She knew just about everybody there and had worked with them as part of the Merchants Association, along with her second-in-command, Vance Ingram and his wife Janey, who were huddled in conversation with the owners of Sassy Sally's Bed & Breakfast, Don Parsons and his husband, Nick Farrell.

The only merchant missing from the party was Andy Rust, who owned Angelo's Pizzeria next door to Artisans Alley. He also happened to be Katie's ex-boyfriend. It wasn't surprising that Margo hadn't invited him. After all, the bulk of Andy's trade occurred during evening hours. It had been difficult to maintain a relationship when Katie and Andy worked opposite ends of the clock, and it became impossible once he admitted he hadn't been faithful. Things had become complicated when another of the Square's merchants seemed to have had a thing for her.

A thing? Ray Davenport, more than twenty years her senior, had made it plain that he would like to date her, but when she'd expressed a desire for friendship only, he'd backed off. Ray was currently seeing the woman who now occupied the position he'd once held at the county sheriff's office—one Carole Rigby, a bleached blonde whose face seemed frozen in a perpetual scowl. Of course, things were complicated at the time when Katie had discouraged his attentions. Ray's children were against him dating after their mother's death, and Katie thought she and Andy might be able to smooth things over. When that didn't happen, Ray had already moved on. But she could at least count him as a friend. Boy, that sounded like a consolation prize, didn't it?

She didn't like to think about it.

An older gentleman crossed the dining room, nodded hello to Katie, and inspected the appetizers on offer. Grabbing a plate, he filled it to nearly overflowing. "Good grub," he said aloud, gave Katie a wink, and wandered off to sample his booty.

"Who's that?" Katie whispered to Brad.

"Beats me. I never saw him before. Ask Margo. I'm sure he didn't just show up without an invitation."

Brad was right, although Katie was pretty sure Margo's local friendships hadn't strayed beyond the confines of Victoria Square.

Grabbing a stuffed mushroom, Katie meandered in the direction of her dead husband's mother. They had a rocky relationship while Chad Bonner lived, but after his death, Margo had reached out to Katie, offering her friendship and more.

Margo conversed with Conrad Stratton, the Square's wine merchant, who held a bottle in his hand, standing in front of a table filled with empty glasses. "Are you in need of some liquid refreshment?" he asked Katie, his eyes twinkling.

She laughed. "I am just a little thirsty," she admitted, and Conrad poured her a glass of something white and bubbly. She tasted it and smiled. "Lovely," she said, approvingly.

"I can give you a discount on a case," Conrad said, smiling brightly.

"I'll think about it," Katie said, and laughed.

Conrad glanced around the room. "It seems that more of your guests need refreshment," he told Margo. "I think I'll help them out."

"Go right ahead," Margo encouraged, her smile wide.

Katie studied her business partner. Margo looked at least ten years younger than her actual age, and dressed in a little black cocktail dress, black tights and pumps, with a triple-strand pearl choker decorating her neck, she looked positively dazzling.

"You've pulled off an amazing party," Katie complimented her.

"That only happens when you hire the best," Margo said modestly. Although she owned a half interest in Tealicious and could have just commandeered the kitchen and ingredients,

Margo had insisted on hiring the firm, as well as the cost of ingredients and Brad's time. And every bottle of wine on offer had been purchased from Conrad's store, The Perfect Grape. As much as she hated to admit it, Margo's arrival on Victoria Square had had a positive effect on just about everyone—even the ill-tempered owner of the Square's quilt shop, Nona Fiske.

Katie and Nona had butted heads on a number of occasions, and when the woman had shown up at the party, Katie felt more than a little miffed.

Margo seemed to notice Katie's disapproval. "I *had* to invite her."

"I understand," Katie said blandly. She didn't approve, but she understood Margo's motive to be inclusive.

Soft music played from the stereo system. Katie sipped her wine and listened, feeling herself begin to relax. That's when she saw the older gentleman, with a shock of snowy hair and a neatly trimmed matching beard, make another trip to the dining room table to refill his plate.

"Margo, who's that man over there?"

Margo looked in the direction of the dining room. "Maxwell Preston. He owns that last derelict building on Victoria Square." Margo actually blushed. "I may have been stalking him."

Katie turned toward her ex-mother-in-law in alarm. "Stalking? That's a pretty strong description."

"You're right. Sweet talking might be a better term."

Katie turned a jaundiced eye on her business partner. "What are you up to?"

"I hope to convince Maxwell to sell the building to me. It hasn't been rented in years."

"I know. Seth—" Landers—Katie's friend and pseudo-big brother, and the village's only attorney— "has contacted Mr. Preston on a number of occasions, but he's always maintained he didn't want to sell. The building is in such terrible shape, it can't be worth much."

"It's not the building, my girl; it's the land beneath it."

"So it's a total teardown?" Katie asked.

Margo nodded. "Just about. But think of what could be built in that space. I have this vision of a little Victorian cottage —think of the houses at the Oak Bluffs Campground on Martha's Vineyard. Those adorable little homes are featured during the Illumination Night."

Katie had never seen the spectacle for herself, but she'd heard about it from friends who had and her own searches for photos on the Internet.

"Is Mr. Preston likely to sell the space?"

"I have no idea. But I figured it wouldn't hurt to put out some feelers. He seemed absolutely delighted when I invited him to the party."

Katie looked over to take in the short, squat gentleman with the close-cropped, snowy beard and dark, shiny suit. Of all those assembled that evening, he seemed to be enjoying himself the most.

"When do you propose to talk turkey with him again?" Katie asked.

"In a few days. I want to give him time to think about what a wonderful evening I've given him."

Everything was fair in love and war—and business was often considered war.

Katie drained her glass. She figured she was good for one more glass and still safe to drive if she accompanied the beverage with a few more appetizers. She'd made the curried chicken balls because they were one of her favorites, and surely she deserved several of them after all her hard work—hang the calories.

Katie glanced at her business partner, who was taking in the guests, a smile gracing her lips. "Everyone seems to be having a wonderful time," Margo said, sounding pleased.

"As am I," Katie said. "But I'm still hungry. Time for me to raid the eats table."

"Fill up, darling girl. I don't want to have a lot of leftovers."

"I'll do that," Katie said, and laughed.

She started toward the dining room again, but Mr. Preston had already disappeared. Too bad. She wanted to engage him in conversation to talk about the building he owned on the Square. Not that she had any ideas of undercutting Margo's desire to purchase the site, but more to discover its history and why it had sunk into ruin despite the resurrection of McKinlay Mill's quaint little business section during the previous three years. It was something Katie was determined to discover.

But that night, she wanted only to relax and have a little fun. After all, nearly all her local friends were at the party. The only one missing was Seth Landers. Had Margo forgotten to invite him, or had he had a prior commitment that kept him from attending? She'd have to ask Margo—but not that night.

Taking a plate from the dishes on loan from Tealicious, Katie chose several appetizers—heavy on protein to counteract the alcohol she'd consumed—and glanced around the home's open-concept spaces, wondering who she should next seek out for conversation.

Her eyes lighted on Ray Davenport. He was smiling, looking happy. Was it the company or because he had Carol Rigby by his side? Katie looked away and popped one of the Buffalo deviled eggs into her mouth, suddenly feeling fat and unattractive. She'd chosen the wrong dress. She no longer liked the shoes on her feet. And her hair! She should have gotten a trim, which was long overdue. Suddenly, every choice she'd made during the past few weeks felt clumsy and wrong and….

Katie stuffed a curried chicken ball into her mouth, chewing as though she'd been starved.

"Are you okay?"

Katie turned to face Moonbeam Carruthers, the newest merchant on Victoria Square and owner of The Flower Child florist and boutique.

Katie forced a smile and swallowed before answering. "Yes, fine. Thanks for asking."

Moonbeam squinted, pursing her lips. "If you say so."

"I do." Katie ate the last chicken ball from her plate before setting it down on the living room's coffee table and dusting off her fingers. She nodded in the direction of Maxwell Preston. "Do you know that older man?"

"Max? Oh, sure. He's a regular at my shop. He comes in every week to buy pink carnations to put on his wife's grave."

"Oh, my," Katie said, instantly feeling sorry for the old man. "How long has it been since he lost her?"

"Twenty years."

Katie blinked in astonishment. "Wow." She'd been a widow for a little over four years, and she seldom visited her husband's grave. Perhaps it was because they'd been estranged at the time of his death. Maybe it was because she'd already burned through one relationship and the possibility of another since his passing. Or maybe it was that when it came down to it, she and Chad just weren't compatible. They'd wanted different things from life and he had acted on his independently. Katie hadn't risked their financial future to try to follow *her* dreams. Still, she felt she must have been an inadequate partner to have moved on so quickly after Chad's death while Mr. Preston still pined for a partner who'd been separated from him by death for so long.

These days, Katie seldom had a thought that wasn't self-deprecating. It needed to stop.

"I'm looking forward to the next Merchants Association meeting to decide the warehouse's fate," Moonbeam said. "I've got so many ideas that keep me awake at night." Katie wished her friend's enthusiasm was contagious.

Moonbeam glanced at the analog watch on her wrist. "Oh, my! Gotta go. Lily," her dog, "will be pining for me—as I am for her."

"I'm glad you could make it. Let's plan to get together soon," Katie said.

"Call or come by my shop anytime," Moonbeam said.

"I will," Katie promised and waved good-bye as her friend sought out Margo to say good night.

Conrad made another circuit around the room. "Can I top off your glass?"

Katie figured one more glass wouldn't hurt. "Of course."

Conrad poured the wine. "Great party," he said, grinning.

"Yes, it is."

"But winding down," he said, not only indicating Moonbeam, who headed for the door, but Don and Nick were saying their good nights to Margo, as well. They, too, had a dog waiting for them at home.

As the sky darkened, more and more guests said their good-byes until the only ones left were Katie, Margo, Ray, and Carol.

"Great party," Ray told Margo. Carol didn't seem impressed.

"I enjoyed connecting with everyone." Margo glanced at the table of finger foods. "We've got a lot of leftovers. Do you think your girls would like some?"

"That's incredibly generous of you," Ray said. "I'm sure they'd love it."

Brad appeared. "Let me put them in containers for you."

"Thanks."

"I wouldn't mind a few," Carol said, perturbed. To Katie's mind, she always sounded sour.

"Of course," Brad said, always accommodating.

"I'll scope out the deck for glasses and whatnot," Katie volunteered, and left the group for her quest.

Sure enough, she found several glasses—some with soggy

9

cigarette butts—on the deck. On impulse, she left the deck to check out the dock. After all, the glasses had been rented, and she wanted to account for all of them.

The expanse of lawn that separated the home's large deck and the stairs to the dock had to be at least twenty feet long.

Katie descended the ten steps from the bank's top to the dock. Despite the big sodium vapor lamp that came on at dusk, Katie felt a little nervous—probably because she was more familiar with the dock at the Marina at Thompson's Landing where her friend, Seth, moored his sailboat, *Temporary Relief*. This dock was much narrower. Margo had been encouraged to lease a boat for the summer, but she balked at the idea. "Too much upkeep," she decided. It would have been fun, but Katie understood her reluctance. Living on the water brought a sense of peace, but there were drawbacks, such as bugs. Lots of bugs. Icky spiders, in particular.

Katie walked the length of the dock, happy none of the guests had left glasses or plates. But something floated some five or so feet from the end of the wooden structure. Something rather...large.

Katie's eyes widened in horror when she realized just what was floating.

Without another thought, Katie jumped into icy water that took her breath away. Adrenalin gave her the impetus to move, and she hoped whoever it was was still alive.

The water was only about four feet deep, and Katie half-slogged/half-swam toward the dark jacket she'd seen earlier.

Snagging the collar, she pulled old man Preston's head out of the water. When he didn't take a breath, Katie feared the worst.

"Help!" she hollered, pulling the dead weight through the gently lapping waves. "Help!"

The others were still in the house. Katie could see their

silhouettes through the wall-to-ceiling windows that faced the lake.

She'd never done CPR before. She wasn't sure it could be done in the water—and she had no idea how long the old man had been there.

"Help! Help!" she screamed, and was unable to pull Preston's dead weight out of the water and onto the dock.

"Help! Oh, please help!"

Katie dragged Preston as close to the breakwall as she could, thankful an aluminum ladder was attached to the wooden dock.

"Help!" she hollered yet again. Her limbs were already going numb and she could no longer see the house from her new vantage point. If Preston hadn't drowned, he was probably suffering from hypothermia—something Katie was well acquainted with after she'd jumped overboard from a sinking boat some eighteen months before. She lost precious minutes trying to get Preston's arm out of his left jacket sleeve, thinking she could somehow tie him to the ladder when she heard a voice call her name.

"Katie?"

"Ray! I'm in the water. Help!"

She heard the ex-cop yell something, and then, seconds later, Ray and Brad hurried down the steps to the dock.

"What are you doing in the water?" Ray called, and then he saw that Katie was not alone and he, too, jumped off the dock.

Brad yanked his phone from his slacks pocket and punched in three numbers. Seconds later, he practically hollered, "A possible drowning."

Ray helped Katie keep Preston's form above the water, but at her panicked look, he shook his head.

Mr. Preston was dead.

Chapter Two

Margo loaned Katie a pair of flannel pajamas and cloaked her former daughter-in-law in a chenille throw that had previously been artfully draped over the south end of the living room's large sectional. It hadn't stopped Katie from shivering. Was it the shock of Lake Ontario's chilly water or finding Preston's body?

Carol Rigby paced in front of the room's huge fireplace that could have held half a cord of firewood had it not been fitted with a gas insert. Katie pulled the throw closer against her skin and wished she knew how to ignite the flames.

"And you saw *nothing*?" Carol practically shouted, directing her ire at Katie.

"I spent nearly the entire evening here in the house, same as you," Katie reminded the detective.

Carol pivoted her malevolent gaze toward Margo. "I'll need a list of everyone you invited to the party."

"I can give it to you," Margo said calmly, but then her gaze hardened. "But does it have to be right. This. Minute?"

"Of course not," Ray said, stepping in to quell the tension that had been building since Preston's body had been pulled from the water. After shucking his shirt, pants, and socks, Margo had outfitted him with a wool blanket while his and Katie's clothes tumbled together in the rental home's dryer.

Margo turned a jaundiced eye on Carol. "Why do you assume Mr. Preston's death was sinister? I hosted an open bar. My guests were welcome to pour whatever they wanted. I have no idea if he over-imbibed and simply fell off the dock."

"Or was pushed," Carol said acidly.

"I know everyone who was at the party. I refuse to believe any of them would have a reason to hurt a complete stranger," Margo said firmly.

"Ah, but what if he *wasn't* a stranger?" Carol countered.

Margo had no answer for that, but Katie was grateful the older woman had deflected Carol's ire away from her. And why was Carol so angry anyway? Katie had jumped into the lake to *save* the old man.

Katie glanced in Ray's direction, hoping for a sign of support, but he merely shrugged. Well, what did she expect?

That was a loaded question. He'd wanted more than just friendship with her and she hadn't been open to it because of her complicated relationship with Victoria Square's pizza meister. Katie could forgive a lot of foibles, but cheating wasn't one of them. If that branded her old-fashioned, so be it.

The county medical examiner arrived, and Carol left the living room to confer with her.

Katie couldn't stop shivering. Margo noticed.

"Darling girl, would you like a hot drink? Coffee? Tea? Cocoa?"

"Cocoa would be nice."

"I'll second that," Ray said.

Margo nodded. "I'll be back in a jiffy," she said, pivoted, and headed for the kitchen. That left Katie and Ray alone in the large room.

An awkward silence ensued. It was Katie who broke it.

"Will the girls be worried about you?"

The girls were his three daughters, although one of them was still in school downstate, soon to return for the summer. The younger two, Sadie and Sasha, were still in high school. They'd lost their mother four years before and were still mourning her loss. Despite their animosity toward her, Katie still had a soft spot in her heart for the girls. She'd lost her mother at an even younger age, and while her great aunt had taken her in and raised her from the age of six, and although Katie loved her Scottish Aunt Lizzie with all her heart, it just wasn't the same as having a mom—or mum, as Aunt Lizzie had called Katie's mother.

"Why is Carol so angry?" Katie asked.

Ray heaved a heavy sigh. "We had plans for later this evening."

Katie wasn't interested in asking just what they were.

"I'm sorry."

"What have you got to be sorry about?" Ray asked.

"For ruining your evening."

Ray shook his head. "You didn't ruin it."

She gazed into his blue eyes. Ray was not a handsome man. He wasn't muscled like Andy or Brad, or even as buff as her friends Nick and Don, but there was something about him that....

Katie looked away. She wasn't about to entertain thoughts of what might have been. Not that evening, anyway.

It wasn't long before Margo returned with a couple of mugs topped with whipped cream from a can that was quickly disintegrating into the steaming liquid.

"Thanks, Margo," Ray said, accepting a mug and wrapping his fingers around it as though to absorb its warmth. Katie did likewise.

Margo plunked herself on the far end of the sectional. "I'm

sure Mr. Preston just fell off the dock—maybe hit his head—and died."

Ray pursed his lips but said nothing. His expression hadn't gone unnoticed.

Margo scowled. "And?" she demanded of him.

"How well are you insured?"

Margo's eyes widened in distress. "Are you saying I could be sued?"

"I guess that depends on the old man's blood alcohol level."

Margo drew in a breath, looking horrified.

"Perhaps the old man had a medical emergency," Katie suggested, hoping to diffuse Margo's unease.

"An autopsy will confirm or disprove that," Ray said matter-of-factly. Sometimes, Katie hated his logical pronouncements. She didn't comment and sipped her cocoa.

An awkward silence followed before Ray broke the quiet. He turned his gaze toward Margo. "So, I heard you're renting out a portion of the old warehouse behind Victoria Square."

"Two portions, actually," Margo said, her voice subdued. She'd been so excited to sign the leases just weeks before, but now she sounded cowed. "I'm the first tenant to renovate one of the loft apartments, and I intend to open an art gallery."

"Chad's art will be on display," Katie piped up.

"And for sale?" Ray asked.

"That's to be determined," Margo said. As Chad's only beneficiary, Katie owned every piece of the florals and landscapes her husband had painted. Since his death, she hadn't sold any of his paintings. She wasn't sure she wanted to. Chad wasn't a gifted artist, but he'd been more than competent. Margo wanted to display his works, and Katie was agreeable, but they hadn't spoken about selling any of them. Yet. But at some point....

"When do you think you can move into the warehouse?" Ray asked.

Margo shrugged. "I have a six-month lease on this house. I hope to be in my loft by the time it lapses."

"Just in time for the festive season," Katie said, trying to sound cheerful. "Hopefully, by then, we'll have rented out a portion of the retail space." She paused. "I guess the partners should start thinking about decorating for the holidays."

Katie took her last sip of cocoa and placed her mug onto the boomerang-shaped teak coffee table before her. It wasn't her style—she was more into shabby chic, rustic country, or Victoriana, depending on the day—but it fit the house.

Ray finished his hot chocolate and did the same.

"This has been an awful experience for you, Katie. You're welcome to stay the night," Margo said sincerely.

After what she'd experienced that evening, the last thing Katie wanted was to sleep in a strange bed. Luckily, she had a good excuse not to. "Thank you for the generous offer, but I really need to get home to take care of Mason and Della." Her two cats. Truth be told, they'd been fed, had plenty of fresh water, and could have made it through the night alone. And yet…after what had transpired, perhaps she should stay to keep Margo company.

"I could stop by and make sure the cats are okay," Ray offered. "If you trust me with your keys."

Katie frowned. "Of course I trust you. Why wouldn't I?"

"Just sayin'," Ray said defensively.

"Then you'll stay the night?" Margo said with just a hint of desperation in her voice.

Katie forced a smile. "Of course I will."

Margo reached out a hand to clasp Katie's. "Thank you, darling girl."

Katie felt ashamed for nearly denying the poor woman company after being traumatized.

Carol chose that moment to reappear. It was apparent her

mood hadn't improved. "They're loading the body into the vehicle. An autopsy will be performed tomorrow morning."

It was more information than Katie wanted to know.

"We're free to leave," Carol told Ray with a glare.

"I'm waiting for my clothes to dry."

As if on cue, the dryer let out a resounding *buzz*!

"They should be dry by now," Margo said and leapt up from her seat to retrieve them.

Carol turned her unfriendly gaze on Katie. "You'll need to make an official statement."

"Which doesn't have to happen tonight," Ray piped up.

Carol glared at him. "We need to go," she said, her tone conveying that it was an order, not an option.

Katie eyed her friend and fellow Victoria Square merchant. She wouldn't have thought Ray would take kindly to such an edict. But he stood and took off in the direction of the home's laundry room.

Once he was gone, Carol spoke to Katie. "You seem to attract trouble."

"I assure you, I had nothing to do with Mr. Preston's death. I'd hoped to save him."

Carol shrugged. "So you say."

During the party, Katie hadn't ventured out on the dock. She had almost a score of fellow invitees who could corroborate the fact. Carol's adversarial attitude bothered her. It seemed the older woman had a grudge against Katie simply because she and Ray were friends. That was it. They were *friends*. Okay, Ray had kissed her, and more than once, but that was the extent of their intimacy, if that's what you'd could call it. His daughters disliked Katie almost as much as they disliked Carol, but Katie had affection for the motherless girls when she was sure Carol did not.

"I'd be glad to make a statement. Just tell me the time and place." And maybe she could share the ride downtown with

Ray, as he, too, would be expected to provide an official statement. It would probably be better if she and Brad made the drive together, as he, too, would probably be asked to make an official statement. Or maybe the three of them could go together to save on gas—to save the planet.

Yeah. Maybe.

After a couple of long silent minutes later, Ray appeared in his newly dried clothes. Carole eyed him. "Ready to go?"

Ray nodded, giving a sidelong glance in Katie's direction. She got the message. They'd talk again…and soon.

"Your keys?" Ray asked.

"Oh, yeah," Katie said, and rose from her seat.

"Keys?" Carol demanded.

"Yes. Katie's going to stay with Margo tonight, and I'm going to check on her cats."

"Surely they can take care of themselves." Carol grated.

"They have paws, not fingers. They can't pour themselves fresh water," Ray replied flatly.

So, Katie wasn't the only one annoyed by Carol's demeanor.

Katie removed her car key and handed over the rest. "Thanks, Ray. I'll pick them up in the morning." She might have to borrow Margo's key to Tealicious, the tea shop they jointly owned and located on Victoria Square, as she helped Brad with some of the baking and making the tuna, egg, and chicken sandwich salads.

Katie let out a sigh. She had a feeling the next few days would be difficult, thanks to Mr. Preston's death.

An uneasy feeling settled into Katie's gut. Difficult? That was probably an understatement. The idea of disaster flittered through her brain, and she had to fight the urge to panic. She couldn't afford that reaction just then. She'd wait until later to succumb to it.

While Margo's rental home was adequately furnished, it wasn't necessarily comfortable—or at least the bed in the guest room wasn't. That night, Katie tossed and turned, missing her cats and her creature comforts. The covers felt hot. Her back ached, and she vowed never to leave her comfortable bed to be a guest elsewhere ever again—well, unless it was at Sassy Sally's Bed & Breakfast on Victoria Square. She knew the beds there were cozy and snug because she'd chosen them herself.

It was early the next morning when Katie dragged herself to the ranch house's mid-century kitchen in search of coffee. She hadn't intended to wake Margo before she left to start her day at their tea shop, but Margo was already up, had a pot of coffee brewing, and was putting everything together to make a batch of French toast.

"Margo, you spoil me," Katie said, although she was not displeased.

"Darling girl, I have no one else *to* spoil."

A wave of affection coursed through Katie, and she stepped forward to embrace her dead husband's mother. They hadn't gotten along while Chad was alive, but during the past year or so, they'd become more than friends or business partners.

Katie pulled back, looking at the feast before her. Not only was there the making for the breakfast entree, but Margo had assembled a host of out-of-season fruits, from strawberries to blueberries and raspberries. "I sure hope you can use all this fruit before it goes bad," Katie said.

Margo smiled. "I planned to have a smoothie for lunch. That is, if I don't have to show up at some dreary sheriff's office to give a statement. Either way, they will not go to waste."

Katie poured herself a cup of coffee, doctoring it to her liking. "And I'll have to do the same."

"Same?" Margo asked, confused.

"Go wherever Carol dictates to make a statement."

"Maybe we can go together and save gas."

Saving gas was the last of Margo's worries. She picked up her own cup, warming her hands around it. "I don't like Carol."

It wasn't the first time Katie had heard Margo make such a blunt statement, but this one interested her.

"And why not?"

"She's all wrong for Ray."

"Why?"

"Because she's a bitch."

As always, Katie felt she had to play devil's advocate. "Why, because she's a competent detective?"

"Even when she's not on duty, she's always so...so...*awful*. Ray's a good man. He deserves someone with a kind heart. He deserves someone who would look out for his best interests. He deserves someone like...."

But then she didn't elaborate. Did she have someone in mind for Ray? Several of the women merchants on Victoria Square were eligible, and at least two of them were about Ray's age. Any one of them would have made a good companion for him in his old age. Not that he was at that stage of life. But he had weathered a long career in a business that had to be soul-shattering on so many levels. And he'd lost the love of his life—his wife Rachel—when they should have grown old together, playing with and enjoying their grandchildren.

"Who were you thinking of? Charlotte Booth? Or Sue Sweeney?" Sue owned the Square's candy shop.

"No, silly. *You.*"

Katie blinked. "Me?"

"He adores you," Margo said. "And it's *not* news to you, either."

He didn't adore Katie. He had a brief infatuation with her, but then he'd moved on. He and Carol had been an item for about six months. Nope. Ray was far too old for Katie, and even if they did have a number of things in common, the one thing that would always come between them—or anyone he dated—was his children. They'd made that quite clear. And she had no plans to ever come between any man she dated and their offspring because she knew, from the bitter experience of friends and former co-workers, that children from a previous relationship were often the death knell of a relationship. She thought of Ray as a friend. Nothing more.

"Besides the night's terrible end, the rest of the evening went well," Katie said, watching as Margo settled a piece of bread saturated with a beaten egg onto a hot skillet.

"Yes," Margo said, but she didn't sound at all pleased. "I'm ready to move on with my loft build and getting the gallery set up to display Chad's paintings."

"We should talk about that," Katie said, hoping she wasn't about to anger her late husband's mother.

"Do you want to sell his paintings?" Margo asked. Her tone had chilled.

"There are quite a few of them. If we *do* sell any of them," and as Chad's widow, it was Katie who owned them, "I would like the proceeds to go to charity."

Sudden tears filled Margo's eyes.

"I think that's what he would want," Katie elaborated. "Maybe a scholarship. Chad loved his students. He always wanted the best for them."

"I would hate to part with any of them, but I think you're right," Margo reluctantly agreed. "When do you want to go through them?"

"There's no point until you're ready to open the gallery — and maybe not just then. We might want to divide the paintings by category, and do a couple of shows to get the art world used to Chad's style, and *then* put up a few for sale."

Margo nodded. "Sound advice from a marketing major."

Katie didn't comment and instead nodded toward the bread in the pan. "You might want to flip that."

"Goodness!" Margo explained, grabbed a spatula, and flipped the bread, which was golden brown on one side.

Katie was more familiar with Chad's paintings than Margo,

and she described them all in detail. Margo made notes, and by
the time the last piece of French toast had been eaten, they had
a rough plan on how they'd best display Chad's paintings and
their least favorites—of which there were few—that they might
put up for sale.

"I'm excited about the exhibition. Chad would be absolutely
thrilled," Katie said.

Margo nodded, her eyes brimming with tears.

"But have you thought about vetting other artists?"

Margo nodded. "I've been putting out feelers for months.
Now to get the space renovated. The lighting will be key."

Katie nodded. "What's of bigger importance to you? The
gallery or the loft apartment?"

Margo frowned. "I have to be out of this place by November
first. So, the apartment has to come first, but I don't see why I
can't be working on both. The gallery may actually be easier to
finish. Right now, it's a crapshoot."

Again, Katie nodded. She glanced up at the kitschy black
cat clock on the wall with its plastic tail waving back and forth,
ticking off the hours. "I need to get to Tealicious to help Brad
with the day's salads. I gave Ray my keys."

Margo grabbed her purse, which hung on the back of one of
the kitchen chairs, extracted her keys, twisted off a set from the
main bunch, and handed them to Katie. "I'll collect them later
this afternoon when I visit the warehouse. I've got an appointment to talk to the contractor who's handling the renovations of
both the loft and the gallery."

Something in Margo's demeanor caught Katie's attention.
She squinted at the older woman. "Are you sweet on this guy?"

"Sweet? Me?" Margo shook her head vehemently. "I've
given up on love." Still, her cheeks betrayed her by coloring a
rosy shade of pink.

"As have I," Katie lamented. Still, she would make it a point
to get better acquainted with said contractor. As head of the

Victoria Square Merchants Association, it was her duty to be acquainted with the contractors working on the latest renovations to the warehouse.

"Oh, darling girl, no!" Margo protested. "I'm sure Chad wouldn't want you to be alone."

"I guess," Katie sort of agreed. Would they have gotten back together if Chad hadn't died? The answer was...probably. Katie *had* loved him. Was disappointed by him, sure. But she *had* loved Chad for all the things he was and had been. He hadn't betrayed her with his heart—at least with another woman. And she had made peace with the idea that he had invested in Artisans Alley because he thought it would ultimately benefit them. He couldn't know that it would take the death of his partner for that idea to be realized. And Chad—who was considerably younger—had died before Ezra Hilton.

Revisiting those thoughts was not conducive to a happy day, and Katie was determined to abandon them.

"If I'm meant to find someone else, it'll happen," she said succinctly. "If not...well, I've kind of resigned myself to the idea."

Margo shook her head. "Darling girl, you're far too young to give up on the idea of love."

"And how about you?" Katie asked, eager to know the answer.

Margo hesitated before answering. "Like you, I believe if it's meant to happen, it'll happen. But, if warranted, I might just give fate a little push."

Katie smiled. "You go, girl."

BRAD WAS ALREADY PREPARING fare for that day's Tealicious customers when Katie arrived at the tea shop's back entrance. She hurried inside and grabbed an apron, calling out a hello as she checked the list of specials on a piece of paper attached to one of the shop's fridges by a magnet Katie had purchased at the village's apple festival the year before.

Brad appeared from the shop's dining room. "I wasn't sure I'd see you this morning," he said as he returned to the long wooden counter where yeast dough had already risen.

"Why wouldn't I be here?"

"Oh, I don't know. After what happened last night...." He let the sentence hang.

He reached into his jeans pocket. "Ray dropped these off. He said to tell you the cats were fine. He fed them last night and made sure they had plenty of water."

Katie accepted the keys, shoving them into her slacks pocket. "He must have been on the Square awfully early." It was only just eight o'clock, and Wood U, the gift shop Ray owned, wouldn't even open until ten.

Brad shrugged. "If you ask me, he didn't want to be seen talking to you. The man's positively pussy whipped by that bitch Carol."

"Brad!" Katie admonished.

"Just sayin'," Brad said, turning his attention to the antique yellowear pottery bowls filled with dough, scrutinizing their volume. "That lady detective has got to be the most insecure woman I've ever encountered the way she wants to control Ray. What I don't understand is why he lets her treat him that way."

Katie had an inkling. The man—a widower—was lonely. Brad had arrived at Victoria Square, taking the job at Tealicious after the end of an unhappy relationship. He hadn't gone out of his way to find female companionship. As she measured the ingredients for the shop's most popular scones, she contemplated asking him about it, ultimately deciding against it—at least just then. Katie was sure he would probably turn around and ask her the same question. The whole situation was sad. So many people on the Square were lonely, and none of them seemed able to find the route to companionship, love, and happiness.

Perhaps the Merchants Association should change its name to Misfits Not-so-Anonymous or something along those lines. What a sad community, Katie decided, and yet there was nothing she could do about it—or have ideas to soften the blow of such misfortune. Instead, Katie turned her attention to the lemon scones she was preparing.

"Speaking of the Davenports," Brad said, "the shop got another email from Sophie asking when she can start her summer internship with us."

"You don't sound exactly happy about it," Katie commented.

"I've got nothing against her skills. She's obviously talented when it comes to pastry, and I see a bright future for her professionally."

"But?" Katie asked.

Brad punched down the dough in one of the big bowls. "It was really irritating to put up with her tortured sighs and the wistful looks she gave me when she interned here after the holidays."

"She's got a crush on you," Katie said reasonably.

"And if she was ten years older, I might be tempted to date her. But she's only a year out of being considered a child. That's too young for me."

"I all but promised her back in January that she could return—and this time as a paid employee for the summer."

Brad scowled. "That's up to you. But please, you've got to tell her she has no future with me and to cool it."

That would be an awkward conversation, but as the primary owner of the tea shop, Katie would have to have it with Sophie. "Okay, I'll do it," she said reluctantly.

"Thank you." And with that, Brad began to form the raw dough into balls for rolls and a second rise.

After finishing prep for Tealicious's lunch crowd, Katie

ascended the stairs to her studio apartment over the tea shop. As she placed the key in the door's lock, she paused, reluctant to enter the space. She'd enjoyed living in tight quarters over the Square's pizzeria owned by her former lover. But when she'd learned he'd been unfaithful—and more than once—she'd made it a priority to move out. She thought she could be happy in a studio apartment, but she'd been wrong. Everything about it felt cramped. She'd had to put half her possessions in storage, and sleeping on a Murphy bed wasn't exactly the lap of luxury, nor was washing in the tiny shower, not to mention the lack of a washer and dryer. Her kitchen space consisted of a tiny stove, a mini fridge, and a two-foot counter space, which wasn't exactly conducive to the kind of cooking she preferred. She could accommodate one or two guests max. Frowning, she decided it was time to admit defeat.

Entering the apartment, Katie was greeted by her cats, who seemed desperate for affection. The kitties also had a few problems since moving to a much smaller home. Sometimes, Della, who had been a rather nervous Nellie when Katie acquired her, missed using the litter box. She was obviously stressed by her new living situation.

Katie petted her kitties and sprinkled treats into their empty food bowls, feeling even more guilty for leaving them alone for such a long time. She leaned against the counter and addressed the felines. "I'm not happy here." The cats ignored her, chomping on their treats. "We've got to do something about it."

Still no reaction.

"And soon. Any suggestions?"

Mason looked up, hoping for more treats.

"You guys are not at all helpful."

Della finished eating and began to lick a paw.

"Well, I'm going to take my walk and think about it," Katie said.

Before she could move toward the door, Mason wandered off in search of a warm place to nap. Della soon followed him.

"Traitors," Katie muttered, grabbed her keys, and headed out the door.

She had a lot to think about. The one thing she didn't want to contemplate was Maxwell Preston's death.

Chapter Three

K atie was on her second circuit walking Victoria Square's
perimeter when she saw a woman standing outside the
last building to be leased on Victoria Square. The one owned by
Maxwell Preston.

Katie decided to approach the woman. "Hi, I'm Katie
Bonner, the head of the Victoria Square Merchants Association.
Can I be of any help?"

The sad-eyed fifty-something woman turned and shook her
head. "Not unless you can raise the dead."

Katie blinked. "I beg your pardon."

The woman nodded in the direction of the dilapidated
building before them. "My dad owns this building." She
frowned, and when she spoke again, her voice cracked.
"Owned it."

"Was your father Maxwell Preston?"

The woman nodded, wiping the back of her hand across her
damp eyes.

"This building used to house my mother's ceramic shop. It
was her dream. She held classes in the front. It was quite the

rage back when I was just a toddler. Lots of stay-at-home moms desperate for some outside connection would bring their babies with them and share their ups and downs while painting green-ware. My mom would fire those pieces in a kiln in the back so that when the moms returned, they would be ready to be used as decor or as gifts for family and friends."

"What was your mom's name?" Katie asked.

"Linda." The woman managed a watery smile. "She had a gift for painting. It was unfortunate that not all her clients were as skilled. But apparently they had fun."

"I understand the building has been empty for a long time," Katie said.

The woman nodded. "At least twenty years. After we lost mom, dad rented it out for a few years, but he wouldn't sell it, despite the offers he received, especially these last couple of years since the Square has had such a renascence."

The women were silent for long seconds before Katie broke the quiet. "First, let me say how sorry I am for your loss. It was me who found your father in the water. I did my best to save him, but it was already too late."

The woman turned anguished eyes on Katie. "Did he suffer?"

Katie bit her lip. "I'm sorry, but I don't know. I hope not."

The woman swallowed. "The police told me he likely drowned. What was he even doing near the lake?"

"There was a party," Katie began, but she didn't want to elaborate. Didn't want to mention Margo and the whole reason for inviting Preston.

The woman shook her head. "My dad wasn't exactly a social butterfly. Who'd invite him to a party—and why?" And then the penny dropped.

Before the woman could speak, Katie spoke. "I'm sorry, but I don't know your name."

"Phoebe Preston." She turned her gaze back toward the building which looked like a good gust of wind might blow it down.

"Would you be open to selling it?" Katie asked.

Phoebe shrugged. "As I understand it, probate could take six months to a year, so I guess I have a lot of time to think about it."

It sounded like she'd already been thinking about it. Had she consulted a lawyer as soon as she'd heard of her father's death, or had she been planning for such an event?

"On behalf of the Square's Merchant Association—" of which Phoebe's father was *not* a member, "—please feel free to contact me if you need help finding someone to lease or buy the building."

"Thank you. I'll keep your offer in mind." Phoebe looked at the creaky old building and heaved a heavy sigh. "Daddy should have sold this old building when things started picking up on the Square. He wanted to wait, seeing it as a boon to supplement his retirement. And now his retirement has been cut short." Phoebe's lips quivered. "Damn," she cursed. "Just…damn."

Katie resisted the urge to hug this stranger, who was obviously racked with grief.

"I'm sorry," Katie said again, lamely. "I'm so sorry."

Phoebe straightened. "Thank you for trying to save my dad. I really appreciate it."

"I just wish I'd gone out on the deck sooner. Then I might have been able to—" And that's when Katie's breath caught in her throat. By chatting with Margo, she had taken far too long to look for the rented glasses. But, she told herself to assuage her guilt, she had no idea anyone had fallen off the dock. Logic said she had no reason to blame herself for the old man's death, and yet some part of her did.

If circumstances had been just a teensy bit different, Maxwell Preston might still be alive.

What if the roads hadn't been icy that night in March when Chad's car slammed into a tree?

What if Ezra Hilton hadn't been pushed down Artisans Alley's main staircase?

What if Katie had decided to trash Artisans Alley instead of turning it into a thriving concern that would bring prosperity to the rest of the Square?

What if?

"I'd better go," Phoebe said. "I have a funeral to plan."

This time, Katie placed a hand on the grieving woman's shoulder. "I'm so sorry," she said again.

Phoebe nodded, and Katie watched as the older woman walked toward and got into a rusted blue Dodge minivan that had seen better days. She watched Phoebe drive away, heading east out of the parking lot.

For some reason, Katie felt like something about her conversation with Phoebe might come back to bite her on the butt. It was an absurd idea…but she'd learned to listen to those vibes.

Still, at that time, she had other concerns. Managing Artisans Alley, Tealicious, and attending to the concerns of the Merchants Association. She'd just have to wait for all hell to break loose.

KATIE FINISHED HER WALK, returned to her apartment, washed in its coffin-sized shower, and dressed in clean clothes before crossing the sea of asphalt between Tealicious and the arts and crafts arcade she managed. Thankfully, her assistant manager, Vance Ingram, had opened the place so that their vendors could restock their booths before the business opened for the day.

After the trauma of Maxwell Preston's death, Katie hoped

she'd have a peaceful day taking care of the administrative tasks associated with running two businesses. But it was not to be.

No sooner had she flopped into her office chair than Nona Fiske arrived at her office door with a sour look plastered across her face. Nona owned The Quiet Quilter, a shop specializing in quilting supplies and fabrics that sat next to Maxwell Preston's derelict building. Calling Nona the B-word was an understatement, not that Katie had ever used that descriptor, but plenty of the other merchants on the Square were fine with that characterization. Nona was not nice. That was as much as Katie was willing to say in polite company.

"Katie!" Nona said, her voice an octave higher than her usual tone.

"Nona," Katie sighed. "What's wrong now?"

"Wrong?" Nona sounded surprised. "Why should anything be wrong?"

"Because you only seem to contact me when you've got some grievance."

Nona frowned. "I came to see you because I've had a brilliant idea on how we can promote Victoria Square."

Katie bit her lip so that she wouldn't laugh aloud. "And that is?"

"We need a summer extravaganza. We need to host the Great American Picnic for the Fourth of July."

Katie's eyes widened. So far, she didn't hate the idea. "Go on."

"I had the TV on last night, and watched the old Disney movie *Pollyanna*. In the movie, as opposed to the book—books and movies are *never* the same—the town held a bazaar. It happened at night, which I certainly wouldn't want to participate in, but I thought we could hold something along the same lines; maybe a picnic. One of the merchants, perhaps Tanners, could sell hot dogs. Somebody else could sell lemonade. I'll bet Sweet Sue could sell pink cotton candy from her confectionery.

Your own Tealicious could sell sandwiches and iced tea. Meanwhile, the other merchants could hold a sidewalk sale. Some of your Artisans Alley vendors might want to participate. Things can get pretty dead on the Square in the heat of July. I thought this might bring in people."

Katie hated to admit it, but Nona might just be right.

"The Merchants Association monthly meeting is on Tuesday. Would you like to pitch your idea to the members?"

"Me?" Nona asked, aghast.

"Well, it *is* your proposal. I'm sure you'd want everyone to know that."

For a moment, Katie thought Nona might take offense, but then the woman's expression softened, and more than a hint of a smug smile quirked her lips. "Why, yes, I would."

"Great. We're only two months out from a July date. It might be more feasible to plan for August, but that can be discussed. Well done," Katie praised the woman.

Nona stood just a little taller. "Thank you."

Katie glanced at the old analog clock on her wall. "Hadn't you better get back to your shop? It'll soon be opening time."

"You're right. And in between customers I'll write up my presentation." Nona looked absolutely pleased with herself.

"Once we cover old business, you'll be the first on the agenda for new business."

Nona nodded. "I'll see you — and the rest of the merchants — on Tuesday evening." And with that, Nona pivoted and strode away.

Katie sat back in her creaky old office chair and stared at the now-empty door frame. That was the first time in nearly four years that she'd actually enjoyed a conversation with the older woman.

Her gaze shifted to the grubby carpet that covered the floor in her office, something she'd never gotten around to replacing. She wouldn't speak about Nona's idea to anyone until it was presented to the Merchants Association in two days. However, she *could* mention it to Margo. In fact, she'd make it a point to do so. In the interim, she'd brainstorm a few ideas of her own on how her Artisans Alley vendors could participate, along with the logistics of pulling off such an event in such a short time. They'd done it with the Square's first Dickens Festival with approximately the same timeline—they could probably do the same now.

Katie reached for a yellow pad of paper and a pen, noted what Nona had said, and started jotting down her own ideas. The Square needed a mid-summer kick in the butt to boost sales. This could just be it. Too bad it had been old sour puss Nona who came up with the idea.

The rest of the morning went smoothly...except for receiving an email from Carol Rigby asking Katie to make an official statement concerning Maxwell Preston's death. She could do that on Monday. Monday. Katie's only day off. Even that wasn't true because on Monday, she ran the Alley's accumulated sales through her computer, sorted them by vendor number, and prepared more than sixty checks, which took several hours to complete.

Still, it was with trepidation that she joined Margo at a table in the back of Tealicious where they had a lunch of tuna salad on the rolls Brad had baked earlier in the day, along with Katie's lemon scones.

"Have you recovered from your ordeal last night?" Margo asked sincerely before taking a sip of her tea.

"I suppose." Katie then related her encounter with Preston's daughter. "Refresh my memory. You said you tracked down Maxwell Preston to try to get him to sell you the property."

"Not exactly," Margo hedged. "I *did* make a point to track him down—and, yes, it was to find out if he was amiable about selling his property. But I never had an opportunity to ask him about it."

Katie nodded. "You wanted to gain his confidence."

"Well, yes," Margo admitted. "But I didn't even speak to him about selling it. It would have taken many more conversations before I dreamed of broaching the subject. Time, darling girl. It sometimes takes time to gain that kind of trust. I wasn't even sure he'd show up at my house-warming party. He told me he had an emotional attachment to the property on the Square."

"I gathered that because of what Moonbeam and Phoebe said."

Margo nodded. "He seemed like a nice, lonely man."

"And you decided he was nice on the basis of how many conversations?"

"Well, two or three. Are you suspicious of him?"

"Not exactly. But his death might have been awfully convenient for someone who wanted him to sell the property—someone with something to gain."

"His daughter?" Margo asked, looking pensive.

"Or someone who wanted to own the property."

"Don't look at me," Margo demurred.

Katie shook her head. "But as Phoebe said herself, if Preston was going to sell, it should be when the property was at its most valuable. The building is in a terrible state of repair. It'll be a total knockdown, selling for less when it finally goes on the market. I think Phoebe realized that."

Margo shook her head. "I'm sorry you had to speak to her."

"Better me than another merchant on the Square—especially Nona Fiske. Which reminds me," Katie began and related her discussion with the older woman.

Margo's eyes widened. "Why, darling girl, I hate to admit it, but Nona's notion is spot on. Just what the Square needs to beat the midsummer doldrums." Margo looked thoughtful. "This could push me—or at least our contractor—to get my gallery up and running months sooner than anticipated. I absolutely *love* having a goal. And, it would be the first commercial enterprise to open in the Victoria Square Annex."

The Square merchants who'd joined forces to buy the site hadn't yet voted on an official name for the structure, but they would soon need a sign to advertise the building to fill the retail and loft spaces. It reminded Katie of her most recent decision. She hesitated to bring it up, but now that she'd decided that she needed more space, she needed to run it by her business partner, who'd put a lot of money into the apartment, constructing it to Katie's exact specifications.

"Um…we need to talk about what could be a potentially sore subject," Katie began.

Margo picked up her teacup and took a swallow, as though to fortify herself. "Go on."

Katie took a breath to perhaps prepare for battle. "Despite all my thoughtful plans, I'm not happy living in the tiny apartment above Tealicious." She braced herself for a blast of negativity but was surprised when the older woman merely shrugged.

"I wondered when you'd come to that conclusion."

Katie blinked in surprise. "After all you invested in the property, I thought you might be upset."

"It's a lovely space—perfect, in fact. But I was sure it wouldn't be the right space for *you*."

"Why didn't you say something?" Katie asked, puzzled.

Again Margo shrugged. "I figured when you came to that conclusion you'd let me know. And we *did* discuss the possibility of renting it out at some future date and make a profit on the space." Margo leaned closer, her eyes wide with interest. "Now, tell me what you want in a house. You do want a *real* house, don't you?"

Katie nodded. "I'm not sure. I mean—I do and I don't. I haven't even looked at what's available in the area, but six hundred square feet just isn't enough room for me and my cats."

Margo nodded thoughtfully.

"It's probably going to take me a few years to qualify for a mortgage, so I guess I should start looking at houses for rent near the Square. Ray Davenport found that lovely little cottage when he relocated to the village. Hopefully, I can do the same."

Margo's expression turned somber. "I'd be more than happy to co-sign a loan for any home you want to purchase."

Katie shook her head. "You've already done far more than I could ever expect. I couldn't ask you to do that."

"You didn't," Margo declared. "I'm offering."

Margo's considerate proposal would allow Katie and the cats to land in a home relatively soon as opposed to years stuck living in a two- or three-room apartment—if she could find a place that allowed pets.

"That's very generous of you, Margo."

"It's what Chad would have wanted for you."

Katie swallowed. Yeah. And with that statement came a lot of guilt. But in the last year, Katie and Margo had bonded. They were no longer at odds vying for Chad's love. Now, they were connected because of their love for the boy Margo had raised and the man Katie had married.

"It might be that any bank we contact could find both of us ineligible, thanks to our investments on the Square."

"You let *me* worry about that," Margo said, settling back in her chair. "Now, let's talk some more about how we want to display dear Chad's paintings and which ones we might be willing to part with."

Despite their evolving relationship, their conversations always seemed to revolve around Chad. That was okay, for the most part, but Katie longed for the day when the women could be friends without the specter of the dead man hanging between them. She understood Margo's grief. She accepted that it might be years before Margo could move on. And, again, she felt guilt because she *was* ready to move on. She'd always have a soft spot in her heart for Chad, but he was gone, and—hopefully—Katie had a long life ahead of her. Still, the idea that she might be alone for decades haunted her. If there was someone out there she was destined to be with, she hadn't yet met him.

At least, she didn't think so.

Chapter Four

That night, Katie went online and was able to stream the movie that had inspired Nona Fiske's idea for a summer extravaganza. She'd never seen the film before and was charmed by the wholesome goodness of the protagonist and the effect she had on her adopted hometown. But the film's inspiring tale of love made her ache for a time long past when the world seemed a lot simpler. Kinder.

And it was the sequence at the bazaar that also held her attention. Highlights included a kiosk selling cake. A kiosk selling watermelon. A live band played while people danced— some with joy, some with military precision. And the sweet voices of children singing 'America The Beautiful.' Could the Victoria Square Merchants Association replicate that on the Square in the scorching heat of summer? Nona didn't want to participate in an evening event, but perhaps others in the vicinity might. She'd bring that up at the Merchants Association meeting.

The next morning, it was with trepidation that Katie battled rush-hour traffic and steered toward the greater Rochester area and to the sheriff''s depot to make her statement on Maxwell

Preston's death, grateful she didn't have to interact with Carol Rigby. As she had plans to visit the city later that day, Margo decided she'd make her statement then, and Brad planned to do so after his hours at Tealicious. Once that was done, Katie drove back to Victoria Square to fulfill her duties for her Artisans Alley vendors. She parked her car beside Tealicious and, seeing lights on at Wood U, decided to cross the Square's parking lot to visit Ray.

The door was locked, but Katie rapped on it and several long seconds later Ray arrived wearing a grubby work apron, with the family dog, Belle, in tow. The apron meant he'd been in back working on his latest carving project.

"Hey, Katie, what brings you here?" he asked as he motioned for her to enter his shop.

"Gratitude," she said, letting Belle give her a warm greeting, the dog's tail wagging cheerfully.

Ray looked at her for a moment, puzzled.

"I'm grateful you took care of my cats on Saturday night. I'm sorry I didn't come by to thank you sooner."

Ray waved a hand in dismissal. "Totally unnecessary." But she knew he appreciated the gesture. "Want some coffee?"

"I wouldn't say no," she said, and followed him to the back of the shop where the coffee pot was half full.

Ray pulled a clean mug from under the counter and filled it, waving a hand for her to help herself to powdered creamer and sugar. He sat at his bench, with Belle settling down beside him, and Katie sat on the upholstered love seat his daughters used when hanging out in the shop. "What's new?"

"Not much. If you discount giving my statement to the sheriff's office this morning."

He nodded, picked up his carving knife, and attacked the piece of balsa wood that was evolving into a Santa figurine.

"Are you already starting on your Christmas inventory?" she asked.

"It's a new design. I thought I'd make a couple, give them different paint jobs, and let the girls decide if I should make more."

Katie nodded, sipping her coffee. Ray had a great relationship with all three of his daughters.

He worked in silence for several long moments before he looked up again. "Is everything all right?"

"Do you mind if I vent?" Katie asked.

"Anytime," he offered.

"Well, not really vent. It's just... Mr. Preston..." she began.

Ray nodded. "I'm sorry he was too far gone. You did a good thing trying to save him."

"That's the thing. I *didn't* save him. If I'd only gone outside to look for glasses and plates a few minutes earlier."

Ray paused from his work, looking straight at her. "It's not your fault. You have no reason to feel guilty."

Katie frowned. "It's not exactly guilt. It's more like—"

"Guilt," he said again.

"More like remorse."

"Same thing," he said and flicked off another wood chip.

"Not really," Katie muttered. She wasn't going to argue with him. Her feelings were hers. As a homicide detective, Ray had seen the worst of humanity. It had hardened him. But he wasn't the curmudgeon Katie had labeled him during the first year of their acquaintance—before she could call him her friend. He was a man of deep feelings and convictions, and she admired those traits in him. But maybe he wasn't the right person to speak to about her feelings. That could develop into an uncomfortable situation.

"Are you planning to attend tomorrow's Merchants Association meeting?" Katie asked, changing the subject.

"Should I?"

"If you're interested in participating in a big summer event on the Square, you might want to be there."

Ray looked up from working on Santa's hat. "I'm intrigued. What's the deal?"

"A Square-wide promotion. I'm just putting feelers out to see if it's something the merchants want to invest in. The time-line's pretty tight if we want to pull it off in July or August."

Ray shrugged. "Didn't you set up the Square's first Dickens Festival with only two months' notice?"

"Well, yes, but that was for the Alley—not the whole Square."

"It's grown into something just about all the merchants participate in, though."

That it had.

"What have you got in mind?" Ray asked.

"It wasn't my idea. Of all people, it was Nona Fiske's suggestion."

"Nona had an original thought?" Ray asked, incredulous.

Katie bit her lip to keep from laughing. "Actually, she was inspired by a movie. *Pollyanna*."

"*Pollyanna*? Does she want us to play the glad game?"

"You know the film?"

"And read the book as a kid in grade school as a class assignment. It's just my opinion, but I thought the film was better—if overly long. My girls have the DVD. Sophie must have played it half a million times back when she was in grade school."

"Nona thinks we should emulate the bazaar, only call it a picnic. She's given it a lot of thought."

Ray shrugged. "I'm open to it. I love hot dogs and beer."

"I highly doubt there'll be beer."

"Why not? Conrad Stratton has a liquor license."

Katie hadn't thought of that. It could be a real draw, especially if he reached out to one or more of the local craft breweries.

Ray grinned. "Did I just see a light bulb go off over your

head?"

"Ha-ha," Katie deadpanned. "What do you think?"

"Sounds like it could be fun."

"So you'll come to the meeting?"

Ray squinted at her. "Do you sound just a little desperate?"

"Only three people came to the last one," Katie lamented. She and Brad had made a lot of food, thinking they'd be feeding twelve or more.

Ray nodded. He'd been one of those who'd skipped it. "Okay, count on me."

Katie finished the last of her coffee and rose from her seat. "Great." She offered him her mug. "Want me to wash this?"

He shook his head. "I can get it."

For the briefest of seconds, their fingers touched as they made the exchange. Katie's gaze rose to meet his, and she fought the sudden urge to kiss him, wondering if he felt the same—and instantly felt ashamed.

She forced a smile. "I guess I'll see you tomorrow, right."

"Yup."

They stood there for several long seconds before Katie pivoted and turned to enter his showroom, with Ray following right behind. She waited for him to unlock the door.

"Bye."

"*Auf wiedersehen.*"

Katie exited the shop, heard the door close behind her, and trundled down the short flight of steps to the asphalt. As she headed toward Artisans Alley, she wondered if he was watching her and why the idea sort of pleased her.

Back in her Alley office, and while printing out the weekly checks, she received a text message from her friend Nick Farrell, inviting her to dinner that evening. Cooking for oneself was a bummer and often led to easy but unhealthy choices—so she enthusiastically texted back her acceptance. Besides, both men were excellent cooks.

And perhaps other male company might give her respite from thoughts and regrets that could lead nowhere.

~

KATIE ARRIVED at Sassy Sally's at precisely 6 o'clock that evening, ready for a lovely dinner, wine, and even more, a sense of camaraderie. She knew they'd chosen the time to give her a chance to finish her work and close Artisans Alley, and she appreciated their thoughtfulness.

"Welcome, fair lady," Nick called as he gestured Katie to enter the bed and breakfast's foyer with its antique reception desk and Victorian charm. After exchanging a quick hug, and petting their dog, Ru, Katie followed him to the kitchen, where Nick's husband, Don, stirred a pot on the stove.

"Something smells heavenly," Katie remarked.

"What? This pot of slop?" Don asked. "It's just something I was cooking up for Ru. We're having lobster tails."

"Wow—you sure know how to impress a guest."

"It would be more impressive if he caught them himself," Nick teased, giving Katie a wink.

"But first," Don said, turning from the stove to the stainless steel industrial-sized fridge where he extricated a bottle of Zinfandel.

"Who wants to do the honors?"

Nick raised a hand. "Mind your manners. You should never ask our guest to work."

"Guest, schmest. Katie's family," Don asserted.

Katie's throat tightened, and she felt her cheeks grow warm at his words. "The feeling's mutual," she said.

"Cut out all this mushy talk," Nick said gruffly. "Some of us are thirsty."

"Then pour," Don encouraged.

Three glasses sat on the counter, and Nick cracked the

bottle's cap and poured, handing them to Katie and Don before picking up the last and tilting in their directions. The three clinked glasses and sipped.

"Thanks for inviting me tonight. Instead of lobster, I was destined to have a couple of stale scones and a cup of tea."

"Ah, the hazards of living over a bakery. Someone's gotta eat those leftovers," Don said.

Don set his glass on the counter and opened the fridge again, this time taking out a tray, which Katie could see contained the lobster tails. This dinner was going to be good. She and Nick took seats at the wooden farm table, and Don turned on the oven to preheat it.

"I guess you heard about what happened at Margo's after all the guests left on Friday," Katie said, working to keep her voice neutral.

"We'd have to live on the moon not to," Nick said. His eyes narrowed, and his voice softened. "Are you okay?"

Katie nodded and sighed. "I just wish...."

"You could have saved the old man? Yeah, that's a bummer. But you tried. That counts for something," Don said sympathetically.

Something? Too bad that something hadn't been enough to change the outcome. But then Katie had a thought. Ray had voiced the same opinion.

"I don't suppose you knew him, Nick?" Katie asked. Nick had grown up in McKinlay Mill.

Nick shook his head. "Not personally. He ran the drugstore up on Main Street, but I'll bet Seth did. As the only lawyer in the village, he knows just about everyone."

Katie should have remembered that about the man she considered to be not only a close friend, but a pseudo-big brother.

"I suppose you've checked into the old man's past," Don

commented, tinkering with the salad he'd prepared to go with the shellfish.

"Not really. I mean … it *was* an accident. I'm just sad it happened. I met his daughter this morning. She came to check out Mr. Preston's building on the Square."

"And?" Nick nudged.

"Of course, she was sad to lose her father, but from the way she spoke, it was just one more hurt after a lifetime of them."

"That's too bad," Don said, picking up his glass once again. "Ru—" their Australian Shepherd mix dog "—and I stopped by this morning to inspect the building on our first circuit around the Square. It seems to me that the village should have condemned that building a long time ago. I wouldn't be surprised if a good gust of wind sent it flying in the air like Dorothy's house in *The Wizard of Oz.*"

"Did you ask if she was willing to sell?" Nick asked.

"Yes. She said she urged her father to sell it when the Square started taking off after the first Dickens Festival. Apparently, he was emotionally attached to the building." she explained.

"That's sad," Nick said.

"Yeah," Don agreed and took a long pull on his glass of wine.

"But her misfortune will be someone else's delight," Nick said.

Katie gave her friend a quizzical look. "You aren't thinking of acquiring the spot, are you?"

"Well, Nick and I *have* talked about opening a little antique shop as a side hustle," Don said.

"Yeah, but we wouldn't want to be too far away from Sassy Sally's," Nick said.

"We've thought about renting space in the warehouse behind the Square," Don added.

"Really?" Katie asked.

Nick nodded. "I don't suppose you'd want to be a picker for us, would you?"

"If only I had the time," Katie said and laughed.

"Don't tell me you're going to pitch to the our merchants consortium to buy Preston's building, too," Don said.

"No. But speaking of pitches, tomorrow night Nona Fiske is going to make a proposal at the Merchants Association's monthly meeting.

Nick rolled his eyes. "Spare me."

"No, I've encouraged her to do so." Katie told them about Nona's idea.

"I'm actually intrigued. Not that it's anything we'd be interested in participating in," Don said.

"I don't know about that," Nick countered. "If nothing else, we could set up a table—under a tent; I don't need to get sunburned—and hand out brochures. Maybe we could put together a short video on our place instead of giving guided tours—we don't need a load of strangers traipsing through the house."

"If you didn't want to sit there all day, I'll bet one or both of the Davenport girls would love the opportunity to sing its praises. Those girls are born entrepreneurs," Katie said.

Suddenly, Don wasn't so skeptical. "It's a thought."

"Then you'll come to the meeting?" Katie asked eagerly.

"We wouldn't miss it," Don said, with a complete attitude reversal.

"Great." Katie picked up her glass and tipped it in the men's direction. At least there'd be five people—including herself—in attendance. To up the odds, she decided she'd hint at Nona's proposal in her reminder email that she usually sent out the day of the meeting,

She was beginning to get excited about the prospects of a big summer promotion. And she hoped she wouldn't be the only one.

Chapter Five

Katie awoke the next morning thinking about and looking forward to that evening's Merchants Association meeting. Hearing stirrings from the bakery below, she hurriedly got ready for the day, feeding the cats before she headed down to help Brad with the day's baking.

"Hey, Lady," Brad called as he shoved a big tray of muffins into the largest of the shop's ovens.

"Hey, Sir," Katie countered. "What do you want me to do?"

"You can start on the tuna salad."

"Will do."

Katie headed for the pantry and returned with two 66-ounce cans, dipping into the utility drawer for a can opener.

"Anything new?" Brad asked.

"As a matter of fact," Katie began, and launched into her spiel about Nona's proposed picnic. "I thought it might be something we could participate in. We could sell sandwiches, iced tea, maybe lemonade, and, of course, desserts. Cookies, at least."

"Sounds like a plan."

"You wouldn't want to attend the meeting tonight, would you?" she asked hopefully.

Brad shook his head. "I think one of the shop's representatives should be enough," he said, referring to her. "But I'd be glad to put together a sample menu if you want."

"I want," Katie said. And with that, she decided she should take time out of her day to try to hit all the shops on the Square to personally invite their owners to the meeting.

"Do you want me to prepare a full meal for the merchants this evening?" Brad asked.

After the last disastrous meeting, when they ended up with tons of leftovers that couldn't be given to the local food pantry, Katie wasn't inclined to do that again. She shook her head. "From now on, we'll only offer whatever is left over that doesn't sell in the shop."

"That's kind of a risk, isn't it?"

Katie shrugged. "I'll ask if they want to return to Del's Diner for meetings. I'm fine with it if they decide that's what they want."

Brad nodded. "I don't suppose you turned on the news before you came down."

From the tone of his voice, Katie could tell whatever he had to say wasn't going to be good news. "No. Why?" she asked warily.

"The medical examiner has pronounced old man Preston's death a homicide."

"Homicide?" Katie echoed. "Did they give a cause?"

"Blunt trauma."

Preston had had a gash on his head, but Katie thought he must have hit it on the edge of the dock when he fell into the water. She swallowed. Fell—or was pushed?

"I suppose you'll want to check with Ray to see what he knows about it," Brad said.

Yes, she would. But maybe she'd wait until after—or

perhaps just before—the meeting that evening. The anticipation she'd allowed herself to feel had utterly drained away, and the reality of Preston's last moments gave her a chill.

Someone at Margo's party had killed the old man. Someone she *knew*—another of the guests—had killed him.

Or was she being melodramatic? What if Preston's killer had tracked him to the party? Lured him away from the rest of the revelers and—*WHACK*—smacked him on the back of his head with something hard enough to send him flying off the dock. Had the old man been dead before he'd even hit the water?

Suddenly, Katie had a lot more questions to ask Ray Davenport.

KATIE STARTED the second part of her day at Artisans Alley with a heavy heart. Her lieutenant, Vance Ingram, had once again opened the building for vendor restocking, and a fresh pot of coffee awaited in the vendors' lounge. She deposited her quarter into the slot of an old coffee can, doctored the brew, and retreated to her office to fire up her computer. Not long after, Vance appeared in her doorway.

"Hey, Katie, what's up?"

Katie swiveled her chair to face him. "It turns out the man who died at Margo's party didn't die by accident."

"Yeah, I heard it on the news this morning. Will you be in trouble for it?"

"Me?" Katie practically squeaked.

Vance's expression soured. "That detective, Carol Rigby—she's got it in for you."

"What for?" Katie asked, confused.

"Because Ray has the hots for you," Vance said nonchalantly.

"Vance!" Katie chided him.

"Well, everybody knows it. I don't know why he's wasting his time with that bi—"

"Vance," Katie interrupted, her tone a warning.

"I'm sorry. I thought you always wanted me to speak my mind."

Yeah, regarding things pertaining to Artisans Alley—not when it was specifically about *her*.

Vance prattled on. "Anyway, if you need to take some extra time off to consult a lawyer or anything, I'll be available to cover for you."

"Thanks," Katie said, not hiding the sarcasm in her voice. Consult a lawyer? She'd planned to talk to Seth Landers. Perhaps she shouldn't put off her call to him. She could invite him to lunch, grab something from Tealicious, and they could talk privately in her apartment above the tea shop—that is, if he could fit her into his schedule.

"What's this about a big bazaar coming to the Square this summer?" Vance asked.

Katie blinked. "Who told you?"

He shrugged. "The rumor is going all around the Square."

Katie hadn't even mentioned it to the rest of the merchants. But she supposed Nona might be out there touting her proposal to ensure that she, and not Katie, would get full credit. As if Katie would try to pull such a stunt. Unlike Pollyanna, who saw the good in everyone, Nona expected the worst of man—and woman—kind. Katie squelched the rising tide of anger that threatened to course through her and concentrated on feeling pity for a woman with such a sour outlook on life and her fellow travelers in it.

"So, what's the story?"

Katie sighed, grabbed a butterscotch candy from the jar on her desk, unwrapped it, popped it into her mouth, and crunched it. Then, she told Vance the same things she'd told Ray, Nick, and Don. And it occurred to her that she ought to mention it to Margo before she, too, heard it anywhere else. She'd do that—and call Seth's office—as soon as she finished her conversation with Vance.

Katie had only been awake for a few hours, but she already felt exhausted. And what had promised to be a good day had already soured.

Swell. Just swell.

Chapter Six

After calling Seth Landers's office, his secretary informed
Katie that there was nothing on his calendar during the
lunch hour—consulted with him—and he agreed to meet Katie
for a quick lunch just after noon. After that, Katie texted
Margo, who was already at the Victoria Square Annex. Katie
walked across the parking lot and into the warehouse, winding
her way through to the vast space where Margo's gallery was
already being worked on. Eventually, there'd be a separate
entrance from the outside of the building, but that would come
later.

"Margo!" Katie called.

"In the back," the older woman called.

Katie was pretty familiar with the proposed layout, which
was mostly studs with some Sheetrock to form the walls at that
point.

Margo stood in what would be a small commercial kitchen.
She intended to host parties in the gallery, offer hors d'oeuvres
to people with deep pockets, and rent out the space for cocktail
parties.

Margo never thought small.

Katie gazed around the room. Blue painter's tape outlined the workstations, while Margo consulted a myriad of brochures on a makeshift table made of saw horses and plywood. "Picking out the appliances?" she asked.

Margo smiled. "Yes. I was never much of a cook, but I can plan one a hell of a good cocktail party."

Katie's gaze dipped. The party on Saturday had been a terrific success—until Maxwell Preston had been murdered.

Margo wasn't thinking along those lines. "I'm thinking about what a caterer might need to pull off a good party!"

Katie was sure her dead husband's mother would have never made a pronouncement if she knew Preston's death wasn't an accident.

"Have you checked the news this morning?" Katie asked.

"No, why?" Margo asked, distracted. Her mind was obviously still concerned with the contours of the new kitchen.

"It seems that Maxwell Preston's death has been ruled a homicide."

Margo looked up, her eyes widening in horror. "No!"

"Yes," Katie confirmed. "Vance seems to think I should hire a defense attorney."

"Don't be ridiculous," Margo said firmly. "You'd never even met the man before the party. Why on earth would you have a motive to kill the old man?"

"I dunno. I'm having lunch with Seth Landers. I'm going to run that idea past him."

"You should talk to Ray, too," Margo asserted.

"Well, that's another thing Vance had an opinion on."

"What does he think?"

"That Ray has—" She wasn't about to say that he might have the *hots* for her. "—some kind of affection for me."

Margo threw up a hand in dismissal. "Oh, well, that's a given."

"Margo!" Katie admonished her.

"Oh, Katie, the man practically lusts after you. He's done a good job of hiding it since he took up with that awful woman, but he sings your praises to anyone who'll listen."

Katie hadn't known that, and now she felt embarrassed. Her gaze remained riveted on the concrete floor.

"Katie, darling girl, Carol Rigby is a stopgap in his life," Margo explained. "His girls are still hurting from the loss of their mother. They hate Carol with a passion."

"How do you know that?" Katie asked.

Margo looked at Katie with pity. "I talk to them on a regular basis."

"You do?" Katie asked.

"Of course. Sadie, Sasha, and I have had a number of lunches at Tealicious to talk shop. Mark my words, those girls are going to be millionaires before they hit twenty-five. But between shoptalk, they've spoken about their home lives and their opinions on many subjects."

"Well, there's nothing between Ray and me," Katie lied, thinking about how she'd longed to kiss him earlier the day before. Hell, the man was old enough to be her father. And yet....

Katie shook herself. "I came here to tell you about Nona Fiske's idea for a summer extravaganza for the Square."

Margo frowned. "Nona had a thought that wasn't filled with malice?"

Katie ignored the sarcasm in her former mother-in-law's tone. "Oddly enough, yes." And Katie told Margo about the whole Pollyanna bazaar scenario.

Margo nodded. "It might be something we should consider."

"So, you'll be at the Merchants Association Meeting this evening?"

"I wouldn't miss it."

"Eat dinner before you come because Brad and I have decided it'll be snacks only after the last debacle of a meeting."

55

Margo nodded, probably remembering the fiasco of the previous month's meeting.

"Scratch that. Come a little early, and I'll make sure there's enough for sandwiches for the two of us."

"Will do," Margo said, turning her attention to the blank slate that was to be her gallery's galley kitchen. She smiled. "I have such a good feeling about the gallery. About the whole Victoria Square Annex."

She'd said the name again. Katie was really warming to it. She needed to talk to all the partners, but she was sure they'd all agree it was the perfect name for the structure that had so much potential to be a business, retail, and residential mecca in the little village of McKinlay Mill.

Was Katie prideful in thinking that she'd been responsible for the resurrection of the village's main business district? Probably. But as long as she didn't brag about it, maybe it was okay. Goodness only knew how many days she'd struggled during the past couple of years when her self-esteem was in the toilet. She'd let herself revel in the idea for a few moments. And then, it would be time to get back to work...and worry.

Katie had no doubt her talk with lawyer Seth would bring her down to earth—but hopefully not with a nasty crash. After leaving Margo, Katie returned to Tealicious.

She prided herself in setting a fine table, even if the fare was only tuna on homemade rolls. She'd assembled a plate of them. Seth wasn't a big eater—but under stress, Katie could shove way too much into her piehole. And it didn't take a lot of introspection to realize she was worried about how her conversation with Seth would go.

Katie was a nervous wreck by the time she heard a rap on her door. She rushed across the small expanse of her apartment and flung open the door.

"Hey," Seth began, but was cut off when Katie practically flung herself at him, clutching him fiercely.

"Hey—hey, what's wrong?" Seth asked, patting her back as only a pseudo-brother would.

All the emotion Katie had bottled up since speaking with Vance earlier that day exploded, and suddenly, she was sobbing into Seth's suit coat.

Wrapping his arm around her shoulder, Seth led Katie back into her apartment, closing the door behind him and towing her to the love seat.

A tissue box sat on the end table nearby, and Seth grabbed a handful. "Here. Blow your nose and tell me what's wrong."

Katie accepted the paper hankies, blew her nose loudly, and wiped away the tears still leaking from her eyes. "It seems like everything in my life has fallen apart."

Seth scowled. "I don't believe it. You are one of the strongest women I've ever met."

"Not today," Katie simpered.

"Yeah, but how about tomorrow?"

Katie coughed and laughed despite of herself. "Okay, maybe I'm having an unnecessary meltdown. But if nothing else, I could use a sympathetic ear."

Seth shrugged. "Why else would I be here?"

"Because you hanker for tuna fish on homemade rolls."

"Damn! You've unlocked my secret ambition in life," Seth joked.

Katie couldn't help but laugh. "Yeah. I have."

Seth frowned. "I'm sorry, but I have an appointment at one, so break out the grub, woman, and let's talk about what's eating *you*."

Katie told Seth about Vance's assessment of her finding the late Maxwell Preston.

Seth shook his head. "I think Vance is encouraging paranoia on your part."

"Really?" Katie asked, sounding unsure.

"Absolutely," Seth said with confidence.

A rush of relief coursed through Katie.

"If anyone from the sheriff's office contacts you about the old man's death, you just refer them to me. We'll work this out. I promise you."

"Thanks, Seth."

"Not a problem. Now, where's that lunch?" he asked.

As Katie pulled out the diminutive sandwiches she'd made for them, a side of pasta salad, and some wavy potato chips, she told him about her desire to find a home for her and her cats.

"I really don't want to go back to an apartment, but I'm not sure I'm a good credit risk for buying a home since I have so much invested in the Alley, two other properties on the Square, and now the warehouse annex."

"That actually might give you a leg up on acquiring financing. But you've already got a lot on your plate."

Katie nodded. "I thought I could live in what now feels like a closet," she said, waving a hand to take in her tiny apartment. "I can't. It's not fair on me, and it's not fair on the cats."

"I hear you," Seth said.

"Margo is willing to co-sign a loan for me, but I don't feel like I can impose upon her to do so."

Seth frowned. "Listen to what you just said. Margo is *willing* to co-sign for a loan. Why don't you just let her do so?"

An amalgam of emotions coursed through Katie and she once again felt close to tears. "Because I'm a grown-up. I'm supposed to be able to navigate by myself at this stage in life."

Seth squinted in Katie's direction. "Even billionaires get bank loans."

"I guess," Katie agreed. "But I also don't want to be mortgaged to the hilt, either."

"You could sell your shares in the building on the Square and in the warehouse. Would that make you feel better?"

"Well, no." Did she want to admit the truth? Yeah, she

could do that with Seth. "It turns out I'm a bit of a control freak."

Seth shook his head, and it looked like he was trying mightily to tamp down a smile. "You don't say."

Katie's eyes widened in distress.

"Yeah, you *are* a bit of a control freak, but your heart is in the right place," Seth explained. "All you've ever wanted for the Alley, its vendors, and the merchants on the Square is to make their lives better—and that extends to the people who visit and shop there, too."

Katie wanted to believe him. But on that day, the ugly shadow of insecurity kept trying to overtake her.

"If Margo can afford to co-sign the loan," and Katie was pretty sure she could, "then let her," Seth advised.

"But—"

"Her son is dead. All she has left as a connection to him is you. Please don't cheat her out of it."

Katie's throat tightened. She'd never looked at the situation from that point of view. "I'm fond of her. I can't say that was true in the past, but she's been not only a good business partner in Tealicious, but now I count her as a friend."

"Then let her continue to be that friend. You don't have to call her mom, but would it kill you if you did?"

Katie hadn't had a mother since the age of six. She never considered ever calling another woman mom. She'd never called her father's beloved aunt by that moniker. It had never occurred to her—or been suggested by the woman—to call Aunt Lizzie anything but her aunt. But calling Chad's mother mom? That was something entirely different.

Wasn't it?

"Just think about it," Seth advised, picking up one of his rolls and taking a bite. His eyes widened as he chewed, conveying his pleasure. Once he swallowed, he spoke. "I don't know what you do with a can of tuna, but they're always the best of those sandwiches I've ever had. What's your secret?"

"I don't have one. They're tuna, mayonnaise, and chopped onion and celery. Oh, and I grind a little fresh black pepper into the mix. It's probably Brad's rolls that make it special."

"Not a chance," Seth said, and took another bite, letting out a groan of pleasure as he chewed.

For the next half hour, they talked about a myriad of subjects, none of them evoking strong emotional reactions. They were just two friends shooting the bull, feeling comfortable in their friendship, and for that, Katie felt grateful.

Finally, Seth looked at his Rolex watch. "Time for me to head back to the office. The whole afternoon is booked."

"Thanks for taking the time to have lunch with me—and act as a trusted counselor."

"What are pseudo-big brothers for?" he asked, and gathered Katie into a loving hug.

And she hugged back, hoping he realized just how much she appreciated him—for himself *and* his expertise.

Seth pulled away. "We've got to do this again soon. Only next time you'll come to my place and I'll make *you* dinner."

"Not having to cook? Call me tonight."

Seth laughed. "I have plans—but it'll be soon."

Plans? Did that mean Seth was back on the dating scene? She hoped so. Losing the man he thought was his soulmate and finding out that the feeling wasn't quite mutual had been a big shock to the village's only lawyer. That he was willing to risk his heart once more was a testament to his strength of character.

"Pet Oran—" Seth's dog "—for me until I can do it myself."

"I will," Seth said.

Katie led him to the studio apartment's outside entrance. "See you soon."

"Count on it," Seth said.

Katie watched as her dear friend descended the stairs and

got into his Mercedes, waving good-bye before he pulled into the Victoria Square lot and drove away.

Katie swallowed down a pang of regret, or was it resolution? Seth never pulled his punches. He'd always been honest with her. She trusted his advice.

As uncomfortable as it might feel, she *would* let Margo help her. But she also decided she had to find a way to help Chad's mother. Just what that entailed, Katie had no clue.

KATIE SPENT the rest of the afternoon visiting the merchants on Victoria Square to personally invite them to the Merchants Association meeting that evening, only to learn that Nona had already done so—mostly by phone or text—with one exception.

It was with trepidation that Katie entered Angelo's Pizzeria. She rarely spoke to her ex-lover, Andy Rust, and since they worked opposite ends of the clock, they rarely ran into each other on the Square. Still, she seemed to know an awful lot about his comings and goings. Several of her vendors had the best of intentions keeping her informed, not understanding— and Katie wasn't about to voice—why the couple had broken up.

But the worst thing about the breakup—besides her broken heart—was that Katie was now forced to only eat frozen pizzas from the grocery store. They were okay, but nothing like a fresh hot pie with a thick crust, homemade sauce, and loaded with cheese and other toppings. Andy also made and sold to-die-for calzones, and his famous cinnamon buns. Those delicious delights were now denied her, too. She could live with that. What she couldn't live with—and had caused their fallout—was his infidelity. She could have forgiven many other sins, but not that one.

Brass bells attached to a leather strap rang out as Katie

entered the shop. The smell of yeasty dough baking nearly lifted her off her feet. Katie didn't know the boy who stood behind the counter. Angelo's had a lot of turnover when it came to personnel, and Andy's most admirable quality was helping kids at risk by giving them a job and mentoring them to be better citizens. He'd been a troubled teen who'd straightened out and had become a successful businessman. Too bad that hadn't extended to his personal life.

Katie read the name tag on the young man's shirt. "Hi, Chris. Is Andy around?"

"Sure he's in the back."

Katie waited, but the teen didn't offer to call him.

"Do you think I could speak to him?" she pushed.

Chris blinked at her. "Oh." He turned and shouted, "Andy. There's a lady here to see you."

Lady. That made Katie feel *old*.

Seconds later, Andy appeared from out of the back room and for a moment Katie's heart pitter-patted. He looked delicious, dressed in a tank top that showed off his toned biceps covered in a thin sheen of sweat. With the ovens heated to 700 degrees, the place was always toasty warm, and Katie's heating bill had been negligible during the winter in the apartment above the shop. However, the summer was another story.

"Hey, Katie," Andy said, taken aback but sounding pleased. He used to call her Sunshine.

"Hey, yourself."

"What brings you here?" Andy asked. Was his tone hopeful?

"Tonight's the Merchants Association's monthly meeting. We'll be discussing the possibility of throwing a Victoria Square Fourth of July picnic. We'd like all the merchants to participate."

Andy's smile melted. "Pizza isn't exactly picnic food."

"No, but it's probably the country's number one junk food."

Andy's gaze narrowed. "That's a pretty nasty slur."

Katie blinked. "Oh, I'm sorry. I just meant—"

"I know what you meant," Andy groused. His whole demeanor had changed, and not for the better.

"I'd like Angelo's Pizzeria to participate in the festivities. It could be a great opportunity for all the Square's merchants."

"Why would I need to be at the meeting? If I choose to participate, wouldn't I just have to open a couple of hours earlier?"

"Well, yes, I guess so."

"So there's no reason for me to be in on a planning session."

Katie sighed. This was the attitude he'd taken during their most recent interactions. He'd first seemed happy to see her, but then turned on her as though it was her fault they'd broken up.

Katie forced a smile. "I wanted to give you the option of being in on the front end of the promotion."

"Thanks, but nah ... I've got better things to do."

Did that include dating someone new? Probably not. And even if he was, it wasn't Katie's business. And as she looked at Andy with his chiseled muscles and seductive sweat she didn't have to fight the urge to kiss him as she had with Ray the day before. Ray, who was balding and at least twenty years older than her. Ray who had never lied to her. Ray, who had been faithful to his wife during their twenty-plus year marriage.

"Okay," Katie said with a shrug. "I'll keep you informed with emails from here on out."

"You do that," Andy said. It almost sounded like a challenge.

"See ya," Katie said and turned toward the door.

"Count on it," Andy said to her back.

Katie left the shop without a backward glance, but like earlier that day, she felt heat on her back as a man watched her walk away.

Chapter Seven

With the exception of Andy, everyone else on the Square turned up at Tealicious for the Merchants Association's meeting expecting to be fed. The leftover tuna salad sliders, as well as the scones and few cookies from that day's Tealicious sales, were soon gone.

Katie quickly re-capped the Association's business from the last meeting before she asked Nona to step forward and describe her vision for the Fourth of July (or thereabouts) event. Since all those in attendance had been forewarned, the ideas flowed so fast and furiously that it made Katie's head spin. Nona—and not Katie—appointed Sue Sweeney to take notes, and everyone gave their opinions on what they thought the event should entail. By the end of the meeting the rudiments of a plan were in place, and it was decided that they'd continue to brainstorm via an email or text chain and convene again in two weeks.

Katie had little to do with the meeting and running it. And the only job assigned to her was to rally the Artisan Alley vendors, causing her to feel more than a little resentful. Maybe Seth was right. Maybe she *was* a control freak. And just maybe it was long past time for her to step down as head of the Merchants Association. The problem had always been that no one else was interested in taking on the job. Perhaps that had also changed, as Nona seemed more than willing to take on the task as leader. She wasn't a pleasant person. She would rule the Association with an iron fist and the decisions she made would be tilted toward her own best interests rather than for the sake of the Square and its merchants. Maybe this was something she should discuss with Margo, who'd been elected to handle the publicity for the summer event. It made sense, as Margo's expertise was in public relations. Ray was assigned the job of security, thanks to his years as a police officer before he'd become a homicide detective, a role he seemed to be pleased to accept.

On the Tealicious end, Katie and the other food vendors were supposed to duke out the items they'd sell to not duplicate the fare. She'd leave that task to Brad—and perhaps Sophie Davenport, once she started her summer internship.

More and more Katie was beginning to feel less connected to the Square. Was that the reason she felt the urge to find a living space apart from the now-thriving business district?

As the meeting broke up, Katie began to clear the tables, stack plates, and collect stained coffee mugs. It was Ray who stepped in to help, as Nona was lecturing Margo on some point.

"Great meeting," Ray said, following Katie into the Tealicious kitchen with a tray filled with soiled plates.

"Yeah. Great," Katie said, unable to keep the melancholy from her tone.

"Is something wrong?" Ray asked.

Katie shook her head. "I've just got a lot on my mind."

Ray nodded. "Don't worry about what happened at Margo's on Saturday night," he said, totally misunderstanding where her depression dwelt.

"Well, it *is* a worry," she said. It was, but not as much as her diminished role in what might prove to be the second biggest promotion for the year on Victoria Square.

"I never thought of Nona Fiske as a leader, but she sure took control of the meeting tonight," Ray remarked.

"Yeah," Katie said halfheartedly as she rinsed dishes before placing them in one of the restaurant's dishwashers.

"Hey, are you okay?" Ray asked.

"Me?" Katie asked, startled.

"Yeah. You don't sound good."

"Like I said, I've got some things on my mind," Katie admitted.

"If you need someone to vent to, you know I'm here," Ray offered.

Katie managed to smile. "You're a good friend, Ray."

"I like to think so," he said with that goofy, crooked grin that she'd first found annoying but now thought of as endearing.

Katie's answering smile was short lived. Ray was dating another woman. For all Katie knew, he was serious about his relationship with Carol Rigby. But that didn't mean he couldn't be her friend. Adding someone else to that roster could only make her feel better. So, why didn't she unload her thoughts and listen to his counsel?

She changed the subject.

"Is there anything new in the Maxwell Preston case?" Katie asked, steeling herself against an answer she might not like to hear.

Ray looked away. "Carol and I don't talk about such things."

"Don't talk about them—or you do and *can't* talk about them to someone on the outside?" Katie asked.

Ray shook his head. "Since I left the sheriff's office, I'm not in the loop. That's the way it should be," Ray said, but Katie got the feeling he wished it wasn't so.

Katie nodded and needed to change the subject to one more closely aligned with Ray's interests.

"Brad and I discussed bringing Sophie back to Tealicious over the summer."

Ray instantly brightened. "And?"

"I want to bring her back. Brad and I both agree she's a gifted pastry artist. But there is a problem."

Ray frowned. "And that is?"

"Hero worship," Katie said succinctly.

Ray's frown deepened.

"Sophie's got a crush on Brad," Katie said flatly.

"Well, he *is* a big-name chef."

"Yeah, but he's very uncomfortable with her hero worship. He's reluctant to have her back because of it."

"Oh, geeze," Ray breathed.

"I'd like to have her back because I think it would be good for her *and* for Tealicious to benefit from her blossoming talent."

"But?" Ray asked.

"He's just not interested." At Ray's confused expression, Katie elaborated. "Brad is flattered by her attention," she fudged.

Ray's brow furrowed even deeper.

"He was burned by his last relationship and wants to focus on his career," Katie explained, pretty sure she spoke for Brad on that front. "Someone has to speak to her about the situation, whether it's you or me. Brad doesn't want to go there," Katie explained.

Ray's expression darkened. Nobody wants to hear that their baby is ugly, even if they're as pretty as a picture. But ugly was where it was at when it came to talking truth.

They looked at each other for long seconds before Ray cleared his throat before speaking again—and changing the subject. "This summer promotion sounds like it could be something we can use to promote the Square for years to come," he said, handing Katie another soiled plate to rinse.

"It sure could. And who would've believed it would be Nona to suggest it?"

"Amen!" Ray agreed.

It took another minute or two before all the dishes were stacked in the dishwasher, and Katie added the detergent and hit the start button.

"Thanks for your help," she said brightly.

"It was nothing," Ray demurred.

Katie gestured toward the swinging door that led back to Tealicious's dining room. Ray preceded her. By the time they entered the room, they saw that everyone but Margo had already left the restaurant. She sat at one of the tables overlooking the Square with a yellow pad of paper before her, making notes. She looked up as they approached.

"Wasn't that the best meeting we've had in a long time?" Margo gushed.

Katie found it hard to smile but somehow managed to force one and swallowed hard before she spoke. "It sure was."

Ray's gaze flicked between Margo and Katie, and Katie wondered what was going on in his mind. She didn't have a chance to find out.

"Uh, I guess I'd better head for home," Ray said. "The girls were fending for themselves for supper tonight. I wouldn't be surprised if they've roasted a turkey."

Was that a dig at the poor fare on offer that evening? Well, no one else had offered to feed the group for free—and on multiple occasions.

Probably not. It wouldn't be like Ray to even hint at such a thing. But was he likely to scrounge his fridge once he got home?

That wasn't Katie's problem, but she felt bad that he might leave her establishment hungry.

The others? Maybe not.

And she felt like crap about that, too.

"Have a good evening," Ray told the women.

"You, too," they chorused, and watched as Ray left the building. They followed his progress across the parking lot to retrieve his car behind his shop. Once he was out of sight, Katie sat down opposite Margo.

"I'm so excited about the picnic extravaganza," Margo proclaimed, and there was absolute joy in her voice. "But I sense you aren't."

"Oh, I'm pumped for it. It's just—" But then she didn't elaborate.

Margo frowned. "Darling girl, what's on your mind?"

"Well, for one thing," Katie said and swallowed, wondering if she really wanted to say the words aloud. But then, she thought about what Seth had told her earlier that day. But then she decided to just go for it. "I know we weren't exactly friends in the past—"

"And that was entirely my fault," Margo interrupted.

Katie shook her head. "We were both vying for Chad's attention. Isn't that kind of expected?"

Margo sighed. "I suppose."

Katie forced herself to continue. "Be that as it may, I was wondering if you'd be open to me calling you … Mom."

Margo's mouth dropped open in shock and the women stared at each other for long seconds. Then Margo's eyes welled with shiny tears. She had to swallow a few times before she could speak. "I would be honored if you would." She reached out to clutch Katie's hand, giving it an affectionate squeeze.

Katie's eyes also filled and the women sat there for long seconds just staring at each other, smiling. This wasn't the time for Katie to tell Margo that she would accept her offer of helping her finance a home. Maybe that wouldn't come for a year or more. At that moment, Katie was more interested in strengthening the bond the women had been working to establish.

Katie cleared her throat. "I haven't had a mom since I was six. It might take me a little while to fully get used to the idea, but I'd really like us to forge that kind of bond."

"As would I," Margo said, her voice more than a little strained.

Katie grinned. "Then I've not only got a business partner, but a family. It's been a long time since I had a family."

"All it takes is two," Margo affirmed and gave Katie's hand another squeeze.

"Great." Again Katie swallowed. "Now, tell me everything you think will work for the Square's summer promotion and what you suggest we could do to make it work."

"Oh, darling girl, settle in for a long gab fest, because we've got a lot to talk about."

WHEN KATIE RETIRED to her studio apartment that evening, she felt a lot better not only about her relationship with Margo, but the Square's summer promotion. Without realizing it, Margo had talked her down from her fatalistic ideas about the event. Did Katie want the burden of making the gala work? No. If the whole thing were a fiasco, it would be on Nona's neck — not hers. If it succeeded, then all the merchants on the Square would benefit, and wasn't that what she'd wanted all along? Now it was Katie's job to figure out how to turn the bash into a win for the Artisans Alley vendors. She'd invite a few of her top vendors to tea to discuss it. And, of course, Brad would be making the better part of the decisions on how Tealicious could participate. And when Sunday arrived, Katie might just take a few hours away from the Alley to visit houses for sale in the area that were open for viewing — just to get her feet wet.

The next morning, Katie again began her day in the Tealicious kitchen, telling Brad all that had transpired the evening before at the Merchants Association meeting.

"Sounds like this could be a good thing for everyone on the Square," he commented, placing the ingredients for bread dough into the big mixer and hitting the switch.

As Katie measured out the ingredients for that day's scones (apricot walnut), she changed the subject.

"I'm thinking about moving off the Square," she remarked offhandedly.

"Really?" Brad asked, looking up to catch her gaze.

Katie nodded. "If I was living alone, the apartment over the shop would be perfect, but I feel so guilty when it comes to my cats. The only window in the place is a skylight. It brings in a lot of great light, but the cats can't watch birds, squirrels, or even a leaf falling in autumn. Della's had some adjustment problems," she said without elaborating. "They need more than six hundred square feet of living space to be happy. And frankly, so do I."

"Tiny house living isn't for you, huh?" Brad asked.

"I think a tiny house would have *more* room, but you're right. When—" and here her throat caught. She began again. "When Andy and I broke up, and I knew I couldn't live above the pizzeria any longer, it seemed like kismet that I should live over Tealicious. Now, months later, I have to admit defeat. The problem is I'm so overextended with owning the Alley, a half share in Tealicious, and shares in the building on the Square, and the warehouse, I feel like I can't even afford to buy a pack of gum, let alone a home in the village."

Brad looked skeptical. "Surely, with all those assets, any bank would *love* to give you a mortgage."

"Maybe not."

"Because if you *were* to move," Brad said casually, "I'd be interested in living above the shop."

Katie stared at the man, taken aback. "Really?"

"You bet. I'm not happy where I am, and…."

He didn't finish the sentence but Katie could guess where this conversation was about to go.

"But you want to save money to open your own restaurant."

Brad shrugged, looking away. "Some day."

That took big bucks. More than what Katie was paying Brad as Tealicious's manager and chef. And she also knew that his good friends Nick Ferrell and Don Parsons were multimillionaires. They could easily bankroll their friend with anything he wanted to do, whether they were active or silent partners in the deal.

Katie swallowed down a pang of disappointment. Of course, Brad had higher aspirations than making bread, cookies, and scones in a little backwater village like McKinlay Mill. He'd been a master chef in a major metropolitan city in the past and would be again. She'd known when hiring him that Tealicious was just a way station. And, of course, she would wish him well in anything he wanted to do in the future. That he would downgrade his life to just six hundred square feet—even for just a year or so—was a testament to his commitment to reach his goals.

"Maybe you're right," Katie said, trying to sound confident. "I thought I might start looking at what's available locally this weekend. You know, just to get an idea of what the market is like." It was more likely that if she *did* move that Katie would end up in the same apartment complex where she'd lived with Chad when they were saving up to buy the old Webster Mansion on the Square, which was now Sassy Sally's Bed & Breakfast. Could she even afford the first and last months' rent in an apartment when it cost her nothing to live above Tealicious?

"Why don't you talk to someone at the bank to get an idea of what you might be eligible for?" Brad encouraged.

"Great idea," Katie said, her cheerful tone seeming to negate her honest conviction that she was destined to die alone and impoverished. Or maybe she'd end up a millionaire at an old age when she no longer felt the need or desire to travel or take on a great adventure. The thought depressed her. She admired Margo. who had been totally alone in the world until emotionally adopting Katie. But here she was not only taking on a whole new life, but also enthusiastic about opening a gallery. Yes, she'd be featuring her dead son's work, but she had ambitions beyond that—to showcase the work of other local artists. There was no doubt that Margo had a change of heart toward Katie after Chad's death. Was it that she realized she *was* so totally alone and didn't want to die that way, or had something else caused her change of heart? Whatever it was, Katie was glad for it. All her life, she'd yearned for a mom and dad. The dad part would never happen, but she felt hopeful about her future with Margo.

She quietly contemplated this while mixing ingredients and baking. And next up, she'd make her circuits around the massive parking lot, something else she enjoyed about living on Victoria Square. See, there were perks to her current quarters, Katie reminded herself. But in the long run, it wasn't quite enough.

After taking her scones out of the oven, she placed the tray on one of the big rolling racks to cool, leaving the building for her daily walk, glad she wouldn't have to run into Andy. He— or more likely, his assistant manager—might be placing the raised cinnamon buns in the ovens or delivering them locally. She'd never met up with him on one of her walks, but she often ran into Moonbeam Carruthers or Don or Nick walking their dogs. Those were days she enjoyed. Talking and laughing with friends, petting happy canines with wagging tails and pink tongues ready to give doggy kisses. If she moved, would she ever feel that simple joy again?

Of course, with four business interests on the Square, she would always have a reason to return on a daily basis, so her reason for choosing not to live on the Square was spot on.

And, of course, on that day, she didn't run into any of her friends during her walk. But once again, the lights were on in Wood U. What was Ray carving that day? Another Santa? Laminating different kinds of wood for the top of a jewelry box? Fabricating a wooden house like he had for her in the shape of Sassy Sally's—what would have been her English Ivy Inn? It was with a pang of regret that Katie felt as she passed Wood U for the second time and headed for her Artisan's Alley office. It was time to go to work.

Chapter Eight

News of the upcoming summer promotion had already spread among the Artisans Alley vendors. Katie was greeted by a group of vendors who were eager to hear about how they could participate in the promotion.

"Hey, hey!" Katie chided them, "give me a chance to get a cup of coffee, and we can sit around the table and talk."

There weren't enough chairs for everyone around the vintage chrome and Formica table, so several vendors sat on the counter where the coffeemaker and related accouterments lived. Seated at the table were Rose Nash, Vance Ingram, Gwen Hardy, the Alley's resident weaver, Liz Meier, who specialized in stained glass, and Edie Silver, who crafted beautiful faux flower arrangements, among other things.

"Tell all," Rose said. She was a seventy-something woman with blonde curls fortified with a liberal amount of Aqua Net. Her specialty was beaded jewelry. Rose sold well during the holidays. The rest of the year—not so much. However, as a lonely widow, she could be depended upon to work far more than the two days required of each vendor during any given month.

The crowd was quiet as Katie related everything that was discussed the evening before.

"We can't very well set up shop in the Square or the parking lot. There isn't enough room for more than ten or twelve vendors. And it wouldn't be fair if only a few of them were allowed to participate," Vance pointed out. Vance had a neatly trimmed, if lengthy, beard and was often confused with Santa by small children who visited the Alley.

"We could hold a lottery," Katie said. "It's something we should discuss in more detail. I thought we should erect a large sign—and I'm talking up to billboard size—to entice people into the Alley. If it's a hot day, we at least have air conditioning…in most of the Alley," she amended. "We'd have to figure out what kind of graphic to go with the sign."

Heads nodded in agreement, but no one seemed to have any idea of what that graphic should be.

"I guess we should all put on our thinking caps," Rose commented.

"That wouldn't hurt," Katie remarked.

"We should have an Alley meeting to discuss it," Gwen suggested.

"Great idea," Liz seconded. "When can you schedule that, Katie?"

Katie forced a smile. "I'll look at my calendar and let everyone know about it with a sign in the tag room." Every shift, someone worked in the Alley's tag room—where the price tags were taken off each of the items sold and taped onto quarter-pieces of sheets of copy paper, that way vendors could compare the tags with the printout Katie provided. The room also contained a hutch with pigeon-holes where the tags—and the weekly checks—were available for pick-up after each week's sales.

"I think we should start brainstorming now," Rose said.

"That's a great idea. But do you think we should wait until

the meeting with those interested in participating before we do so?" Katie asked.

"Maybe we should," Liz agreed, but she didn't sound confident.

"I think we should start now. Then we'd have something to present to the group," Edie said.

"Good point," Vance agreed.

The group brainstormed for the next hour or so, with some dropping out at opening time to work their shifts on the Alley's sales floor.

Katie took notes, and by the time they broke up, the group had decided to hold one of Artisans Alley's rare vendor meetings so the collective could choose how to proceed. That was fine with Katie. Although....

Was she just a bit petulant because others wanted to take the lead? The idea of possibly (or possibly not) moving, Maxwell Preston's death, and getting the Victoria Square Annex on its feet would be more than enough for anyone to handle—including Katie. She didn't need to prove she was some kind of Superwoman to the world at large, let alone herself.

As Katie left the vendors' lounge, she noticed a tired-looking newspaper on the counter. The main story was about the nation's economy, but the sidebar's headline read M.E. SAYS IT WAS MURDER.

Katie picked up the paper and continued to her office, where she sat down to read the story. The paper was from the previous day, and the story was about Maxwell Preston's death. While it didn't tell her much more than she already knew, two things were apparent in the last lines of the brief update. First, that alcohol was not a factor in Preston's death. The other had a chilling effect on her: *Police have no motive for the murder.*

First, she felt relief that Margo was off the hook for over-serving wine and spirits at her party. But it brought back to mind that someone at the party had probably done the deed, and most of them worked or owned property on Victoria Square.

Katie made a list of the attendees. Margo was, of course, the host, and Katie and Brad were there not only as friends but as the catering staff. Then there was Conrad Stratton, the Square's wine merchant, and his wife, Gilda Ringwald-Stratton, whose gift basket shop joined his; Sue Sweeney who owned Sweet Sue's Confectionery; Ray Davenport and his date (that descriptor caused Katie to scowl...just a little) Carol Rigby; Charlotte Booth of Booth's Jellies and Jams; Nona Fiske, Nick and Don from Sassy Sally's B&B; Paula Mathews, owner of the Heaven's Gate angel shop, Moonbeam Carruthers, Vance and Janey Ingram, and, of course, Maxwell Preston. Ann Tanner came alone, as her husband had to get up early to prepare the dough for the morning's pastries at their bakery. Seth Landers had been invited but hadn't attended due to having had a previous engagement.

Katie sat back in her chair and thought about that evening. She and Brad spent an inordinate amount of time fussing over the food, so she hadn't had an opportunity to really speak with several of the guests other than to say hello, including Paula and Ann. As Preston had never been a presence on the Square, did anyone actually know him or had even met him before that evening? Who could have held a grudge against a stranger?

Right off the bat, Nona Fiske came to mind. Preston's building was Nona's next-door neighbor, and it was the Square's eyesore. Nona had bedeviled the owners of the tea shop known as Afternoon Tea, Tealicious's predecessor. She'd relentlessly harassed them over what Nona deemed as parking infractions. Once Katie and Margo bought the establishment, Nona had subsided into silence on that account, probably because she figured out that Katie refused to be bullied. But even Nona wasn't capable of killing someone over something so petty. Then again, Nona *was* petty.

Katie dismissed the notion. There had to be some deeper motive for killing the old man.

The only person who'd attended the party and admitted knowing Preston was Moonbeam Carruthers. She'd spoken about the older gentleman with admiration, relating to how, after decades, he still mourned his dead wife, regularly buying flowers for her grave.

Katie thought about what Preston's daughter, Phoebe, had told her the morning after the murder. Her mother had held ceramics classes in the building decades before, and his emotional attachment alone kept her father from selling the building. However, for all that sentiment, Preston hadn't kept the building in good repair. And as had been mentioned, it was probably too far gone to save. The building would likely be razed—before or after it was sold—post probate.

Could Preston have made enemies when he owned the drug store up on Main Street? That didn't seem likely, but it wasn't something she could rule out, either. His tenure in that capacity was well before Katie took up residence in the charming village. Did he still live in the village or had he moved away before his death? She hadn't thought to ask his daughter that question.

Katie wondered if the local newspaper had ever written about the man. That little rag had been available only in an online edition for the past few years, but she wondered if the office—or perhaps the local library—would have archived the older issues. She'd make it a point to find out.

Katie needed to speak with Margo about the dead man. She wasn't clear on how Margo had tracked him down. Yes, to talk about the property's future—but the invitation to the party had been made just to soften the man up. When Margo turned up the charm, men paid attention. Margo had that gift—something Katie knew she'd never possess.

Taking out her purse, Katie retrieved her phone and texted

LORRAINE BARTLETT

Margo, asking to meet her at Tealicious for lunch near the end of the day's service.

See you there, Margo texted back.

Good.

With that scheduled, Katie turned her attention to her computer. Just then, a soft knock on her door interrupted her musings. *Now what?* she thought, but she opened it, surprised to see the younger Davenport sisters. Their demeanor toward her had softened since winter, and while they didn't yet call her a friend, they were at least cordial, which was a lot considering their ages.

"Can we talk?" Sadie asked, sounding timid. Sasha, her younger sister, stood behind her, looking just as cowed.

"Sure, come on in, girls."

The office was too small for more than Katie's office chair and a metal folding chair, so Sadie sat while Sasha leaned against one of the khaki-colored file cabinets Katie had never gotten around to painting a softer tone.

"Shouldn't you be in school?" Katie asked.

Sasha rolled her eyes. "There's some kind of teacher's meeting today. We've got the day off."

"Good for you. Now, what can I do for you?"

"Well," Sadie began. Apparently she'd been designated the sisters' spokesperson. "Dad said there's going to be a big promotion on the Square this summer, and we want to be a part of it."

"In what way?" Katie asked.

"Well, that's the thing. We're not exactly sure. Since you know just about everything that goes on around here, we figured you might be able to find a place for us."

The girls had started their own business as window dressers. They hadn't exactly been successful at it, but they did have an eye for design, and Katie was sure one day they'd own a fantastically successful enterprise dedicated to interior design. But for now, they were just a couple of high school kids who were looking to gain experience.

Katie thought about Sadie's query for a few moments. "You know, I think I might have an idea."

The girls' eyes widened in anticipation.

"The Artisans Alley vendors are going to participate in the promotion, and we've discussed making a big sign to promote it. We're talking something *really* big on canvas—perhaps ten or twelve feet in height—and longer in width. We haven't come up with a concept yet, but once we do, I'd be willing to work with you girls to pull it off. Would you be willing to call outside vendors who make vinyl signs that can be staked, get prices, and present it to the group at a meeting?"

The sisters exchanged excited glances. "We're good at that kind of stuff. We've contacted vendors to find bags and other stuff for our dad's shop. We could do that. Not a problem," Sadie said excitedly, although Sasha didn't look quite as convinced. Perhaps her older sister had done more of that work. In any case, Katie wanted to encourage the girls' entrepreneurial spirit.

"Great. So, I'll let you know when the meeting is, and after the vendors decide on a concept, I'll work with you girls to figure out what we need. I've seen sketches you've done, and been tremendously impressed, so don't worry about having to sell yourselves to the vendors. I feel confident you can pull this off."

Sadie's smile was wide. Sasha's wasn't.

"But in the meantime, I have another job for you girls—if you want it."

"A job?" Sasha asked eagerly. "For real money?"

Katie nodded. "The library has bound volumes of the local Penny Saver, old newspapers, etcetera. I want to know if any of them have articles concerning Maxwell Preston, the former owner of the pharmacy on Main Street."

Sadie frowned. "That was the guy you tried to save at Margo's party last week, right?"

"Yes," Katie said sadly.

"Dad said you'd tried your best but that it was too late. That he drowned."

The girls obviously hadn't read the news stories that proclaimed the man had been murdered.

"Yes," she said succinctly. "I'd be willing to pay you girls to read through those volumes to find anything you can about Mr. Preston."

Sadie gave her sister a sideways glance. Sasha nodded. These girls really were business-minded.

"How much?" Sasha asked.

Katie named a price.

Once again, the girls glanced at each other and seemed to be communing telepathically before Sadie turned and faced Katie. "We'll do it. When do you want the results?"

"As soon as you can do it."

"We've got the rest of the day free," Sasha said. "We can start today."

"Great," Katie said.

Katie found herself feeling antsy after the girls left her office. The best remedy for that was a walk around Victoria Square. She didn't wear a pedometer, but she had a feeling she'd already met the ten-thousand-step goal that people who tried to keep fit used as a benchmark. Still, she was the boss, and if she wanted to take a break, who was going to criticize her?

Don't answer that, Katie thought as she snuck out Artisans Alley's back door.

As Angelo's Pizzeria wouldn't open until four, she decided to pass by it first because then she wouldn't see or be seen by Andy. She always felt a pang of sadness when she thought about him. They'd shared so much in the three years they'd been together. Sometimes it felt like they'd made a better couple than she and Chad, until he'd cheated on her. Once a cheater, always a cheater her beloved Aunt Lizzie used to say. Had that phrase colored Katie's thinking and hardened her heart? Maybe, but the words rang true, too.

As Katie approached the angel shop, which was recently renamed Heaven's Gate, she wondered if she should stop in to speak with Paula Mathews. She hadn't said more than a hello to the woman at Margo's party.

On impulse, Katie mounted the steps and entered what some on the Square called a death shop.

Paula had lost her daughter a few years before and had found comfort in the idea of angels, which was the impetus for her owning and stocking the shop. In a way, it *was* a death store because Paula offered many ways one could remember a loved one who'd passed.

Paula waited on a customer but waved as Katie entered. While Paula was busy, Katie studied the shop's inventory. There were one-of-a-kind cremation urns, which seemed a little macabre, but there were also many angel figurines, plaques with platitudes, framed poetry, and a year-round Christmas tree adorned with angels of glass, wood, and resin. And the displays didn't just favor humans, for there were ornaments and remembrances for lost dogs and cats, too. A one-stop shop for grief, Katie thought sourly. The things on display didn't make her feel any better about the losses she'd suffered, but she could see how they might give comfort when given by a loving soul who wished only to help heal a broken heart.

Finally, Paula wrapped a figurine in paper, stowed it into a gift bag, and sent her patron on her way.

"Hey, Katie, how can I help you?"

Paula belonged to the Victoria Square Merchants Association but missed most of their meetings. She didn't mix much with the other merchants but paid her yearly dues and sometimes sent an email after the monthly meeting to comment on one point or another after receiving the meeting's minutes.

"I'm sorry I didn't get a chance to connect with you at Margo's party on Saturday," Katie said. "I'm glad you could attend. We don't see you often enough."

Paula brushed a lock of her shoulder-length gray streaked blonde hair behind one ear. "I'm a pretty private person. Especially since…." Her teenage daughter's death some five or six years before. "But recently, I've decided that I need to get out more. I truly enjoyed the party. It turns out I have more in common with several of the other merchants on the Square than I thought. I might even come to the next meeting."

"We'd love to have you. I don't think you've even seen the inside of Tealicious."

"You're right. So many of my customers have sung its praises, I really should make the effort. It's just been hard," she explained.

There was no timeline for grief. Katie was a child when she'd lost her parents. She'd been devastated, but her sense of loss hit even harder when her Aunt Lizzie passed, the woman who'd stepped up to raise her. The elderly lady was brusque, old-fashioned, and Katie had loved that old woman unconditionally. Sometimes, she blocked out memories of her aunt because such an intense sense of loss would wash over her like a tidal wave. Other times, that were happening more often these days, she remembered the old lady with a swell of unbridled affection.

These days, her grief was over the death of her relationship with Andy. But he wasn't dead. And Katie knew she'd get over that loss—and hopefully sooner rather than later.

"I was so sad to hear about poor Mr. Preston's death. Another soul lost," Paula said, shaking her head.

"Did you know him?"

"Oh, sure. I've lived in the village my whole life. He

dispensed prescriptions since I was a child." Paula's expression turned pensive. "He always seemed so focused. I was kind of afraid of him when I was little, but later when I couldn't get a quick appointment with my primary care physician for myself, or needed advice for my sick daughter and I couldn't get in to see the pediatrician, I could always ask him for recommendations on how to handle Mandy's fevers or other minor ailments."

These days, it seemed a lot easier when Paula spoke about her daughter, Amanda. That hadn't always been so.

"What was so scary about him?" Katie asked.

Paula smiled. "His beard. It wasn't like Santa's—more like the devil's, or at least from the pictures I'd seen as a child. It was pitch black with a V of white right under his lower lip. But as he got older, his beard went snowy white—more like Santa. And, like a guardian angel, I don't think he ever turned away a customer who couldn't afford a prescription. That may have been a reason he ended up selling the pharmacy. He cared that much about the people in the village."

Katie frowned. That description diverged from what Preston's daughter had conveyed. Or had age softened the old man? Lots of fathers and daughters clashed—especially during the teen years. Often, those conflicts resolved themselves, but sometimes they didn't. And, after all, there was no owner's manual when it came to parenting.

"Did you speak with him during the party?" Katie asked.

Paula's expression darkened. "Only to say hello."

"Oh?" Katie probed.

"Yeah," Paula said flatly.

Katie wasn't sure how to proceed. "Did he say something that upset you?" she guessed.

Paula's mouth twitched. "Well, kind of," she admitted. "I knew he was a widower. The whole village knew it. He could have used counseling over it—like so many of us who've suffered the loss of a loved one."

"But?" Katie pressed.

"I asked him how his daughter was." She stopped and swallowed.

"And he said?" Katie asked.

Paula's voice trembled. "I don't give a shit about that bitch." Paula's eyes filled with tears. She'd lost her daughter, and Preston hadn't cared for his, which only confirmed what Phoebe Preston had told Katie.

"Wow," she said quietly.

"I'd sell my soul directly to Satan himself if I could have my baby girl back for even one minute," Paula choked, "and the vitriol with which that man spoke about his daughter...." Her voice caught in her throat, and her eyes filled with tears.

"I met her," Katie said.

Paula looked up.

"Her name is Phoebe. She seemed like a perfectly nice woman, but she did say she'd had a difficult childhood."

"How sad," Paula said with a shake of her head. Katie was positive Paula had given her daughter a lovely life and that it wasn't guilt that had caused her to open Heaven's Gate, but more in tribute for the love she felt for her lost child.

But then it occurred to Katie that the bad blood between Preston and his daughter could have inspired Phoebe to —

Did Katie dare think the woman could commit patricide?

Her impression of Phoebe was that the woman felt more regret than animosity toward her father after years of apathy — if not neglect. But then sometimes people were great actors. They could say one thing and feel — and act out — something entirely different.

Could Phoebe have smacked her father on the back of the head and pushed him over the dock and into the lake?

First, she'd have needed to know her father was attending the party at Margo's rental home. She'd have had to approach the old man surreptitiously and then attack him from behind, sending him to his doom.

For all the bitterness Phoebe Preston had spouted against her parents, Katie didn't sense the woman was a murderer. If nothing else, Katie got the impression Phoebe had longed to receive even the slightest gesture of affection from her father. And now she would never get it.

But now, knowing how Preston had spoken ill of this daughter to others, would Carol Rigby consider Phoebe a possible suspect in her father's death?

Much to her chagrin, perhaps Katie should do the same.

Chapter Nine

Katie's pace was considerably slower after leaving Heaven's Gate and continued east on the Square, passing Tealicious, The Quiet Quilter, and the derelict building Maxwell Preston had owned, before coming face-to-face with Tanner's Cafe and Bakery. As it was mid-afternoon and after the lunch crowd, Katie hoped she could speak to Ann Tanner, who'd also been at Margo's housewarming party. Katie wasn't exactly sure what she'd say but figured she'd come up with something.

Upon opening the door, Katie was enveloped with the heavenly aroma of baking—yeasty and sweet, like Angelo's pizzeria when Andy baked a batch of his cinnamon buns to deliver to the village's grocery store. She hadn't had one of those buns in months. They were hard on the waistline but passed so easily over the tongue.

No one stood behind the large refrigerated glass counter, so Katie called out, "Hello!"

"Be right there," came a female voice. Ann Tanner burst through the swinging door separating the kitchen from the shop's retail space. "Katie! Hey, what can I get you?"

Katie eyed the case before her. "How about one of those decadent-looking brownies topped with walnuts."

"Sure thing," Ann said, donned a plastic glove, plucked one of the confections, and reached for one of the white bakery bags. She'd correctly guessed that Katie wouldn't eat it on site.

Katie reached into her pocket, where she always kept a few bucks—just in case—and paid for her selection.

"That was some party Margo gave on Saturday, wasn't it?" Ann said.

"Yes and no," Katie remarked.

Ann's expression soured. "Yeah, I guess it ended kind of brutally for you, but I left before all the drama, so I can honestly say I had a great time." She let out a sigh as she gave Katie her change. "I so seldom have a chance to attend anything that approaches a party that I was glad when Jordan said he'd take care of the shop so I could attend. Other than the Merchants Association meetings, I haven't had a night out of harness in years."

Katie had too often heard that complaint. And, since her break-up with Andy, she'd felt the same way. Although in her case, because of their work schedules, they'd had to connect at Del's Diner for lunches instead of romantic dinners.

"Did you have a chance to speak with Maxwell Preston at the party?" Katie asked.

Like Paula Matthews, Ann's facial expression took a downward turn. "Kind of," she admitted.

"Oh?" Katie asked innocently.

"I acknowledged his presence," Ann said coldly. Did she have a beef with Preston?

"It doesn't sound like you were friends," Katie ventured.

"Definitely not!" Ann said vehemently.

"Can I ask why?" Katie asked.

If possible, Ann's expression turned even darker.

Ann seemed to weigh the request before answering. "Mr.

Preston wasn't the only pharmacist on duty at his store, so I can't say it was *him*, but I once brought a prescription to be filled and a mistake was made."

That didn't sound good.

"What happened?" Katie asked.

"I had a violent reaction that landed me in the emergency room. I looked into filing a lawsuit, but this was before everything was computerized, and it was argued that the doctor's poor handwriting was to blame for the pharmacy's interpretation of the dosage."

It must have been quite a while ago, Katie reasoned, since now all prescriptions in New York were required to be filed electronically.

"Did you blame Mr. Preston personally for your reaction?" Katie asked.

"I got the prescription from *his* pharmacy. He owned the place. If nothing else, he *should* have accepted the blame." she said adamantly.

Was her one bad experience with Preston's Pharmacy enough to hold it against the man—and a strong enough motive—to kill him for it?

That didn't seem likely, as Ann hadn't died, nor suffered any long-term negative effects.

"I'm sorry you had to go through that," Katie said sincerely.

"Yes, well...it *was* a long time ago," Ann remarked. "But I don't appreciate that awful woman detective from the sheriff's office continually interrogating me about my interactions with Mr. Preston."

"Continually?" Katie asked.

"Yes, she's called or stopped in to speak with me three times now. It's almost as though she wants to pin his death on me."

It was an unusual admission. Carol hadn't contacted Katie since she'd filed her official statement. That either meant she believed Katie's version of the events of that night or she was plotting to arrest Katie at the earliest possible moment. Katie didn't trust Carol Rigby as far as she could spit—which wasn't far. And she didn't for a moment believe that anything Ray Davenport might say in her defense would be taken seriously. On the contrary, Carol came across as extremely jealous. And it probably didn't help that the younger Davenport girls, who didn't want *anyone* dating their father, did everything they could to annoy the detective—even if that meant throwing Katie under the bus as some kind of sacrificial lamb just to grate on Carol's nerves.

"Well, at least you had a good time at Margo's party," Katie said.

Ann immediately brightened. "You bet. I studied everything you and Brad did on the catering end. Don't be surprised if you see me try to replicate some of those dishes for our party tray customers."

Katie wasn't happy to hear that admission, but she wasn't about to get angry over Ann potentially poaching Brad's menu. Ann was a talented baker, but she was no Brad Andrews. And she wasn't even as accomplished as Sophie Davenport, who had an incredibly bright future ahead of her in the culinary world.

"I take it as a compliment that you'd want to emulate us instead of coming up with your own recipes," Katie said sweetly.

Ann's expression darkened. "We have plenty of unique recipes."

"Of course you do. Like the marvelous brownie I'll be devouring as soon as I get back to Artisans Alley and make myself a pot of tea. Everything tastes better when you've got a freshly brewed cup of tea to go with it."

"Coffee, in my case," Ann said offhandedly.

"We must get together soon to decide what Tealicious and

Tanner's should sell on the Square during the big summer promotion. To shine, we should each have unique items on sale to entice customers to our respective businesses."

"Yeah," Ann said simply, but her tone negated her positive answer.

So, Ann felt Tanner's competed with Tealicious. Well, may the best business win. This only enhanced Katie's already competitive nature. If this was to be a race between the two businesses, she was determined to win. She and Brad had a lot to think about during the planning process for the summer extravaganza.

"I'm looking forward to ironing out the details for the Square's summer picnic. I think it could be a boon for all our businesses."

"I'm for anything that brings attention to Victoria Square."

"As am I," Katie remarked. "We'll talk again soon," she promised.

"Amen," Ann said.

Katie exited the building and didn't look back.

As Katie continued on her walk, she dipped into each of the other establishments on the Square to do a little nosing around.

Katie entered Sweet Sue's Confectionery and the aroma of chocolate practically lifted her off her feet.

"What can I do for you?" Sue Sweeney asked.

"Just checking in to see what you think about the idea of a summer extravaganza."

"If it bring in customers, I'm more than fine with it. People seem to think a candy shop only deals with chocolate—which melts in the heat, but I can offer them so much more," Sue asserted. To prove her point, she directed Katie to take in her handmade gum drops, hard candies, and toffees. Katie bought a half pound of her favorite butterscotch candies to put in the jar on her desk before moving next door to speak to Charlotte Booth, of Booth's Jellies and Jams.

"Hey, Katie," Charlotte greeted her, but she seemed anything but jolly.

"Are you okay?" Katie ask, noting Charlotte's bloodshot eyes.

The woman sniffed. "Just seasonal allergies. They make my eyes—and nose—just a little red." She sniffed again. "Now, what can I do for you?"

"Just wondering how you feel about the Nona's big summer promotion."

"I'm all for it. I usually do quite well in July, but then the August slump arrives."

"I hear you," Katie said in commiseration.

They spoke for a few minutes about the event before Katie bought a jar of gooseberry jam, which she'd never had before. There was no harm in culinary experimentation!

Bypassing Wood U and The Flower Child, Katie headed straight for Gilda's Gourmet Basket. Gilda's most lucrative sales came at Christmas. Still, she kept her business going throughout the rest of the year by depending on made-to-order wedding and baby shower baskets, and preparing elaborate birthday gift baskets, too.

Sue Sweeney had been contacted by Detective Rigby. Charlotte Booth had not. Gilda Ringwald-Stratton had been indignant, annoyed by Carol Rigby's annoying questions. Conrad Stratton had brushed off Carol's investigation as an indignity that had to be endured but not dwelled upon. He was more interested in enticing Katie to try a new Cabernet Sauvignon, a bottle of which she dutifully bought. She'd gift it to Nick and Don, as it wasn't her favorite. They could always offer it to their guests if they didn't care for it.

By the time Katie arrived back at Artisans Alley, she felt

weighed down by everything she'd purchased. No way was she sharing her brownie or the jam she'd bought. The latter could go on one of the leftover Tealicious scones for a number of breakfasts.

As she gazed at her purchases, Katie wondered if she should have dropped by to speak to Ray and Moonbeam. Gut feeling told her neither of them could possibly have a grudge against the former pharmacist, as they were relatively new to McKinlay Mill. It was doubtful Ray met the older man before Margo's party. Still, the next time she bumped into either of them, Katie figured she should ask—just in case.

Katie shook herself. Why was she appointing herself as an unpaid investigator in the Preston murder case? Because it had happened at Margo's party, and her affection for the older woman grew every day. That was something Katie would never have believed two years before, but now she hoped she could feel good about calling her dead husband's maternal parent by the title of mom. It hadn't yet happened and Katie wondered if the moniker would feel artificial when she spoke to Margo or introduced her to others that way. Maybe she should have waited and tried it out without first mentioning it to Margo.

The whole plan now seemed like a bad idea. And now Margo would expect to be introduced as a mother, the title she'd cherished most among all her many accomplishments.

Katie shook herself and was contemplating what she'd learned during her circuit around the Square when Vance Ingram poked his head around her office's door jamb. "Hey, Katie, got a minute?"

"For you? Always. What's up?"

"We've got a slight problem." When Vance said that phrase, he was usually trying to break some unhappy news—like a roof leak or a blocked toilet.

"What now?" Katie asked with dread.

"Nothing horrible. It's just—"

"Don't tell me some vendor is annoyed with a newcomer because..."

"What? Are you psychic?" Vance asked with raised brows.

"No, but I've been at this long enough to get the vibe. Tell me more."

"Ida—" Vance began, and Katie lifted a hand to stave off an explanation.

Ida Mitchell had to be the most unattractive person Katie had ever encountered. The large, wobbly wart on her face gave Katie the heebie-jeebies. But it wasn't just the woman's less-than-lovely features that were a turn-off. Ida, one of the Alley's most senior vendors, rented a single shelf in a showcase to exhibit and presumably sell (although Katie knew that was a rare occasion) her handmade lace. The woman, who probably sat somewhere on the autism spectrum, was a stickler for rules and when she felt they'd been violated she caused a big stink.

"What's she complaining about *this* time?" Katie asked wearily.

"Our newest vendor—" Of course. "—Treena Jarvis embroiders vintage linens. Ida thinks that because she does it by machine and not by hand, that her wares aren't handcrafted."

After renting Treena a booth, Katie went online to watch videos on machine embroidery. Learning the machine's program wasn't as easy as one might suspect. When Katie had taken over Artisans Alley after the death of its founder, Ezra Hilton, she'd allowed crafters to rent space because that was the only way the place would ever break even, let alone make a profit, and her hunch had paid off. People now flocked to Artisans Alley for unique—mostly—handcrafted items. And, honestly, one had to be well acquainted with the program that propelled the machine to make the intricate patterns Treena offered to customers, as well as the custom orders she accepted.

"Don't tell me; Ida won't accept your defense of Treena's products, and only I can calm her down."

"You got it," Vance said. Katie would bet Vance had done his best, but Ida was such a pill when it came to such things that Katie would have to devise a reasonable explanation to appease the old lady.

"Is Ida still here?"

Vance nodded. "She's in the tag room."

"I suppose I have to go speak to her," Katie said, feeling suddenly drained.

Vance shrugged. "She wouldn't listen to reason from me, so —yeah, I guess you probably should."

Katie was as eager to speak to Ida as have a healthy tooth pulled. She let out a weary breath. "Okay," she said, rising from her chair, "I'll give it a shot."

"Great. And while you do that, I'll tidy up the vendors' lounge."

Katie knew Vance despised that job, which could only mean he loathed the idea of having to soothe Ida's ire.

"Great. Be back in a jiffy," she said, not feeling the zeal with which she'd said the phrase.

Katie dawdled as she made her way through the Alley's main showroom and headed toward the tag room. She found Ida huddled over the table, diligently placing sales tags onto the papers that were numbered 41 through 50.

Katie forced herself to speak in a positive tone. "Hey, Ida, Vance said you wanted to speak to me."

Ida looked up, eyes narrowed, her expression one that could only be called extreme annoyance. "You bet I do," the old woman grated, and practically exploded with vitriol toward Treena Jarvis and her work.

"Whoa-whoa!" Katie proclaimed in a placating voice. "I don't understand why you're so upset."

"Because she has no real skill. A computer does all her

embroidery while I make my lace the old-fashioned, painstaking way."

Yes, and machine-made lace had been around for over a hundred years, Katie thought.

"I appreciate your workmanship," she said, "but you need to understand that Artisans Alley welcomes artists and craftspeople of all types and celebrates their creativity."

"Well, it's not fair to us *true* artists."

Ida's handmade lace *was* exquisite, but it was so labor-intensive that few (any?) wanted to pay the prices she assigned to her work.

"What is it about Treena's work you object to?" Katie asked.

"I already told you. A machine does it for her. Anybody can turn on a machine and churn out crap."

But what Treena produced was, in its own way, just as enchanting as Ida's lace. And Katie knew that not everybody would have the dedication to learn how to master the embroidering machine's intricacies. Katie knew she wouldn't have the patience to do so.

"You need to tell Treena she *has* to leave," Ida insisted.

"No," Katie said firmly. "Treena creates beautiful products she's doing well with, and Artisans Alley is in business to sell well-crafted items."

Ida squinted at Katie. "What you really mean is that as long as she pays her rent, she can stay."

Katie bit her lip so as not to explode and point out that as long as she'd managed Artisans Alley, Ida had seldom made her rent. And yet, Katie hated to say the words. "That's pretty much it."

Color rose up Ida's neck, her cheeks darkening. "Well, that's a pretty reprehensible statement."

Katie was surprised Ida even knew the phrase. "I'm sorry you think so."

Ida nodded, looking grim. "I may have to rethink staying in a place where real craftsmanship isn't appreciated."

Katie hadn't said that at all. And she was sure that if Ida *did* leave Artisans Alley, there'd be no one to mourn her absence—the woman made herself that big a pain in the butt.

"I'm sorry you feel that way, but I completely understand if you wish to give up your shelf and no longer be a part of Artisans Alley."

Ida's eyes widened. "I didn't say that."

"Well, yes, you did. I have a waiting list for those wishing to rent a shelf. Please let me know before the end of the month if you'll be packing up your lace and leaving."

Ida's eyes blazed. "Are you kicking me out of here?"

"Not at all," Katie said reasonably. "You're the one who said you weren't sure you wanted to stay."

"Well, I—" Ida began, but then didn't elaborate.

Katie decided it would be best to de-escalate the timbre of their conversation. "I appreciate your dedication here in the tag room and your artistry as a lacemaker, but if you feel you'd be happier selling your wares somewhere else, I completely understand. Again, if you decide to leave, please let me know before the end of the month so I can rent your shelf to another budding artist."

"Is that all you have to say?" Ida demanded.

Katie nodded. "Pretty much. We'd miss you, Ida," Katie lied. She was pretty sure more than half the vendors would rejoice if the older woman no longer darkened the Alley's doors, but she wasn't about to voice that opinion either.

Ida's gaze dipped to the table and the pile of tags that hadn't yet been taped to the various vendors' papers. "I'll have to think about it."

"You do that," Katie said, turning to leave the windowless room, feeling unsettled. Ida had been a thorn in her side since the day she inherited Artisans Alley, but she also knew that the older woman had virtually no social life outside Artisans Alley. Still, Katie had a business to run. And yet ... sometimes, the decisions she had to make didn't always set well.

This was one of those times.

Chapter Ten

After her conversation with Ida, Katie spent the rest of the afternoon feeling agitated. Still, she wasn't about to let one vendor decide who could and couldn't rent space in the arts-and-crafts arcade.

However, Ida's complaint wasn't the only thing on Katie's mind. Her thoughts kept returning to the night of Margo's party. Yes, she'd been preoccupied with making sure that things ran smoothly and that the food she and Brad had prepared was presented beautifully. And why was that? Did she really need to sell Tealicious and what it could deliver to the other merchants on the Square? After all, it wasn't like they'd be referring any of their customers to the tea shop. When it came to business, it often seemed like it was every man—or woman—for themself. That wasn't the way Katie thought. Like her deceased husband, she wanted to buoy all the merchants on the Square, to ensure all their businesses thrived. She wasn't sure she could count on them to feel the same way, which saddened her.

But then, that was why she remained the head of the Victoria Square Merchants Association and hadn't actively pursued finding a replacement. No one else seemed to have that generous streak. She couldn't count Nick and Don among them, since as the only hospitality business on the Square, they had no competition. They offered products from Sweet Sue's Confectionery, The Flower Child, and especially Booth's Jellies and Jams in their B&B. They supported the Square's wine merchant, the Perfect Grape. And though Katie hadn't known the men for an abundance of years, she trusted them. They might like to open an antiques store on the Square, but she was sure neither would contemplate murder to acquire a spot. As Don had said, they might just rent a space in the up-and-coming Victoria Square Annex. It would still be close enough that they could walk to their side hustle from their home and probably pay less for a bigger retail space than a building on the Square itself.

Maxwell Preston was either a saint or a sinner, depending on who Katie spoke to. He was kind to his customers and unkind to his daughter. He fiercely loved his wife but not their only child.

Katie scowled. She didn't have only Phoebe's word for that. Paula Matthews had backed up that claim. Despite the second opinion, Katie wasn't sure she believed that story. But who else could she ask about it?

She wished she had someone to bounce her ideas off. She knew Margo would find such a discussion distasteful. Margo had had her fill of death. First, with the loss of her husband Charles, and then her son.

The only person Katie would feel comfortable speaking to about it was Ray Davenport, and he was off limits.

Katie frowned. Why did she feel that way? If nothing else, she *did* count Ray as a friend, *and* he was a former sheriff's detective. He hadn't welcomed her opinions when he was still on the job, but that seemed to have changed upon his retirement. Did he see talking about such things as a hobby—or was he only placating Katie when she wanted to muddle over such things?

There was only one way to find out.

Katie glanced at the clock on the wall. Just about every shop on the Square called it quits at five o'clock on a weekday —and Wood U was among them. She still had time to speak to Ray before he closed for the day. If nothing else, she could break the ice by mentioning her visit from his daughters earlier that day.

With that in mind, Katie left her office and strode with purpose toward Wood U. Mounting the steps, she threw open the door and was confronted by the sight of Carol Rigby standing in front of the sales counter.

"Oh," Katie blurted.

"Oh?" Carol inquired with a side eye.

Katie laughed nervously. "Great to see you. I just stopped by to talk to Ray about the upcoming summer extravaganza."

"Yes, I hear it'll be a good time for all," Carol deadpanned.

"I sure hope so," Katie said with a forced cheer.

"Well, then I guess I'll let you two get to it," Carol said, and turned her attention to Ray, giving him a meaningful look. What that meaning was escaped Katie.

"We'll talk later," Carol said, leaning across the counter and capturing Ray's face in both her hands, giving him a kiss that was meant to send a message to Katie that Ray belonged to her. Finally, she pulled back, leaving Ray with a confused expression.

"Until tonight," Carol said, which sounded more like a command than a promise. Katie watched as Carol sauntered out of the shop, noting how tight the pencil skirt fit the lady detective. Perhaps tight wasn't the proper description. Form-fitting was probably a kinder representation.

Carol closed the door behind her, letting it shut with a bang.

Katie and Ray looked after her for long seconds before Katie spoke.

"Wow," she said flatly.

"Yeah," Ray echoed. For such a passionate kiss, he didn't sound all that enamored.

Katie shook herself and ambled over to the counter that separated the two.

"What brings you here?" Ray asked mildly.

"The Preston case, of course. I don't suppose Carol mentioned any new developments."

"We don't talk shop," Ray replied.

Katie wondered what *did* they talk about when they were alone.

Ray's eyes twinkled. "But that doesn't mean I don't have my own thoughts about what happened last Saturday night."

Katie raised an eyebrow. "Do tell?"

"I'm more interested in your take."

Katie shrugged. "Someone smacked Preston hard on the back of his head, and he drowned."

"No possible suspects?" Ray asked.

"Well, it wasn't me. I hadn't even been formally introduced to the man during the party. And I would never suspect my— my…." But then Katie couldn't say the word "My mother-in-law of murder."

"I thought you always referred to her as your *former* mother-in-law."

Katie scowled. "That makes it sound like Chad and I divorced, which we certainly hadn't."

Ray quirked a smile. "You've grown fond of her," he accused.

Katie stood just a little straighter. "And why wouldn't I? She's shown me nothing but kindness this past year or so and is now my business partner."

Ray nodded, his expression bland.

"Anyway, my list of suspects is short. It had to be someone on the Square. I mean, there weren't any others at the party. And I don't know about you, but I didn't see any strangers crashing the event or skulking around the property. Did you?"

"I was out in the yard for a good portion of the party, but no —I didn't see any strangers. In fact, Carol was probably the only stranger there, and she was with me the entire time."

Yes, she was.

"I've spoken to most of the merchants and nobody stands out," Katie said. "Well, except for Nona—who complained about the state of Preston's building, but I hardly think she'd kill him over it."

"Did you speak to her about it?"

Katie shook her head. "Nona seems much more interested in the Square's summer promotion. Dare I say it—she actually seems excited about it—especially since she came up with the idea. And she's sure taken a shine to taking the lead on organizing it. Honestly, I didn't think she had it in her. She's been such a sour old biddy."

"Anyone else on the Square have a beef with the old guy?" Ray asked.

Katie related her conversations with Preston's daughter, Phoebe, Paula from Heaven's Gate, and Ann Tanner.

"Interesting," Ray observed.

Katie eyed him critically. "I've spilled my list; now it's your turn."

Ray scowled and heaved a sigh. "I concur that it was probably one of the party guests. Some have been on the Square a lot longer than you—and long before Ezra Hilton put Victoria Square on the map by opening Artisans Alley. Did you know that Conrad Stratton's wine shop recently celebrated its twentieth year in business here on the Square?"

Yes, Katie *had* been aware of it. Conrad held a big anniversary sale a few months before, and she stocked up on her favorite white wine. Not a lot, but a case. She wasn't one to drink alone, and in fact had so far only opened one bottle—which she hadn't yet finished.

"I'm betting Conrad knew Preston—or at least his wife when she ran her ceramics shop."

So, Ray knew even that fact about Mrs. Preston.

"Anyone else?" Katie asked.

"Charlotte Booth."

Katie frowned. "And what's her connection with old Mr. Preston?"

Ray gave a side eye-roll.

Katie's jaw dropped. "They were lovers?"

Ray nodded.

"But—but—" Katie sputtered. "His wife! According to what I heard, Preston was devoted to his wife. Up until his death, he was still putting flowers on her grave every week."

"Yes. But the affair happened *after* her death."

Katie scowled.

"His wife was gone. No matter how much love you share with your life partner," Ray said, apparently speaking from experience, "one does get lonely."

Was he speaking about Preston or himself?

"Who told you about their affair?" Katie demanded.

Ray seemed to mull over the question before answering. "Sue Sweeney."

Why had Sue confided in Ray and not with Katie? Was it because he'd been a former detective and was skilled at wheedling information out of witnesses, or had that other never-married older woman on the Square been jealous of the relationship Charlotte had with Preston and wasn't going to admit it to yet another woman? Sue and Charlotte were cordial with each other but didn't appear to be friends.

"Were Charlotte and Preston still an item at the time of his death?" Katie asked. "Because when I spoke to her, Charlotte looked like she'd been crying."

Ray nodded. "Apparently, they'd been together for years—but not so many people noticed," Ray said. "They didn't flaunt their relationship."

"So then, how did Sue know they were dating?"

"Her shop *is* next to Charlotte's. She noticed that Preston often arrived at the jam shop at the end of the day and that he and Charlotte would leave together."

"But not lately?" Katie asked.

Ray nodded.

"So, what recently caused a riff in their relationship?" Katie asked.

"Sue didn't have an opinion on that subject," Ray said.

"And you didn't confront Charlotte with that information?"

"It's not my place to do so," Ray explained.

"Did you mention it to Carol?"

Ray hesitated before answering. "Uh…not as yet."

So when *would* he spill the tea to his … Katie hated even to think the word *lover*.

"Don't you think that information might be pertinent to her investigation?"

"She's a smart woman. I'm sure she'll come up with that information on her own."

"And if she doesn't?" Katie pressed. "I mean, she doesn't exactly have a warm personality that one would bare his or her soul to."

"You think so?" Ray asked.

Katie nodded.

"Have *you* kept any information from her?"

"Of course not," Katie said, bristling. "I didn't even know Preston, and I did my damnedest to try to keep the old guy alive. As you well know, he was literally dead in the water when I found him. I was just too late to save him."

"Yeah," Ray said, his voice clipped. Did he suspect *her* of killing the old guy?

Katie decided to ignore the last thread of their conversation.

"Did you notice Charlotte and Preston speaking at Margo's housewarming party?" Katie asked.

He shook his head. "I can't say I did. But then, I wasn't paying attention. I was there to enjoy the company and the food."

She nodded. "So, do you think Charlotte could have killed the old guy, and if so, why?"

"Well, as the saying goes, 'hell hath no fury like a woman scorned.' Maybe Charlotte told the old coot to shit or get off the pot when it came to their relationship. Maybe she wanted a ring around the third finger of her left hand."

"And you think if he didn't offer it she might have *killed* him?" Katie asked, aghast.

"It wouldn't be the first time it happened," Ray said blandly.

Katie liked to think she knew Charlotte enough to trust the woman wasn't capable of murder. But then ... one never knew.

"Any other suspects?" Katie asked.

Ray looked thoughtful. "Not as yet."

Katie scrutinized his face. "And where would you look for other suspects?"

"That would involve talking to everyone who knew the man."

"And where would one start to *find* those people?" she asked.

"That's Carol's job—not yours or mine."

Except that Katie had a stake in this investigation—or at least Margo did, since it had happened on the property she was renting—*and* had apparently been perpetrated by one of the guests who'd attended her housewarming party.

"You shouldn't be so concerned," Ray warned, sounding

more like the no-nonsense cop she'd met a few years before and not the friend she'd come to know.

She chose her next words carefully. "Is it wrong of me to want to suss out a killer on the Square—and perhaps stop them from killing again?"

Ray shrugged. "I'm betting whoever killed the old guy had a personal beef against him. It's going to be as simple as that."

Much as she wanted to believe him, Katie wasn't so sure.

Ray squinted in Katie's direction. "I know you, Katie Bonner," he said quietly. "You're not going to trust Carol to solve this, are you?"

"Why do you say that?"

Ray laughed. "Because I know you, lady. Sometimes, I think I know you better than you know yourself."

Ha! Fat chance of that, Katie thought, and caught Ray's unwavering look in her direction.

Katie looked at the carved sunburst clock on the wall of Ray's showroom. It probably had a battery-operated quartz movement, but he'd used woods of different shades to mimic the sun's rays. It was a beautiful piece of art, like everything else he'd made in the shop. The man—who sometimes drove her bonkers—was a skilled craftsman and artist. Everything he made was beautiful, right down to his three daughters.

"What are you thinking?" Ray asked.

Katie shrugged. "How someone's act of revenge will ultimately scar poor Margo," she fibbed.

Ray raised a quizzical eyebrow. "Really?"

"Yes!" Katie said emphatically.

"Somehow, I think Margo will come through this okay. She's a pretty strong lady. She knows what she wants and how to obtain it."

That was a pretty cynical statement, but not something Katie wanted to challenge, at least at that moment.

Again, Katie glanced at the clock on the wall. "I'd better get going. We've both got businesses to close for the day."

"Feel free to drop by anytime you want to talk," Ray said with what sounded like sincerity.

"I will," Katie answered, with just an edge of defiance in her voice. No matter what, she and Ray *were* friends, and she wasn't about to let Carol Rigby ruin that.

"We'll talk again soon," Katie promised.

"I'll count on it," Ray said with a crooked smile.

For a moment, Katie fought the urge to say something more —but she couldn't think what. Then she turned and crossed the showroom for the exit, quietly closing the door behind her.

Chapter Eleven

Ray had given Katie a lot to think about that night as she locked the doors to Artisans Alley and walked across the tarmac to her apartment over Tealicious. Twilight was arriving later and later, something she appreciated. The Square often felt spooky when she'd leave the Alley to go home, knowing she'd be the only one on that part of the Square after Angelo's Pizzeria closed at midnight. Who knew what—or who—lurked in the shadows? *You're catastrophizing,* Katie often told herself, when she'd walk up the icy steps to her apartment during the winter months. But this was May—spring—when the sun lingered at the horizon just a little longer every evening, so that now the lot was bright as she approached home and her cats.

As Katie fumbled for her keys to unlock her apartment door, her phone pinged: a text message from Moonbeam Carruthers.

I just made a big batch of vegetable soup. Want to join me for supper?

Katie smiled and texted back. *You just saved me from stale scones and cocoa. Are you at your shop?*

Yes.

See you in a jiffy.

Katie pocketed her phone once more and trundled down the stairs. It only took a minute or so before she stood at the front entrance to The Flower Child. Katie rapped on the door, and in seconds, Moonbeam threw it open. "Come in, come in," she said with a welcoming wave of her hand. Lily barked a joyful hello, demanding Katie's attention and giving her lots of canine kisses.

Moonbeam laughed. "She remembers her savior."

"You think so?"

"It's been proven."

Lily's big doggy smile seemed to substantiate Moonbeam's claim. Katie had saved Lily from being sent to a kill shelter after her first adopter had decided she was too much trouble.

A minute later, Katie was seated at the little bistro table in one of Moonbeam's back rooms with Lily at her feet, her tail thumping on the plank floor. The room was set up as a kitchenette. Sometimes Moonbeam cooked there; other times, she created fragrant homemade soaps that she sold in her shop—and often gave as gifts to friends. She made small bars for Sassy Sally's, which enticed guests to seek out her shop when Don or Nick told them where to find larger versions.

Moonbeam ladled soup into deep, handmade pottery bowls, placing them on the table before turning to grab a plate of rolls that Katie recognized as coming from Tanner's Cafe and Bakery. They were just as good as the ones she served at Tealicious. A covered glass dish held a slab of butter.

"Thanks for inviting me. As I said, my dinner was destined to be pretty pedestrian."

"You haven't tried the soup yet," Moonbeam warned.

Katie lifted her spoon, tasted the soup and closed her eyes. Hmmm…heavenly. "Would you be willing to share the recipe? I'd love to include it on the Tealicious menu this fall."

Moonbeam waved a hand in dismissal. "I'm sure Brad makes a far superior version. Besides, I just throw in everything from the fridge—or the garden—and hope for the best."

"Well, it's pretty fabulous."

Moonbeam beamed, which Katie found humorous.

"These bowls are gorgeous. Did you make them?"

Moonbeam hesitated a beat before answering, looking just a little uncomfortable. "I've had them a long time. You see, I took a class right here on the Square with—"

"Maxwell Preston's wife?" Katie supplied.

"Yes," Moonbeam admitted.

Katie took another spoonful of soup, savoring it, before swallowing. "I thought her ceramics classes only entailed slipware. Scrape it, paint it, fire it."

"Yes, those customers *were* the majority of Linda's clientele. But she also held classes for those who wanted to make pottery from wet clay." She laughed. "Do I dare age myself by telling you I was influenced by the movie *Ghost* with Patrick Swayze and that sexy scene with Demi Moore where she was throwing a pot and his spirit hovered around her?"

Katie hadn't seen the film since she was a teenager but she remembered it was quite sensual.

"And Linda taught you how to make pottery?"

Moonbeam nodded, her gaze dipping to focus on spooning her soup.

Katie plucked one of the rolls from the plate, cut it in half, and buttered one side. "How well did you know Mrs. Preston? I mean, I didn't think you even had a link to McKinlay Mill before you opened your shop."

"Heavens, no!" Moonbeam declared. "I grew up here in the village. But I didn't want to hang around a place where nothing was happening…until it *was* if you catch my drift."

Katie wasn't sure she did. She didn't comment.

"I was rather at loose ends at the time I met her. Struggling might be a better descriptor. I was looking for something to do with my life, and met Linda at just the right time. You know what her name means, right?"

Katie frowned. "Spanish for beautiful?"

Moonbeam nodded. "She wasn't especially pretty but she *was* a lovely friend." But then Moonbeam frowned. "She just had one pretty big flaw."

"That she didn't place her daughter as one of the most important aspects of her life?" Katie asked.

Moonbeam nodded. "So you've heard?"

"Yes, and from the woman in question."

Moonbeam nodded. "I always thought the relationship her parents had with Phoebe was weird." Suddenly, Moonbeam's expression darkened, and her gaze dipped to the floor. "I was only privileged to be pregnant once, and...my little girl wasn't viable. It broke my heart," Moonbeam said, tears filling her eyes and her voice breaking. "Worse, my partner abandoned me when he learned of our misfortune."

It must have been decades before, but Katie was sure the pain of that betrayal had left a terrible scar on Moonbeam's soul. "Anyway, that experience ended my days of casual sex. It was fun while it lasted, but while *he* wasn't interested in being a dad, it was always my life's dream to be a mom." She stopped and, waved a hand as though to erase what she'd just said before continuing. She took a breath and swallowed. "I found peace in identifying with the natural things of this world, like arranging flowers—and making pots and bowls from the clay of the earth. You can't possibly know how many bowls I threw. I got rid of or broke most of them years ago, but I still have a few."

"Like these," Katie said, indicating the bowl before her.

Moonbeam nodded. "Because of our professional association, you know my given name," she said matter-of-factly.

Katie did. Her name was Jane.

"It was Linda who started calling me Moonbeam. She told me about the three moon goddesses of ancient Greece, Selene, Artemis, and Hecate, but didn't think they were exotic enough to define me. At the time, the name Moonbeam really appealed to me, as I'd always hated being called Plain Jane. And things were different back in those days. Everything felt so much more creative back then. Not so much now."

"So you thought of Linda Preston as kind of a mentor?"

Moonbeam nodded.

"But what did you think of her husband?"

Moonbeam sighed. "If nothing else, he was devoted to Linda."

"But?" Katie asked, studying her friend's face because she wasn't sure if Moonbeam would answer truthfully.

"He was okay," Moonbeam said, but it was a pretty ambiguous answer.

Katie frowned. "It doesn't sound as though you liked him."

Moonbeam shrugged, but avoided Katie's gaze. "What's not to like?"

"That's what I'm asking," Katie said.

Moonbeam lapped up another spoonful of soup before answering, and even then, Katie felt like the older woman was guarding her speech. "I've heard he was generous to people who couldn't pay for their meds."

Confirming what Katie had already heard.

"But…?"

Katie waited. Moonbeam plucked a roll from the plate, sliced it, and buttered both halves.

"But?" Katie prodded.

"I don't like to spread gossip," Moonbeam said, still avoiding Katie's gaze.

"*But?*" Katie pressed for the third time.

Clearly, Moonbeam didn't want to speak ill of the dead. But, she finally took what seemed like a fortifying breath before answering. "Max hit on me. He made it clear he wanted to bed me—and it happened more than once."

Katie blinked, confused. "But…but from what you've said, he was devoted to Linda."

"I've often wondered if it was guilt that drove him to buy flowers every week for her grave."

"What made him seek you out as someone who could supply him with those flowers?"

Moonbeam shrugged. "I guess before I opened my shop, he bought flowers from the grocery store in the strip mall behind the big warehouse out back."

Katie had a feeling there was more to the story. "I take it you hadn't seen Preston for years before opening The Flower Child."

"You've got that right. But what unsettled me was once he found out I'd opened for business, he kept coming into the shop. He bought flowers—and with every purchase, he'd flirt with me." And how had Charlotte Booth reacted to that?

Katie raised an eyebrow. "And?"

"I ignored his advances," Moonbeam said adamantly. But then she frowned. "Maybe I should have shown the man a little more compassion. He *had* been without his wife for many years." And bedding Charlotte for a few of them.

But Moonbeam hadn't been the only woman Preston had sought to date after the death of his wife. Twenty years was a long, long time to be without companionship. Katie had been without Chad for months and ached to be with someone she could trust when Andy entered her life. She wanted someone who could fill the empty spaces in her life and be the corresponding person in that man's life. At 34, her options weren't closed, but Katie didn't see anyone she currently knew as being able to step into that role, either.

Some people were just destined to be alone. Like Katie's beloved Aunt Lizzie, whose unhappy marriage ended when she was younger than Katie was now. The poor woman had never

found someone to share her life with—that is, until Katie's
parents died. And then the older, childless woman had had to
step into the role of pseudo-parent to a six-year-old homeless girl.

"How did that make you feel?" Katie asked.

Moonbeam concentrated on the bowl of half-eaten soup
before her.

"I was never interested in Max. And even if I had a smat-
tering of interest, the idea was pretty off-putting. I mean, the
idea of sleeping with a man who'd been my mentor's husband
was a real turnoff."

Katie could understand that sentiment.

"How did you feel the first time he showed up in your
shop?"

Moonbeam mulled over the question before answering.
"Wary. My last encounter with the man hadn't been exactly
positive."

Katie's eyes widened. Did Moonbeam have a motive for
murdering the old man?

"In what way?" Katie asked.

Moonbeam scowled, once again averting her gaze from
Katie's. "He started talking dirty."

Katie's eyebrows rose. "How dirty?"

"*Very* dirty. Using words that aren't in my lexicon. He
seemed confused when I told him I didn't appreciate it." Moonbeam looked thoughtful. "I know some women *like* that kind of
thing, but that isn't me."

Was Katie a prude because she didn't see herself welcoming
that kind of foreplay, either? And what about Charlotte?

"Was dirty talk the only reason you said your last interac-
tion with Preston wasn't positive?"

Once again, Moonbeam's gaze dipped. "Not exactly."

Katie waited, wondering if Moonbeam was about to drop a
bombshell. When the older woman didn't elaborate, she tried
again. "Well?"

Moonbeam shook her head. "I'm embarrassed."

"About what?"

Moonbeam let out an exasperated breath. "I threw him out of my shop."

"That doesn't sound so bad, asking him to leave."

"No, I literally *threw* him out of my shop. He was older than me and a few inches shorter. I circled around my shop's counter, grabbed him by the waistband of his pants and shoved him out onto the asphalt, telling him never to darken my door again."

"When was this?" Katie asked.

Moonbeam still would not look Katie in the eye. "The afternoon of Margo's party."

Katie's eyes narrowed. "Did anyone see that?"

Moonbeam shrugged. "Who knows?"

"Did you interact with Preston at the party?"

"I was shocked to see him there," Moonbeam confessed. "I'd figured—hoped—I wouldn't have to speak to him ever again, and then hours later, there he was right in my face."

"I never saw you and Preston together," Katie said.

"Well, then you weren't looking," Moonbeam grated.

No, Katie had been more obsessed with ensuring that the food was presented in a pretty manner and enjoyed by the guests, oblivious of any tensions that might have existed among them.

"What happened?"

Moonbeam's cheeks colored. "I was standing out on the deck with a glass of wine, enjoying the sunset, when Max came out from the house. I didn't hear him—he snuck up on me and smacked me on the bottom."

Katie's eyes widened. "And how did you react?"

"I turned so fast I spilled my wine and slapped him so hard it sent him staggering."

"Did anyone witness it?"

Moonbeam scowled. "Nona Fiske."

"Oh, dear," Katie muttered. She wouldn't be surprised if the old bat reported the encounter to Detective Rigby, giving it the most unsavory spin she could.

"Did you tell Detective Rigby about the incident and give her the background as to why it happened?"

Moonbeam's gaze drifted downward. "I may have forgotten to mention it."

"Oh, Moonbeam," Katie lamented.

Moonbeam's expression soured even more. "Do you think I ought to call the detective and tell her?"

"Yes, and the sooner the better!" Katie admonished, and then cringed at the forcefulness of her tone. "Yes," she tried again, softening her voice. "I can understand why you wanted to keep the incident quiet, but Carol's looking for a murderer. Our jails are full of people who've been convicted on circumstantial evidence. You don't want to be among them. I urge you to call the detective as soon as possible."

"But what would I say?" Moonbeam asked. Worry had crept into her tone.

"Admit that you were embarrassed by the situation. If you've got anyone who can vouch for you after the episode, tell the detective."

"I tried not to be alone after that. I pretty much clung to Nick Ferrell and Don Parsons."

"Good. Make sure Detective Rigby knows it."

"I'll do that," Moonbeam said, nodding. "Is there anything else I should do?"

Katie thought about how she should answer that question. "Cross your fingers and hope."

It wasn't the most brilliant piece of advice she'd ever offered, but it was the best Katie had to give in this circumstance.

Even more curious...why hadn't Detective Rigby called

Moonbeam on the incident? There was only one conclusion: Nona hadn't reported the incident. But why?

"Did you see Preston interact with any of the other guests?"

"Yes. Just about every other woman."

"Sue?"

Moonbeam nodded.

"Ann?"

Again, Moonbeam nodded.

"Charlotte?"

She nodded once again.

Katie let out a breath. Was the third time the evil charm that killed Maxwell Preston?

Chapter Twelve

Springtime was Katie's favorite time of year. The air was fresh the following morning as she headed out from Tealicious for her daily walk around the Square after once again helping Brad with the salads. She preferred to bake, but why waste a gifted pastry chef if she was going to take on that task herself? Of course, Brad didn't complain about Katie wanting to make the odd batch of scones. Any fool could turn out that tea-time staple. But the sublime little cakes, pastries, and custards he prepared were the things most coveted by their guests.

Katie headed west, walked the eastern perimeter of Artisans Alley, and headed toward the Victoria Square Annex's main entrance. Every day, another little job seemed to have been completed. The big brass sconces on either side of the double plate-glass doors of the building's main entrance had been installed since the last time she'd walked past. By looking north, she could see the alley behind the buildings on that side of the Square and saw Ray's car parked behind his shop. He must have left his home right after his daughters had headed off to

McKinlay Mill High School. None of the other merchants seemed to be in residence at that hour of the day.

Katie walked on and turned east, walking alongside the path above Sweet Sue's Confectionery and then down in front of Sassy Sally's B&B. A line of six or seven people had formed inside Tanner's, and Katie resisted the urge to dart inside to grab a latte and a sticky bun. Nope. If she wanted to buy a home, she needed to start cutting corners. She could grab a cup of coffee in Artisans Alley's vendors' lounge for a quarter, and as always, there were stale pastries at Tealicious she could eat for her breakfast. The rest of them were often crumbled and put out for the birds.

But as Katie approached the ramshackle building owned by Maxwell Preston, a battered minivan pulled up in front with Phoebe Preston behind the wheel. She killed the engine and jumped down from the driver's seat.

"Hey, Katie."

"Hey, yourself. What are you doing on the Square so early on this fine morning?"

"Got some repairs to make."

Katie blinked. "Oh?"

"If I want to get top dollar for this place," Phoebe jerked over her shoulder, "I need to fix it up. I hit the big home improvement store in Greece and loaded up on lumber, nails, and plywood. I figured if I invested a little cash and some sweat equity in the building, it would be worth a whole lot more after probate."

Considering the rocky relationship Phoebe and her father shared, was the woman really sure she would be the *one* to inherit his estate? And what if he had a load of outstanding debt? Preston had apparently sold his pharmacy a couple of years before Katie arrived in the village, but had he made a fortune or taken a loss? Considering he was known to eat the cost of prescriptions for those who couldn't afford it, perhaps the latter was the realistic outcome.

Phoebe opened the van's gate and began to unload the 2x4s and pressure-treated lumber from within it.

"Do you need a hand?" Katie asked.

"I'd sure welcome it," Phoebe admitted. Together, the women quickly emptied the van.

"What's your plan?" Katie asked.

"To make the building safe so that that horrid red X can be wrenched from the siding. Nobody in their right mind is going to want to buy a building that a good stiff wind could take out." The X meant the building was unsafe and that firefighters shouldn't risk life and limb should the building go up in smoke. Katie couldn't argue with that logic, but what DIY skills did Phoebe possess?

"What's your plan?" Katie asked.

Phoebe looked at the building's crumbling facade and frowned. "Pull out any rotten wood I find and replace it."

"Where are your tools?" Katie asked. She hadn't seen a circular or reciprocating saw in the back of the van.

"In the well of my passenger seat." Phoebe circled to the front of her van and flung open the door. Behind her, Katie looked to inspect the woman's inventory before cringing. Phoebe had brought a hand saw, a couple of boxes of nails, a hammer, and a crowbar. She didn't envy the woman who would definitely be trying to transform a sow's ear into a silk purse — or, more likely, to put lipstick on a pig. Either way, Katie didn't see the value of the building rising all that much, although Phoebe might be able to at have at least the dreaded red X removed so potential buyers could safely walk through the building without fear of being maimed or killed.

"You're taking on a lot," Katie commented.

Phoebe turned a worried glance toward the long-neglected building. "I haven't got much choice."

Katie contemplated asking a blunt—and possibly inappropriate question—and decided to go for it. "Have you considered that you might *not* inherit your father's estate?"

Again, Phoebe glanced toward the building before swinging her gaze back to Katie. "Yeah, I've thought about it," she said sadly. "I can't think who else Dad might leave it to, but...yeah. I've thought about it. So far, I haven't been able to find a copy of Dad's will."

"And you're still willing to improve the property?"

"It's a gamble," Phoebe admitted, "and I'm putting myself in hock with the supplies I've bought, but I need to do *something*."

Katie nodded, doing some fast thinking. "Seth Landers is the only attorney here in McKinlay Mill. Have you checked with his office about a will?"

"No, but that's a good idea."

"I can give you his number," Katie said. "And before you cut one piece of lumber, would you like to speak to my friend Fred Cunningham? He's a real estate broker. He knows what properties are going for in this area. I promise his advice is sound. If he says it would be better *not* to make improvements, you could at least return the things you've purchased and not be out of pocket. And Fred won't charge you a thing for his advice."

"You trust this guy?" Phoebe asked, skeptically.

"I've dealt with him on several occasions, and he's never steered me wrong."

"Well, okay," Phoebe reluctantly agreed. "But I'd need to speak to him in the next day or so."

"I'll give him a call as soon as I get back to my office," Katie promised. "Until then, if you've got a key, it might be best to move your supplies inside so they'll be safe from thieves."

Phoebe's mouth dropped in alarm. "I thought that kind of thing didn't happen out here in the boonies."

Boonies? Hardly.

"Better safe than sorry," Katie remarked.

Phoebe's gaze dipped to the rotting boards that formed a porch in front of the building. "Would you help me put them inside?"

"Sure," Katie agreed.

Phoebe withdrew a key from her pocket, unlocked the door, and pushed it open, the rusty hinges groaning in protest. Like the porch outside, the wooden floor was rotted with treacherous holes that threatened to snag and pull down an unwary foot.

Once all the supplies were secured, Katie took down Phoebe's number so that she could connect her with Fred and waved good-bye as Phoebe steered her minivan out of the Square's parking lot.

As Katie made her way toward Artisans Alley, she was thankful she had no interest in the former ceramics shop as she wanted Phoebe to make a decent profit on the property—should she inherit it.

At that moment, that seemed like a big if. Still, as soon as Katie landed behind her desk at Artisans Alley, she called and left a message with Fred Cunningham, asking him to return her call.

It was the very least she could do.

OWNING a business wasn't all rainbows and unicorns, something Katie discovered the day she inherited Artisans Alley. That said, the enormity of data collection was daunting. After a long day of admin work for both Artisans Alley and Tealicious, Katie's eyes were bleary as she stared at the spreadsheet on her computer screen. A knock on her office door jamb startled her into acute awareness. Katie turned to find Rose Nash standing in the doorway. Until recently, Rose had been Katie's favorite vendor. But after the fiasco of Rose adopting a puppy and then considering surrendering the dog to a kill shelter, Katie found herself stepping back from the friendship. She took the stewardship of a pet seriously. It was only because Katie had taken charge of the dog and found it a new home that the pup was still alive. That Rose hadn't taken on the task of finding the dog a furever home hadn't endeared her to Katie. If that was a character failure on Katie's part, she'd accept it.

"What's up, Rose?" Katie asked wearily.

"Sorry to disturb you, but we seem to have a problem out on the floor."

Swell.

As a reflex action, Katie reached for the glass candy jar she kept on her desk, grabbed a butterscotch, unwrapped it, popped it into her mouth and crunched it. The action always made those around her cringe. Katie ignored Rose's reaction. "Go on."

"Bonnie Wozniak is accusing Wanda Baldack of copying her stock—and trying to undercut her."

Bonnie and Wanda were both fine art painters whose booths faced each other. Katie tried to separate like-minded artists, but when a slot came open on the Alley's main selling floor, it could be open warfare for the vendors who'd been on the waiting list to occupy such coveted spaces. Katie tried to be fair, and before she'd moved Wanda downstairs she'd spoken to Bonnie about it. The woman assured her she didn't have a problem with arrangement—until now, apparently.

"Are they both here?"

"They've been duking it out for the past ten minutes, and they're scaring away customers."

A slow burn passed through Katie. Why hadn't Rose, or one of the vendors, come to her at the start of the trouble, instead of letting it escalate to intimidating customers?

"I'll take care of it," Katie said tartly.

"Thanks. I'd better get back to the cash desk. We'll be closing soon and it'll be chaos those last few minutes."

It always was.

Rose turned and walked through and out the vendors' lounge with Katie not far behind. Sure enough. She could hear Bonnie's and Wanda's raised voices as she approached the aisle where their booths were located.

"Ladies," Katie called as she approached, "please use your indoor voices while inside the Alley."

Wanda turned a blistering glare on Katie. "And you can refrain from that condescending attitude."

If Wanda was hoping to garner support from Katie, she'd already shot herself in the proverbial foot.

"What seems to be the problem?"

Both women took a step forward and bombarded her with their overlapping voices, which grew more shrill with each word. Katie held up a hand and said sharply, "That's enough! Please follow me to the vendors' lounge, where we can talk this through."

"But then you couldn't see how this bit—"

"Name-calling is not appropriate," Katie warned the older woman, who was dressed all in black, her hair the same color— and it hadn't been natural for quite some time.

"Then explain what's going on—in quiet tones. Wanda, you go first."

"But I—" Bonnie nearly exploded.

Katie raised a hand to silence the woman, who acquiesced but looked even angrier because of the admonishment.

"This—" Wanda seemed to stumble over how to describe her fellow vendor. "—person seems to think I'm copying her work. I've done no such thing. Is it my fault we visit the same beaches and parks for inspiration for our paintings?"

"Give me an example," Katie said.

Both women entered their respective booths and came back with two paintings each. The first Bonnie held up was of the docks at the marina where Seth Landers kept his sailboat, named *Temporary Relief*. Both had chosen to render the gazebo with the lake in the background. It was a popular spot for wedding photographers to take shots of brides and grooms. However, while the location and perspective of the paintings were nearly exact, the women's styles were certainly different. Wanda worked in watercolors, and her paintings were muted, with colors mingling and complimenting each other, while Bonnie's work was done in acrylics and so meticulously rendered one might have thought they were photographs.

"I don't see the problem," Katie said quite frankly.

"She's copied my work!" the women said in unison.

Katie frowned. "The subject matter is the same, but the works are distinctly different."

"How can you say that?" Bonnie demanded.

Was the woman blind?

"Because your styles are poles apart."

Neither woman was willing to admit that, and they again started haranguing Katie with their complaints. Again, Katie held up a hand to stall the argument.

"What do you want me to do about the situation?"

Wanda glared at Bonnie. "Tell her to leave me the hell alone."

"You leave *me* alone," Bonnie started in again.

"Enough!" Katie said sharply.

"You need to make *her* move," Bonnie said, pointing at her nemesis.

"We discussed this when Wanda was moved to the booth across from yours. You said you had no problem being located across from her."

"That was before she started copying my work."

"Copying?" Wanda cried. "Look at the date of my painting. It was done a full year before yours."

Katie looked at the dates on both paintings. Unless Wanda had fudged the year—which seemed unlikely—it *had* been painted before Bonnie's.

"That's a bad example," Bonnie grumbled. It wasn't.

"I'm not moving," Wanda said, crossing her arms over her chest in defiance. "It's taken me six years to move from the back of the building to a prime location, and now that I'm here, I refuse to leave."

Katie had the last say on that, but she understood where Wanda was coming from. The Alley's main showroom was prime retail space, and the vendors who landed such coveted spots paid a little extra to be there.

"I implore you ladies to find some common ground to get along."

"And if she *can't?*" Bonnie bluffed.

"There are others in line who would be happy to take over your booths."

"Are you threatening us?" Wanda asked, her eyes wide.

"If you look at the rental agreements you signed, you'll find that it can be terminated for a number of reasons. Infighting happens to be one of them."

"Ezra Hilton would have *never* enforced such a rule," Bonnie insisted.

"Well, apparently, he did. Or at least he intended to, because it's part of the agreement *he* drew up and both of you signed during *his* tenure as owner of the Alley."

Suddenly both women looked uncomfortable.

"Well, tell *her* to stop copying my work," Bonnie insisted.

"No, tell *her* to stop copying *mine*," Wanda countered.

"I'll do no such thing. If you want to see different vistas, either use your imaginations or spread out beyond the village landscapes to find your inspiration. Do I make myself clear?" Katie demanded.

"Yes," Wanda grumbled.

"I guess," Bonnie reluctantly agreed.

"And if you have any other beefs, do *not* address them on the showroom floor. Apparently, you've scared off more than a couple of customers. A bad experience means they won't return —and that negative talk to friends and relatives could have a snowball effect."

"Yes, Katie," both women said contritely and in unison.

That was more like it.

"Fine. Now, if you'll excuse me, I have a business to close for the day."

Katie swore she could feel the heat of their anger scorch her back as she made her way to her office. The confrontation left her feeling grumpy and put upon. So did the thought of returning to her cramped apartment upon closing the Alley.

Plopping down on her chair, Katie reached for her mouse and awakened her sleeping computer, pulling up a popular real estate website. Typing in her preferred zip code, she had a look at what was currently for sale in the area. Ten addresses popped up, and she went through each listing. Most of them were to be shown by appointment only. She wasn't in a position —hadn't even done a pre-loan application—so she looked at the two listings with open houses scheduled for that weekend. One was for a four-bedroom Colonial on half an acre with a pool and a hot tub. That was far too big for her needs. And the maintenance on a pool was definitely more work than she was willing to put in when it came to upkeep. The second house was a two-bedroom Craftsman bungalow in the heart of the village, which had been built a century before. The landscaping was minimal, but she could envision ripping out the tired, overgrown bushes and planting a row of beautiful old roses of various colors. It would take a few years to establish, but she could be patient.

The kitchen hadn't been touched in decades, and what had been done to it was a crime. Nineteen-seventies orange-and-brown wallpaper, white cabinets with bullnose oak handles. Yellow appliances that also came from the last century were ugly and not at all energy efficient. It would take big bucks to restore the kitchen to its former glory, but it would be an act of love to do so.

The bedrooms were small, but adequate. It was the living room with its brick fireplace and a darling inglenook that stole her heart. She looked at the asking price and winced. Yeah, she could only afford the place if Margo held the mortgage, and she didn't want that. But it might be fun—or incredibly frustrating—to tour the place during the open house on Sunday.

Katie scrolled through all the pictures another three times before she decided she'd definitely make time to tour the house. Maybe she'd ask Margo to accompany her, too.

Rose's voice came over the public address system. "Artisans Alley will be closing in five minutes. Please bring your purchases up to the front desk to check out. Thank you."

Katie knew that Rose was the only cashier on duty that afternoon, so she rose from her desk to see if she would be needed. Sure enough, a line of people greeted her as she approached cash desk two, which she rounded. "I can help someone over here," she called, and several people scooted over to her counter. She didn't have an assistant to wrap the shopper's items, but she was good at multitasking, and within minutes, the last of the customers filed out the French doors that separated Artisans Alley from the lobby and the rest of the merchants who rented space in the building.

"What are your plans for the evening?" Rose asked Katie as they cleaned out the cash and credit card receipts from the register drawers.

"Nothing special."

Rose sighed. "I'll probably nuke a frozen dinner, sit in my living room with Rose and Walter (her pet goldfish), and read. Maybe later I'll watch a little TV. There never seems to be anything good on the tube anymore," the older woman lamented.

Katie didn't have cable or subscriptions to any streaming

services. She liked to read, but she didn't have a current book or print magazine to pour over. She preferred actual pages of photographs of beautiful homes or of delectable recipes rather than viewing them on a tablet. It was somehow just more satisfying. That evening was a blank slate before her. The thought depressed her, but for some reason, she didn't want to admit it to Rose. "I've got a lot of work to do, what with the summer programs coming up for the Alley and the Square."

"Yes, I hear Nona Fiske is taking charge of the big summer picnic on the Square and that she's angling for your job as head of the Merchants Association."

Katie blinked. "Really?"

"It's the talk of the Square," Rose said nonchalantly.

Well, Katie certainly hadn't heard that piece of gossip. She stood there, her expression blank, as Rose turned to gather her purse, getting ready to leave for the day.

"See you tomorrow?" Katie asked hopefully. Rose had already worked more hours than she was required for that month, but she answered with a cheerful, "Yes."

"Great."

Rose headed for the exit while two of the other vendors approached the cash desk.

"We've done the walk-through. There's nobody left in the place except the three of us."

As Vance opened the Alley two hours before retail hours, Katie's second-in-command had left earlier that day.

"Great."

Katie waited while the women collected their purses from the tag room, followed them out, and locked up for the night. Then she advanced to the back of the building to secure it, too.

But instead of heading out the door for her apartment across the square, Katie sat back down behind her desk and awakened her computer once again, going through the pictures of the little bungalow on the real estate site and examining every picture in great detail. What if—just what *if*—she could possess that house? She could envision the furniture she'd take her time finding that would be just perfect for the living room and the master and guest bedroom. She'd keep the vintage fixtures in the main bathroom, finding appropriate wallpapers—maybe a pattern by William Morris to decorate the walls.

Stop it, she warned herself. *There's no way you could afford, let alone restore this place to its former glory.*

That fact depressed her, but it only made her determined to count the hours—and dream about—the home until she could visit on Sunday.

Chapter Thirteen

Katie returned to her tiny apartment more out of a sense of duty to her cats than a desire to be in a place she had never really called home. As always, the cats were glad to see her—until they decided to punish her for leaving them alone in such a cramped space for so many hours.

"Yeah, and I love you, too!" Katie said as the cats regrouped to sit beside their food and water bowls, letting her know her true role in their lives: servant.

Katie couldn't sit comfortably on the love seat for long. Why had she ever thought it would be adequate? She couldn't even stretch out on it to take a nap on a lazy afternoon—not that she'd experienced one in eons.

Admit it, girl—you're bored.

Here she was on a Saturday night with nothing to do and no one to do it with.

She could always drop by Margo's house, knowing she'd be welcome. But Katie also realized she'd been avoiding Margo, and she knew why. Why had she blurted the little-thought-out request to call Margo "mom?"

Because Seth thought it might be a good idea.

Katie thought she'd be able to do it, but doubt had haunted her ever since he'd brought up the subject. And how was she going to introduce Margo to others? She could do it by using her full name and not mentioning the relationship? Because their last names were the same, people might assume they were mother and daughter, although they looked nothing alike. Perhaps Katie should think about their connection as one of adoption. Without Chad in their lives, the two lonely women had adopted each other. Yes, they were now a chosen family since they weren't tied by blood.

They hadn't spoken for a few days, and Katie realized she actually wanted to connect with Margo. She liked those conversations. It seemed like the longer they knew each other, the less they chafed. And then there was the fact that they were business partners.

Katie didn't want to think about how reneging on her request to call Margo mom might disrupt their working relationship.

Putting those thoughts aside, Katie decided that—although it was short notice—she'd send out a blanket text to her Artisans Alley vendors, inviting them to a meeting the following evening after the Alley closed so they could discuss Nona's extravaganza. She was beginning to think of the event in that term, and it smarted.

After sending the text, and though it wasn't late, Katie changed into her sleep shirt and settled down in her bed, feeling at loose ends, wondering if she should peruse the same stack of decorating magazines she'd thumbed through a dozen times or do something different.

Like what?

Listen to music? Nah.

Draw up lists of things to do? That was work and she was done with that for the day.

Mason and Della soon joined her on the bed.

"I'm bored," she told the cats. There, she'd said it aloud. They merely looked at her.

Katie thought over her options. "I think I'll watch *Pollyanna* again. Would you care to join me?"

Again, the cats looked at her. Mason's expression seemed to say *duh, woman! We're already here on the bed!*

Katie turned on the movie and settled back against her pillows to watch the opening credits. Then the steam engine pulled into the Harrington station and Pollyanna disembarked. Katie closed her eyes for just a second—and was out like a light.

THE DAYS HAD TAKEN on a routine that Katie found both tedious and yet comforting. She got up, fed the cats, got ready for the workday, and trundled down the stairs to the Tealicious kitchen, where she helped Brad get set up for the day's guests. It was after ten by the time she finished cleaning up her work-station—later than usual. But she'd texted Vance and, as usual, he'd opened for vendor set-up at eight, and now it was time for Katie's daily power walk around the Square. She hadn't gotten far when her phone pinged. Katie glanced at the screen to see a text from Sue Sweeney, owner of the Square's candy shop.

Did you know Nona is selling raffle tickets for a quilt—but there's no charity listed?

Katie studied the words. She wasn't sure what the legal rules were for raffles, so she backtracked to Artisans Alley and turned to her computer to find out. It didn't take long. Only non-profit entities could legally hold a raffle in New York State *and* they had to be registered for at least three years to be eligible. That let Nona out.

Before she could head out to continue her walk—with a stop at the Quiet Quilter—Katie was intercepted by Bonnie Wozniak. "Katie we have to talk!"

Oh, dear.

"Yes, Bonnie," Katie said.

"I wanted to talk to you about Wanda—without her interrupting me."

Katie sighed. "Go on."

"What can I do to make her stop copying my work?"

Katie blew out a breath. She had other, much more important things on her mind. "Well," she said, hesitating. "Why don't you do something that's completely different from your usual landscapes?"

"Like what?"

Katie wasn't an artist, nor a critic. Her thoughts whirled. "Well, how about a still life?"

Bonnie wrinkled her nose. "You mean with fruit or flowers?"

"Yeah. Then wait to see if Wanda does something similar."

"Are you talking about setting a trap to catch her?" Bonnie asked, her brow wrinkling.

"No, I'm just saying—" But then Katie didn't elaborate.

Bonnie's expression underwent a dramatic change, her mouth tightening into a crooked smile, her gaze shifty. "That's perfect. Absolutely perfect. I'm going home right now and start working on a new painting," she said gleefully. "I can't wait to see what Wanda hangs in her booth next." She pivoted and headed for the Alley's main showroom, calling over her shoulder, "Thanks for the idea."

Katie sighed, wondering if she'd have a public relations problem should Bonnie tell other vendors that it was Katie's idea to trap Wanda. Technically, it was, but she wouldn't have couched it in those terms.

Katie ducked out the Alley's back entrance before another vendor could detain her. Once outside, she strode directly across the Square to ask Nona about her raffle and to have a look at the prize.

The Quiet Quilter had been open for only fifteen minutes, but already several customers were examining the bolts of fabric that lined one wall. As usual, Nona watched the women like a hawk after prey.

The quilt in question was a pattern Katie was familiar with: tumbling blocks in primary colors. It was pleasant to look at but not something Katie would care to own. She went for more muted shades. As expected, on the counter sat a tall plastic jar stuffed with raffle tickets and no charity listed. Katie crossed the store and approached Nona, who was so intent on spying on her customers that she didn't see Katie approach.

Katie cleared her throat—twice—but Nona took no notice of her. Finally, she spoke. "Nona?"

Nona started, clutching her chest. "Goodness! Are you trying to give me a heart attack?

"Sorry," Katie said, frowning. She crooked her right index finger and beckoned Nona to follow her out of the customers' earshot. Katie stood before the jar of tickets.

"What do you want?" Nona asked testily.

"I understand you're raffling off a quilt."

Nona's expression turned decidedly shifty. "What of it?"

"What charity do you hope to help?"

Nona straightened so she stood just a little bit taller. "None."

"So you're just hoping to profit from the raffle?"

"That's why I'm in business," Nona asserted. "There's no law that says I can't do so."

"Well, as it happens—there is. And you must refund whatever you've collected to everyone who bought a ticket."

"Who says?" Nona barked. Apparently Katie hadn't made herself clear.

"The state of New York. Only registered charities can run a raffle."

"That's ridiculous. They have them all the time at craft shows."

"And who are they collecting for?"

Nona frowned. "Usually the sponsors."

"Yes, like high schools raising money for the band, the art department, or library. You can't legally hold a raffle and keep the money for yourself."

Nona's mouth tightened into a thin line. "Who's going to report me?"

"Well, I think it's safe to say that someone on the Square who's been in law enforcement will definitely notice." And if Ray didn't, Katie would point it out to him.

"Are you threatening me?" Nona demanded.

"No, I'm trying to save you from yourself so that you don't end up with a stiff fine—or worse—from the state."

Nona said nothing.

"As long as I'm here, I'd like to know when you want me to call another meeting of the Merchants Association."

"What for? Can't we just wait for the next scheduled meeting?" Nona asked, clueless. "I can give a report then."

Katie sighed. "If we're going to pull off this event before Labor Day, we need to get the ball rolling. What have you done so far?"

Nona's eyes blazed. "Not that it's any of your business, but I've already looked into buying several hundred Japanese paper lanterns." And then her gaze seemed to lose focus. Slowly, she waved her arm in the air and misquoted a line Katie remembered hearing Hayley Mills deliver in the movie version of *Pollyanna*: "Picture it…bicycles with a hundred Japanese lanterns."

Katie blinked at her. "Where will you get the bicyclists?"

For a moment, Nona looked stunned—like she'd been smacked upside the head. "What?"

"Who will you hire to ride around the Square with the lanterns on bikes? And am I wrong—but didn't the whole bizarre depicted in the movie occur at night? I'm not sure that can be replicated during daylight hours when the Square's businesses are open."

"Well then they'll just have to adjust their hours," Nona declared.

Katie bit her lip, thinking—looking not unlike the young girl depicted in the film. "Have you found a band to play for those who want to dance?" Katie asked, hoping to distract the older woman.

"What?"

"A combo of older ladies who belted out the tunes of the day. Have you looked into hiring someone to fit that bill?"

Nona looked confused. "No. Why would I?"

"I thought you wanted to portray our celebration as something akin to what happened in the film."

"Well, I ..." But then Nona didn't elaborate.

"I thought you said you were spearheading this event. How can you do so if you haven't thought out what needs to happen and the logistics to make it occur?"

Nona looked confused. "Well, I—" she began again.

"What's the budget for the bazaar? So far, you haven't submitted one to the Merchants Association for expenditures. Will you be doing so any time soon?"

"Budget?" Nona repeated, the furrows on her brow deepened. "What are you talking about?"

"Are you going to put up posters, or place an ad in the local Penny Saver or the Rochester Democrat & Chronicle? Or were you thinking more along the lines of using social media?"

"Social media? I'm not even sure what you mean," Nona said, sounding frustrated.

Katie fought the urge to roll her eyes. Instead, she turned a steely gaze upon the older woman. "These are all questions that the merchants are going to bring up the next time we meet. I suggest you figure out the answers."

"Well, *you're* the head of the organization. Why can't you take care of those details?" Nona groused.

"*You* said you wanted to spearhead the event. Well, feel free to do so."

Nona's face twisted into a malevolent glare. "I think you're setting me up for failure."

"Are you kidding me? I've just told you what it will take to make it a successful promotion. And as the one in charge, it's up to *you* to figure ways to make that happen."

For a moment, Nona looked like a deer caught in a car's high beams, knowing oblivion was inevitable. But then she straightened. "You need to help me, guide me."

Katie shook her head. "Not a chance. Especially as you've been touting to some of the Association's members that you intend to take over the Merchants Association. Well, good for you. I've been looking to dump the position since the day it was foisted upon me. But I'll warn you—if you fail at your first foray into leadership, you'll find it hard to rally the troops behind any other initiative you might suggest."

Nona shook her head, her lips curling. "You're so damned smug."

"No, I've earned a degree in marketing and I've got experience pulling off more than a few successful promotions."

"Smarty pants," Nona uttered under her breath.

Katie raised her head defiantly. "I like to think so."

Nona's gaze shifted to the floor, and it was long seconds before she answered. "You've given me a lot to think about."

Good.

"When would you like me to schedule the next meeting?" Katie asked. "With such a short timeline, we'll have to move fast."

Again, Nona looked overwhelmed. "I'm going to need a few days to process what you've told me."

"A week?" Katie suggested.

Nona's expression was fifty percent uncertain and another fifty percent terrified.

"I guess."

"Great. I'll schedule a meeting and ask the merchants to come prepared to ask questions. I suggest you ready answers for any contingency." Katie knew that Nona wasn't prepared to tackle the long list of things that needed to be accomplished to make the promotion a success. Katie had no desire to pull off the Herculean task on her own. But perhaps if Nona—or she—could encourage volunteers among the merchants, the event might succeed despite such long odds.

It was worth a try. Most such proceedings took a year or two to take off. It would probably be the same with this one.

And with that, Katie decided to take a wait-and-see perspective.

She really had no other choice.

Chapter Fourteen

K atie made another circuit around the Square and saw the familiar car parked outside the old ceramics shop. Phoebe Preston had returned to Victoria Square.

Katie jogged closer to the building. "Hello!" she called.

Phoebe poked her head outside the derelict shop's open door. "Katie, is that you?"

"It sure is. What are you up to?"

"I was trying to figure out what it would take to stabilize the inside of the building." By the expression on her face, Katie got the feeling the news wasn't good. "It looks like I'll probably have to rip everything down to the studs; the building is in such disrepair," Phoebe lamented.

"Is it worth it in the long run?" Katie asked.

"Fred Cunningham came out and we discussed what it would take to stabilize the building. He thinks the property would be worth more if it were in better condition. The land is worth a bit, but not nearly as much as a sturdy structure sitting on it."

Katie did a mental assessment. The building needed a new roof, all new electrical, HVAC, and plumbing, plus new floors, insulation, drywall, and paint. Sometimes, it was better to cut your losses and sell a property as is to the highest bidder.

Phoebe seemed to sense Katie's thoughts. "What would you do?"

Katie shook her head. "It's not my place to comment."

"I'm *asking* you for your opinion. I know you own property on the Square and are refurbishing the big warehouse up the hill." Phoebe gestured toward the hulking concrete structure behind the buildings that made up the south side of the Square.

Katie considered her words before speaking. "It might be worthwhile to refurbish the building *if* you intended to run a business yourself, but if not—I'd put the property up for sale as is and hope for a great deal. That might not work for another commercial property, but Victoria Square is experiencing a renaissance. We've become a bit of a destination. It's a hot property. Without putting in much effort, I think you'll get top buck for the site."

Phoebe nodded. "That's more or less what your real estate friend told me."

"Fred wouldn't steer you wrong."

Phoebe nodded and glanced around the decrepit building. "I guess I should return all the wood I bought. I still have the receipt."

"If you need help loading it in the back of your van, I'd be glad to give you a hand."

Phoebe nodded, sadness tinging her features. "Thanks. I'd appreciate it."

They stood in silence for long seconds, not making eye contact. Katie felt bad for the woman. But then she had an idea. "Thanks to probate, you've got a way to go before you can sell the property. In the meantime, it wouldn't hurt to try to gin up some interest in the place."

"And how would I do that?"

"I could give you a free membership to the Merchants Asso-

ciation. Members have been known to team up to buy
properties."

"Oh yeah?"

Katie nodded. "And if they wouldn't want it for themselves,
they often have contacts who might."

Phoebe's gaze narrowed. "Are you among those who might
want it?"

Katie shook her head. "I own Artisans Alley and am in part-
nership on three other properties in the area, but I have no
interest in obtaining your building or land. In fact, I'm considering downsizing my interest in the Square." She didn't explain
why she'd made such a decision.

Phoebe nodded. "I appreciate your honesty. And you're
right. I can't do anything until Dad's estate is settled. And I'll
accept your offer of membership to the Merchants Association."
Phoebe turned her gaze toward the shambles of what had once
been a stable structure. "I wish I had a use for the property. In
my heart of hearts, I really don't want to sell it."

"Is there a way you could use it? I mean, could you be an
entrepreneur on the Square?"

"The only skill I have is sewing. I once worked in a tailor
shop. I make a lot of my clothes." She plucked at the blouse she
wore, which had a rather peasanty feel—made of gauzy blue
fabric, with a floral bodice trimmed in ribbon. Phoebe laughed.
"Would you believe, I made this when I was in high school and
it still fits?"

"It's beautiful. I love it."

Phoebe beamed. It was the first time Katie had seen her
smile.

"You've got a while before you can sell the property. What if
you spent the time—and money you would put in to shore up
the building—researching what it would take to open a clothing
boutique?"

"Isn't there already a consignment shop in the same building that houses Artisans Alley?" Phoebe asked.

"That's true, but they specialize in children's clothing."

Phoebe's eyes widened with interest, as though a whole world of opportunity had just opened for her. "You've given me something to think about. When is the next Merchants Association meeting?"

Katie explained that they held one just days before, but with a big upcoming promotion, there would be more than the usual gatherings to discuss the project.

"If I can't open a shop before then, maybe I could volunteer to help someone out."

"That's a great idea. Several women on the Square work long hours and only hire seasonal people. If nothing else, I'm sure some of them could use help with set-up and tear-down. And it would allow you to meet everyone. For the most part, they're a pretty great bunch of people."

Phoebe's gaze narrowed. "For the most part?"

Katie nodded sadly. "There's bound to be at least one bad apple in every barrel. And it isn't always the same person or persons," Katie amended.

"Nobody's perfect, I guess," Phoebe agreed.

"Yeah." Katie glanced toward the wood pile. "Let's get that wood packed into your van so you can get your money back."

"Thanks. I appreciate your help. And I *will* spend some time online later today to try to find out what I might need to do to make a go of a business. It's never been my ambition, but you make it sound enticing."

"It wouldn't be easy, but it *would* be satisfying," Katie said encouragingly.

It took the women less than ten minutes to pile the wood into Phoebe's van. Upon closing the gate, Katie spoke.

"Why don't you give me your cell phone number and email

address and I'll give you mine. Then I can add you to the Merchants Association email loop. That way, you'll hear about all that we've got going on in planning the big summer promotion."

"Thanks. I'd appreciate it. And by the way, I've got an appointment to talk to that lawyer you mentioned."

"That's great. When will you see him?"

"This afternoon."

Katie nodded.

Phoebe glanced at her watch. "I'd better get going. We'll talk again soon."

Katie nodded and watched as Phoebe climbed into the driver's seat of her minivan, giving Katie a wave before she drove off.

Would Phoebe decide to try to be a part of the Square, or would she sell her property and take the money and run?

Only time would tell.

～

KATIE CONTINUED on her walk and as she rounded the corner near Tanner's Cafe and Bakery, she saw Charlotte Booth step outside her shop with a broom in hand and start sweeping the porch. Quickening her pace, Katie jogged to join her. "Charlotte! Have you got a minute?"

"A minute," she said, and paused her task.

"I understand you and Maxwell Preston were acquainted," Katie said, keeping her tone neutral.

Charlotte stood just a little straighter, taking a step back. "We'd spoken in the past," she said guardedly.

"I understood you did more than speak."

Charlotte's expression hardened. "What are you implying?"

"That you had a relationship with Mr. Preston, and that it wasn't just casual."

"That's none of your business," Charlotte said coldly, turned, and reentered her store.

Katie followed.

"But it *is* Detective Rigby's business. I assume you've reported your friendship with him to the detective."

Charlotte said nothing, setting the broom behind the curtain that hung between the retail shop and the kitchen where she prepared her wares.

"Because if you haven't," Katie continued, "there are others who may have done so. Carol Rigby doesn't strike me as the forgiving type."

Charlotte looked up sharply. "What are you implying?"

"I assume that at the time of his death, you and Preston were no longer in a relationship."

Again, Charlotte said nothing.

"If I've heard about your connection to him, chances are Detective Rigby has, too."

"And?"

"That puts you in a precarious position. If you haven't already disclosed that information to the sheriff's office, it could be construed that you've got something to hide."

"I've got *nothing* to hide," Charlotte asserted.

"Then I urge you to contact the detective and clear your name as soon as possible."

"Or?"

"I don't think you want to end up in the county detention center—even for one night."

Charlotte's eyes widened in what Katie could only assume was terror.

"It wouldn't hurt to talk to an attorney, either," Katie advised.

Charlotte's cheeks darkened and her gaze dipped as the bell above her door chimed and a couple with a small boy entered the shop. With amazing speed, her countenance transformed as a genuine smile crossed her lips and when she spoke, there was no hint that anything could be wrong with her life. "Welcome to Booth's Jellies and Jams. Feel free to look around and don't hesitate to ask if you need assistance."

The couple nodded, and turned to peruse the gleaming jars of jams and jellies on offer.

"I think you'd better go," Charlotte whispered.

"Call Detective Rigby. Today," Katie advised.

Charlotte's gaze was penetrating, but she remained silent.

Katie turned and left the shop, pretty sure that whatever kinship Charlotte felt for her was now gone.

Maybe Nona would have someone in her corner if she challenged Katie at the next Merchants Association meeting.

At that point, Katie wasn't sure she cared.

PHOEBE WAS as good as her word. It was after four that afternoon when Katie's phone rang.

"How did your meeting with Seth go?" Katie asked.

"I just came from his office. You were right. He did have my father's will on file. Apparently, his father drew it up." Something in her tone sounded off.

"And?" Katie prompted.

"It's rather convoluted, but in order for me to inherit, I'm not allowed to sell the property on Victoria Square, and I'm not supposed to make any substantial upgrades and only enough repairs to keep the building standing."

Katie frowned. "That's a strange request. Was there any explanation?"

"Just that my dad didn't want my mother's studio to be defiled in any way."

"It's about to collapse. Is there any provision for that?" Katie asked.

"Mr. Landers said I can and *should* strengthen the building's structure and replace glass in the windows and the roof if need be."

"Is it worthwhile *not* following those guidelines?"

"Oh, yeah. Dad left a fair amount of money, which I'll get after probate. All I have to do is pay the taxes on the property, and I can probably live quite comfortably for the rest of my life —if I invest wisely. Mr. Landers gave me the name of an accountant he said I could trust: Mr. Derek Kline."

"I can vouch for Derek. He's my accountant, too."

"That's good to know. Thanks. Anyway, I guess I won't need that membership to the Victoria Square Merchants Association."

"If you'd like to keep in touch about what's going on you're welcome to come to a meeting or two."

"Thanks. I'll keep that in mind."

"And thanks for keeping me in the loop."

"You're welcome."

"Have you reconsidered doing repairs on the building any time soon?"

"I'll have to think about it. I've got time before I have to return the lumber and everything I bought."

"Well, good luck," Katie said.

"Thanks. It'll be months, maybe a year before I see even a dime of my inheritance, but I'm sure we'll see each other before that happens."

"Feel free to stop by my office at Artisans Alley any time during our sales hours."

"You bet. Bye."

"Bye."

Phoebe ended the call. Katie set her phone down on her desk and sat back in her chair. Why would Maxwell Preston make such a strange proviso in his will?

It was worth pondering—but not just then.

Katie glanced at the clock on the wall. She had half an hour before the Alley's vendor meeting was set to begin.

She crossed the tarmac to Tealicious, let herself in, and perused the day's leftovers in the big commercial fridge. She found a container of tuna salad but none of the wonderful Parker House rolls Brad often made. She settled for whole wheat bread—not her favorite. After making a quick sandwich and chugging half a glass of water, Katie flew back out the door, heading for the Alley.

Vance had set up several rows of folding chairs in the building's lobby—enough seating for at least twenty, not that Katie was expecting that many vendors to attend. She was wrong, and it was standing room only by the time she called the meeting to order, surprised when the group quickly quieted, apparently keen to learn about the summer promotion.

"The Merchants Association hasn't yet set a date, but we're here tonight to talk about how we might participate in—" Katie wiggled her fingers as air quotes, "—the extravaganza. To publicize the event to those attending the day's proceedings, I've arranged for a couple of young entrepreneurs to come up with signage to promote Artisans Alley. Size wise, it'll be big—*very* big. Apart from that, if you have a suggestion on how we can participate, please raise your hands, and I'll call on each of you in turn."

At least a dozen arms shot into the air, some waving madly. Katie nodded at Rose, who sat in the front row. "Will participation be mandatory?" she asked.

The question gave Katie a start. Usually Rose was all in when it came to promoting the Alley. As though sensing Katie's confusion, Rose added, "asking for a friend."

Katie nodded. "That's something we need to discuss. Summer sales can sometimes be as elusive as a cool breeze. I thought it might be a good idea to consider a blanket ten percent off in all booths."

"Are you kidding," came a female voice from the back. "I barely make my rent during the summer months. I can't afford to give away my merchandise."

"I'm talking a straight ten percent," Katie explained. "It's not a lot, and if you end up selling in volume, there's a possibility you'll make your rent *and* a profit."

"Possibility," someone else grumbled.

"That's just one outcome. Who else has a question?"

Again the arms shot up. Katie pointed at Liz Meier.

"I'd just as soon set my own discount. I've found the sweet spot to be between twenty-five and fifty percent."

"It's lucky you're able to afford it," the woman in the back grumbled.

Katie recognized another woman.

"What happens if it rains during the promotion?" Gwen Hardy asked.

"Luckily we're an indoor venue, but I imagine it would considerably reduce attendance," Katie reluctantly admitted.

"Will any of us get to set up in the parking lot?" Joan McDonald asked.

"That's something that needs to be discussed with the Merchants Association members. They may not want to lose potential parking spaces."

"What about behind the Alley?" Edie Silver asked.

"I only own a small portion of that property. The rest is considered a municipal lot."

The questions flew fast and furiously for the next hour. Katie did her best to respond, but this early in the planning stages there were too many unknowns to give definitive answers.

"In the meantime, how about I put together a survey? Everyone will get a copy and be able to give their opinions."

A few of the vendors grumbled under their breaths, but the proposal was voted on by a show of hands supporting the idea.

"Great," Katie said with satisfaction. "Once I've tabulated the results, I'll report back to everyone with a letter that will also update you all on what the merchants decide after their next meeting."

"And when will that be?"

Katie hesitated before answering. "Some," well, one, "of the members want to wait until the next scheduled meeting to discuss the details."

"Are you kidding?" Ben Stillwell asked. "We should already be talking about this year's Dicken's Festival," which didn't begin until November.

"As I said, I'll let you know as soon as I know what's happening with the merchants."

"Aren't you the head of the association? Shouldn't you already know what's going on?" Edie asked.

"I'm not in charge of this event. I'm stepping aside to let the merchant who suggested the promotion take the lead."

"And who's that?" Anne Bard asked.

"Nona Fiske from The Quiet Quilter."

"Oh no," came an anguished female voice from the back. "The whole event is doomed."

Katie concurred but didn't voice the opinion.

"If you have any other questions or suggestions in the coming days, please feel free to drop by my office to discuss them."

And with that, the meeting was over. The vendors rose from their seats, some streaming toward the exit and the front parking lot while a few hung back to speak to one another.

Katie was about to help Vance stack the folding chairs on a cart to be put back into the storage room when Bonnie Wozniak approached Katie.

"Katie, come see the still life I painted. I've already hung it in my booth."

Katie was about to protest, but excitement sparkled in

Bonnie's eyes. She forced a smile. "Sure. Lead the way." Bonnie turned, and Katie shot an apologetic glance in Vance's direction. He merely shrugged and continued stacking the chairs.

Katie followed Bonnie, threading their way through the Alley's main showroom until they came to Bonnie's booth. "I'm surprised you finished the painting so fast," Katie commented as they walked. Chad often worked on a painting for days—sometimes weeks before he was satisfied with the results. Perhaps that was why he'd finished so few canvases.

"Acrylics dry fast, and I had the perfect frame for the canvas," Bonnie explained. Arriving at the booth, Bonnie stood aside to give Katie the grand view. In the center of the wall, surrounded by an ornate gilt frame, was a gorgeous painting of fruit and flowers.

"Wow," Katie muttered, taken aback

"This may be one of my best paintings yet. Once I started working on it, I couldn't stop. I probably worked twelve straight hours on it."

No doubt about it: the composition was well executed, the background looked like gold velvet cloth haphazardly tossed, the folds catching light in some areas, fading to shadows in others. The painting looked like something executed by a Renaissance master; it needed to be displayed and put up for sale in an exclusive gallery, not meager little Artisans Alley.

Katie stared at the work, chewing her lip.

"You don't like it?" Bonnie asked, concerned.

"Oh, no. I absolutely love it."

"But?" Bonnie asked.

Katie chose her words carefully. "Were I you, I'd seek out a more impressive gallery to offer this painting."

Bonnie looked confused. "Why do you say that?"

Katie inspected the price tag on the piece. "Because I believe it's worth much more than you're asking for it, and you'll never get that here in Artisans Alley."

Bonnie looked from the painting to Katie and back again. "You really think so?"

Katie nodded. "I do. You might want to ask my—" and here she hesitated. Did she have the courage to say the word? "You might want to ask my Mom, Margo, about it. She's going to open a gallery in the big warehouse up the hill. She's about to start looking for work to show. I think she'd be very interested in this painting."

Again, Bonnie looked confused. "You really think it's that good?"

Katie nodded. "I do."

"But...but what about Wanda copying my paintings?"

"I wouldn't worry about it. Just keep doing your best work. And, again, talk to Margo. I don't think she'll steer you wrong."

"How can I get in touch with her?" Bonnie asked.

"I'll have her contact you. I'm sure she'll want to include this in her gallery. It won't open until at least the fall, but I'm sure she'll be as impressed as I am." And heaven help Katie if she was wrong about that.

Bonnie smiled. "Okay. I'll take it home—for now. And I'll paint something else to go in its place, but probably not in time for the weekend."

"You're a long-time vendor here. You know what you need to do to sell in this venue."

Bonnie shrugged. "Yeah, I guess I do."

"That said, I urge you to explore what else you're capable of. And if that takes you out of Artisans Alley, you definitely need to go for it."

Bonnie's expression was a mix of awe and puzzlement.

Katie had a feeling that once Margo's gallery opened, Artisans Alley might have another open booth.

The thought pleased her.

Chapter Fifteen

During the winter and early months of spring, Saturdays on Victoria Square took on a sameness that would soon change in the coming weeks when summer finally hit. As usual, Katie started the day at Tealicious, moved onto Artisans Alley, worked on the books, settled petty disputes between vendors, and jumped onto the register when needed. When closing time rolled around, she walked over to her apartment over Tealicious, made herself a sandwich, which she took to her apartment, and killed time until she felt tired enough to go to bed.

Depending on the weather, Sundays were often the best sales days for Artisans Alley *and* Tealicious. Katie was up early, excitement coursing through her at the prospect of touring what had become the house of her dreams during the past few days. She trundled down the stairs from her apartment to Tealicous an hour before Brad arrived to start work for the day. By the time he showed up, she already had scones in the oven and had started chopping celery for the salads.

"You're up bright and early," Brad said as he tied an apron over his street clothes.

"Big day. I'm going to look at a house this afternoon," she said excitedly.

"Get out!"

"Yup. It's an open house. Judging by the online photos, it needs a lot of tender loving care, but it's got great bones."

"How much TLC?" Brad asked, his tone skeptical.

"Well," Katie began, "the kitchen is a total gut. The house is over a hundred years old and doesn't look like it's had much work done since before our mothers were born, but that could be a real bargaining tool."

"Then it's a fixer-upper?" Brad asked, pulling a large sack of flour from one of the cupboards.

"It probably needs all new plumbing and electrical," Katie remarked, hoping the home's flaws would discourage anyone else from buying it.

"Are you sure you want to tie yourself to a place that needs that amount of work?"

"It needs to be saved," Katie said sincerely.

"Yes, but how deep is your well of dollars? This sounds like it could be a real money pit."

"Maybe," Katie admitted. But she wasn't about to let Brad spoil her sense of adventure, either.

"Well, good luck on that account. Hey, have you heard anything else about old man Preston's death?" Brad asked.

"No," Katie said warily. "Why?"

Brad shrugged.

"What have *you* heard?"

"I hit The Perfect Grape last evening to pick up a nice Bordeaux, as I was having dinner with Nick and Don."

"And?" Katie asked anxiously,

"Did you know Conrad's been doing business on the Square longer than anyone else?"

"Kind of," Katie fudged. That must have been before Ezra

Hilton, Artisans Alley's founder, had sold furniture in the old applesauce factory that now hosted Katie's vendors.

"Apparently, he knew Linda Preston."

It sounded right. A number of businesses had come and gone before Artisans Alley started being marginally successful.

"How well did he know her?" Katie asked.

Brad raised an eyebrow. "Very well—if you catch my drift."

Katie's jaw dropped. "He had an affair with her?" she asked, aghast.

Brad shrugged. "I guess, unless it was just boys' locker room talk."

Men often padded their list of sexual conquests. Was this just another example?

"What's your take? Was he giving you a line of bull, or was he being honest?"

"He lowered his voice, just in case his wife was listening, but —yeah—I think he was being honest. Don't forget, he was a bachelor at the time."

"And he seduced Linda?" Katie whispered back.

"According to Conrad, it was the other way around."

Had Maxwell Preston known of his wife's infidelity? That didn't seem likely. And what could that past possibly have to do with the here and now—and Preston's murder?

Katie voiced the question.

Brad shrugged. "Nothing, I guess. Unless there was an old score to settle."

"But if that's true, wouldn't it be Preston who wanted to take revenge against Conrad and not vice versa? I mean, Gilda and Conrad seem to be pretty happy together. And it was Maxwell, not his wife, who was murdered, and decades later."

Brad shrugged, and began measuring the flour for a cake recipe. "Don't shoot the messenger," he said and laughed.

"As if I would," Katie declared.

Brad grabbed a ten-pound bag of sugar and measured out

four cups. "So, what are you going to do before you head out for the open house?"

"Try to concentrate on my job. Either that or keep scrolling through the pictures of the house, downloading them, and examining them with a magnifying glass."

"All you'll see is fuzzy pixels by doing that."

"We'll see," Katie said, and wrapped what remained of the celery for another day. She changed the subject. What could Linda Preston's infidelity have to do with her husband's murder decades so many years later?

Nothing, Katie decided.

And yet ... who knew when a seemingly useless piece of information might just crack a case?

Was this something to bring up to Carol Rigby, or should she keep her mouth shut?

Katie would have to think about it.

KATIE PULLED her car into the bungalow's driveway. A white Kia, probably the listing agent's car, sat in the driveway. It was a good sign. It meant there probably wasn't a lot of interest in the little bungalow.

She glanced across the vehicle to Margo, who stared at the home's stucco facade. "Well, what do you think?"

"That mustard color has *got* to go," Margo said, frowning.

"My thoughts, too. But the fact the curb appeal isn't ideal could be a good sign."

"For whom?" Margo asked doubtfully.

"For whoever ends up with this place."

Margo craned her neck. "It looks like there's a parking pad at the side of the house. Why don't you back up over there? That would make it easier for you to pull out onto the street when we leave."

Was Margo in a hurry to do so? Katie hoped not.

"Good idea," she agreed, and maneuvered into the spot, which left her car hidden from the driveway and street.

The women got out and circled to the front door, which was unlocked. They stepped inside and onto the ceramic tile floor and into the living room, which was devoid of furniture. "Hello!" Katie called, her voice echoing.

"In the kitchen," came a familiar voice. It was Fred Cunningham. Katie should have but hadn't noticed his sign at the foot of the yard—she'd been that psyched about visiting the property.

Katie walked through the living room, the dining room, and into the kitchen beyond. "Hey, Fred. How did I miss this was one of your properties?"

"Carelessness on your part," the older man teased. He wore a dark suit, white shirt, and a dark blue tie featuring bunches of bananas. It was a silly affectation for a man who took his job deadly seriously.

"I didn't know you were in the market to buy a house," Fred said. "You should have called me."

Katie did. "Uh, I *did*."

"Yes, but that was about the commercial site on Victoria Square."

He was right about that.

"I'm not sure I'm ready to buy, but I didn't want to miss out on looking at this one…just in case."

"It's got good bones," Fred agreed. That was real estate jargon for *will cost a lot to bring up to modern standards*. "Why don't you take a walkthrough, and then we'll talk."

"Great."

Fred nodded in the direction of Margo. "And who have you got with you?"

Katie's heart froze. This was the moment. The moment she'd been dreading, and she chickened out. "This is Chad's mom,

159

Margo."

If Margo took offense, she didn't show it and graciously offered her hand to the Realtor. Fred had known Chad. It was the proper way to introduce Margo in that instance. Katie hoped.

"Pleased to meet you," Fred said.

"And you," Margo replied with a smile.

Fred waved a hand toward the home's front rooms. "Well, go explore."

Katie grinned. "With pleasure."

During the ten or twelve minutes the women walked through the home's first floor, they examined cupboards, baseboards, flooring, and ventured into the unfinished basement, which held cobwebs, an ancient furnace, and a relatively new water heater, and the built-in shelves some previous owner had lined along one side of the basement's walls.

Margo sniffed. "Seems a little damp."

"Nothing some water-proofing paint couldn't solve." Katie wandered around the space until she reached a round hole in the concrete floor where a sump pump resided. The hole wasn't even half-filled, which was a good sign. "A dehumidifier would dry this place out in no time," Katie remarked.

"If you say so, dear," Margo said skeptically.

Katie examined the space. The ceiling height was a good eight feet, which meant it could be converted into living space should one decide to do so—and why hadn't that been done before now?

Next up, the women trundled up the stairs to the second floor and the home's two bedrooms and full bath. As she'd been poring over the pictures for days, Katie knew what to expect of the bedrooms, but the dated bathroom was far bigger than she'd imagined. The original tub and tile still decorated the space, but both needed an update. Refinishing for the tub and new grouting for the tile. No way would Katie gut the room as most of its charming original features were intact.

Margo's jaundiced eye traveled around the bathroom. "A total gut job."

"No," Katie protested. "It's perfect."

Margo raised an eyebrow. "Perfect?" she repeated skeptically.

"Okay, it's *not* perfect, but it could be *made* perfect."

"With a lot of work."

"At the price they're asking, it's entirely possible," Katie said. Well, the price *was* high for the changes that needed to be made to bring the home back up to modern standards. But suddenly, Katie wanted nothing more than to rescue this little diamond in the rough.

"Let's go back downstairs and talk to Fred."

Margo nodded but wasn't nearly as enthusiastic as Katie.

However, upon rounding the bottom steps, Katie stepped back into the living room and came face-to-face with Ray Davenport.

"What are you doing here?" they both asked at once.

Katie laughed. "Looking at a house."

"I didn't know you were interested in moving."

"I thought you and the girls were happy in your rental house," Katie countered.

"I'm perfectly fine there," Ray said, "but the girls —" he said, referring to the two daughters currently living at home. "—want a," and here he made air quotes, "bigger canvas to practice their interior design schemes."

"Schemes?" Katie asked. That seemed a frivolous view of the girls' ambitions. Sadie and Sasha seemed pretty adamant that they wanted — and expected — to be professionals in the interior design field.

Katie heard the thunder of steps coming up the basement

steps and whoops of laughter that could only have been made by the Davenport sisters.

"Dad!" Sadie called. "The basement is perfect for a media room.

The teen came rushing into the living room, saw Katie, and stepped dead. "Oh." That's all she said, her voice flat.

Her younger sister practically smashed into her as she, too, rounded the corner into the room. When she, too, saw Katie, Sasha blanched.

"Hello, girls," Margo said cheerfully. The girls liked her, but they were still wary of Katie.

"Hey, Ms. Bonner," Sadie said politely. "You aren't gonna buy this house, are you?" Sadie's tone was distinctly unfriendly.

"Uh, no. I'm having a loft apartment built in the warehouse behind Victoria Square."

"Then why are you here?" Sasha asked suspiciously.

"Katie's interested in the house."

Sasha's eyes widened in either anger or horror; Katie wasn't sure which.

"But—but this is *our* house," Sasha protested.

"Now, honey, you haven't even seen the upstairs. And if we bought it, you and Sadie would have to share a room," Ray said reasonably.

"Like we haven't done that all our lives," Sadie grumbled.

Katie bit her lip, feeling like a rug had just pulled out from under her.

"Why don't you run upstairs and check out the bedrooms and the bath," Margo encouraged the girls. Whose side was she on?

Nodding, the girls raced up the stairs. The three in the living room could hear their heavy footfalls as they dashed into and out of rooms.

"Is this house a contender?" Margo asked Ray.

"I don't know. The girls seem enamoured, but that kitchen," he said and winced.

"Oh, I don't know, strip the wallpaper, give it a fresh coat of paint and some new appliances and it'll look as good as new," Margo said cheerfully.

"Dad!" Sadie called. "Come upstairs and look. This is it — this is the house we've been waiting for!"

Ray glanced in Katie's direction. "Were you serious about making an offer?"

"Uh, no," Katie lied and swallowed her disappointment. "I saw it online and I thought it might be fun to tour, but…." She let the sentence trail off. She loved this place — flaws and all. She wanted it with all her heart. *But….*

"Dad!" Sasha called.

"Coming!" he yelled back, forcing a smile. "We've looked at over eighty houses since we moved to this side of the county. I haven't seen the girls this excited."

Katie forced yet another smile. "It could make a fine family home."

"Dad!" Sophie demanded.

"I'd better get up there before they blow a gasket," Ray said with an embarrassed shrug.

"Sure thing," Katie said.

"Come by my shop and have coffee with me tomorrow. There's something I need to talk to you about."

"Oh. Yeah. Okay. Before opening?"

"Yeah. I'll put on a fresh pot of coffee."

He did that every day. And what on earth did he want to discuss?

"Daaaaaddddd!" Sasha wailed.

"Coming!" Again, Ray shrugged. "Kids. See you tomorrow, Katie."

"I'll be there," Katie said with a forced smile.

As Ray trundled up the home's stairs, the front door opened

and a young couple with a baby entered. They nodded hello and began to inspect the living room.

"Well, what do you think?" Margo asked Katie.

"I don't know," she lied.

"Are you ready to leave?" Margo asked.

"I guess so. Just let me say good-bye to Fred and I'll meet you back at the car."

Margo hesitated for a moment before nodding. "Yes, dear." Then she headed for the front door and exited the home.

Katie walked purposefully toward the kitchen, where Fred sat at the small table, tapping on his laptop. "I take it you've got a hot spot."

"Yes. The heirs cut off the internet when the former owner passed."

Katie nodded.

"So, what do you think?" Fred asked expectantly.

"I love it. I absolutely love it, and I'd make an offer in a heartbeat—"

"But?" Fred asked, squinting at Katie.

"But I have a feeling the Davenports are going to make an offer, and I wouldn't want to deprive them of the house. The girls are so excited about it."

"And Ray?"

"Maybe not so much. But if he doesn't make an offer, I'd like to."

"The market is kind of cool right now, but you never know if interest in a property will heat up fast."

"Well, I don't want to get into a bidding war. I love this place, but I could love another, too."

"If you say so," Fred said skeptically.

Katie knew real estate agents hoped for a bidding war because that would jack up their commission. She couldn't blame Fred if he invited such a scenario, but Katie didn't want to be a part of it. There *were* other houses. This was the first she'd looked at. Ray and the girls had looked at scores of them during the past couple of years.

"Keep in touch," Fred said.

"You know I will," Katie said, forced another smile, and threaded her way out of the home.

Margo waited beside the car. Once inside, Katie shoved the key into the electronic ignition but didn't turn it. Instead, she gripped the steering wheel.

"We probably should have toured the backyard," Margo remarked.

Katie shook her head. "I have a feeling the Davenports are going to make an offer. I don't want to be the one who deprives them of a family home."

Margo frowned. "Maybe not. The girls will be out of school and on their own in a couple of years—be it in college or just wanting to break free. Will Ray want a whole house to himself?"

Katie squinted at the older woman. "Why not? I do."

Margo didn't comment.

"Besides," Katie continued, "the girls aren't going to want to spend bucks on an apartment if it means they'd have put off their dream of opening a real business."

"They're high schoolers," Margo pointed out.

"Who are extremely talented. As you heard Ray say, they want a bold canvas to show off their talents. I don't doubt they think this house could be a stunning portfolio piece."

Margo's frown deepened. "Really?"

Katie nodded.

"Then they've got a better vision of it than me," Margo said with a shrug. "I'd gut the place."

"No you wouldn't, because you'd never settle for a house like this."

"And what makes it so attractive to you?" Margo asked.

Katie let out a weary sigh. "I dunno. But when I opened the

front door, a feeling echoed through me. It said *home.*" She let out another sigh and, with it, a wave of grief.

"If you want it that badly, let's go back in and talk to Fred," Margo insisted.

"I won't make an offer until I know the Davenports can't or don't want to do so."

"Whatever," Margo said with a shrug. "Was there another property you wanted to look at today?"

Katie shook her head.

No. They were situated right next to the home of her dreams—even if she hadn't known it was on the market until a few days before. She'd have to go back on the hunt, but there was no hurry.

Katie's beloved Aunt Lizzie often repeated the old saw that when one door closed, another opened. Sometimes, that saying was right, and sometimes, it wasn't.

This time felt like the latter.

Chapter Sixteen

The rest of the day passed in a fog for Katie. So many ideas and scenarios pressed upon her brain but she tried not to think about the craftsman house and instead concentrated on other matters.

So, Linda Preston had cheated on her husband years before her death. If he'd known, would he still be placing flowers on her grave decades later? And while he suffered grief for the woman he'd loved, he *had* pursued other relationships with women in the years after her death...and who could blame him? Katie had found herself in another relationship less than a year after Chad passed and had been harshly judged in that regard — and mostly by herself.

Margo was having dinner with Nick and Don, and they'd no doubt talk about their plans for spaces in the Victoria Square Annex. It would be gauche to drop in and crash their conversation — let alone look for a free meal. Instead, Katie left her cramped apartment for her even smaller office in Artisans Alley, where she worked late into the evening doing the work that she usually did on Monday mornings.

As she distributed the checks in envelopes to each of the

vendors' pigeon holes in the rack on the wall of the Alley's tag room, she wondered how she'd kill the rest of her day off. Both Artisans Alley and Tealicious were closed on Monday.

She had nowhere to go and nothing to do. That didn't bode well.

After a restless night, Katie dressed and started her day with her usual walk.

After her second circuit around the Square, Katie noted that the lights were on in Wood U. Ray said he had something to tell her. Was it about Maxwell Preston's death? She climbed the steps to the porch and the shop's entrance, rapping on the door before she tried turning the knob. It opened and she entered. "Ray?"

"Come on back," he called.

Katie crossed the shop, noticing it had been rearranged since she'd last been there only days before. The Davenport girls liked to keep things fresh, and Katie knew it also helped quickly turn over the shop's stock. The Davenport's dog, Belle, was happy to welcome a friend and lavished Katie with kisses and a tail that wagged frantically.

A fresh carafe of coffee sat under the coffeemaker, filling the workshop with its heavenly aroma, and a box from Turner's Cafe and Bakery sat next to it. Ray had gone all out.

"What are you doing here on your day off?" Katie asked.

"If we're going to have a big summer sale, I've got to increase my inventory. Sit, sit," he encouraged, grinning. Hearing the command, Bell promptly plunked onto the wood floor.

"My, you're in a good mood," Katie said, planting her butt on one of the cushioned bar stools that Ray had pulled away from his workbench.

"We did it."

Katie's gut tightened. "Did what?"

"Made an offer on that house we saw yesterday."

Katie swallowed, her heart sinking. "How—how," she stammered. "How wonderful."

"You weren't seriously looking at it, were you?" Ray asked.

Katie shook her head, schooling her features. "No. I thought it might make an interesting project, but it wouldn't have been something I'd have seriously considered," she lied and bit her lip to keep from tearing up. "The girls seemed really happy as they raced through the place."

"After all the houses we've looked at, it's a relief to find something we all fell in love with."

"All?" Katie asked. "What about Sophie? I mean, it's only a two-bedroom home. Will the girls have to be stacked in bunk beds?"

"Well, maybe at first. But then Sophie will be at school for the next couple of years, and she might intern in another city between semesters. It's something we can work out. And if nothing else, we could put a bedroom in the basement."

With all the spiders? Katie thought.

"You've got options," she agreed and nodded toward the coffeemaker. "Aren't you going to offer me a cup?"

Ray grimaced. "Oh, sure—sorry." He jumped up from his seat and poured coffee into mugs, doctoring one just how Katie liked it. As a former homicide detective, he noticed such things.

"I don't suppose you've heard from the sellers."

Ray shook his head, handing Katie a cup and then seemed to remember the bakery box. He bent down and retrieved a couple of paper plates and napkins from a drawer under the bench, handing a set to her, then opening the box and offering the contents to her. He'd ordered a variety of things: a scone, a chocolate-covered eclair, a doughnut covered in confectioners' sugar, and a cream puff.

"Wow—how am I supposed to decide on just one?" Katie asked.

"One? Have them all if you like," Ray said and laughed.

Katie shook her head, gazed at the offerings, and plucked the cream puff from the box.

"Ha! I could have predicted it."

"Why?"

"Because I saw you have one at Tealicious at one of our Merchants Association meetings."

He must have been paying attention because she could claim everything in the box as her favorite.

"Thank you," she said, placing the puff on her plate. "When will you know if your offer is accepted?"

"Fred said we could hear as early as this evening, but I'm not going to hold my breath. I have a feeling we might go back and forth a time or two before we come to an agreement."

That meant he'd offered a price lower than asking. What if they rejected the offer? Would Ray up the ante? Was there a chance Katie still might be able to obtain the home?

"Are you prepared to go higher?"

Ray nodded. "We got a good price for our house in Penfield. Prices are a lot lower out here in the boonies. I think we'll reach an agreement."

Again, with the boonies.

"I'll cross my fingers for you," Katie said, picking up the cream puff and taking a savage bite of it, chewing vigorously. Ray didn't seem to notice.

Once she'd swallowed, Katie spoke again. "So, you said you had something to tell me. I'm assuming it has to do with Maxwell Preston's death."

Ray selected the eclair from the box and placed it on his paper plate. "Why would you think that?"

"Well, because…." But then she didn't elaborate.

"No, I wanted to warn you that Nona Fiske is after your job as head of the Merchants Association."

"You know I've been trying to unload it ever since I got roped into taking it on," Katie said, picked up her cream puff and this time took a more reasonable bite, savoring the smooth, sweet center.

"Yeah, but we both know what a disaster that would be. She'd ruin all of the hard work you've put into the organization."

"If that's what the members want, then I'd have to stand aside and keep my peace. Besides, I have my hands full with the two businesses I own, plus part-ownership in a building on the Square and the warehouse behind us."

"I agree," Ray said respectfully. "But would you be okay with her stepping into that role?"

"I'd feel sorry for the rest of the merchants, and I'm sure she'd make my life a living hell, but what am I supposed to do if the other members vote her in?"

"You *could* remind them of everything you've done on their behalf."

"If they can't remember on their own, then they're — " Katie wanted to say *idiots* but refrained from doing so. "Forgetful," she finished lamely.

Ray nodded, taking a bite of his eclair, a dab of custard clinging to his bottom lip.

"Besides," Katie continued. "Someone — other than herself — would have to nominate her. Who do you think might do that?"

Ray nodded. "You're probably right. No one in their right mind would want Nona to lead the group."

Unless they held a grudge.

Katie had campaigned against Sue Sweeney's request for her niece to rent a space in the Victoria Square Annex for a reduced rent based on her relationship with one of the partners. Charlotte Booth had been upset when Katie had rejected her request to rent a shelf at Artisans Alley for her jellies and jams. Yes, her product was unique, but as a food item, it didn't fit the criteria of an art or a craft. As she thought about it, several of the merchants on the Square might have a petty beef against her for sticking to the rules that had been established for the group years before Katie had become the head of the organization.

"I can't worry about it," Katie said, and took another bite of her rapidly diminishing cream puff. But as she chewed, she grew more and more depressed. It seemed like everything was falling apart around her.

"I don't think you have to worry," Ray said, and took another bite of his eclair.

"I'm not. But if I'm to be replaced, I'd like it to be by someone who won't destroy the organization."

"Amen," Ray agreed. "But I don't see anyone else stepping up to take your place."

The best and the worst of all worlds.

Katie polished off the last of her cream puff. She should speak to Brad about offering them more often to their guests as part of an afternoon tea or on the à la carte menu.

Ray eyed her critically. "You came here this morning expecting to hear something about the Maxwell Preston case. I'm sorry if I made you think that."

"You didn't say a word about it. I just assumed."

"And you know what happens when you assume?" Ray said with a twinkle in his eye.

"Yeah. I make an ass out of you and me."

"I think it's an ass out of me and you, but…yeah."

"Well, as I understand it, the old boy thought of himself as quite appealing to the ladies. And his late wife wasn't exactly the epitome of faithfulness during their marriage."

"And where did you hear this?" Ray asked, his brow furrowing.

"Around. It's something I heard third-hand, and so far in the past it couldn't possibly pertain to this case."

"You'd be surprised how past events contribute to current murder investigations."

"Well, I'm not going to spill the beans because, as far as I'm concerned, it's hearsay."

Ray nodded, but he didn't exactly look happy about it. Perhaps if they'd been on more intimate terms, Katie *might* have told him what she knew, but that wasn't likely, either. While Brad hadn't specifically asked her for confidentially, if Carol Rigby came sniffing around, asking Conrad about his prior relationship with Linda Preston, he would know that Brad had committed a breach of trust.

Katie sipped the last of her coffee and stood. "Thanks for the invite and the cream puff. It was delicious."

"Thanks for the company. It gets lonely around here when the girls are in school. Belle's great, but she's not the best conversationalist. I don't know what I'll do with myself once Sadie and Sasha are off designing home interiors for the rich and famous—or whatever they end up doing."

"Well, first, they'll have to decorate their new home. I'd love to see it in all phases of completion."

They both knew that wouldn't happen—not the way the girls felt about Katie. But then Sadie and Sasha weren't shy about posting their projects and triumphs on social media, so their videos and still photos would have to be good enough.

"So, I guess I'll see you around the Square," Katie said.

"I'm here almost every day," Ray said with a note of finality.

Katie got up from her stool, set her mug on the workbench, and headed into the shop's showroom. Ray walked her out.

"Talk to you soon," Katie said in farewell.

"I'll hold you to it," Ray said, giving her a grin.

Katie's return smile was half-hearted.

As she walked back to Artisans Alley, Katie couldn't help but feel a cloud of depression descend upon her, she truly wished the Davenports well in what could be their new home. But if that were the case, she'd be stuck in that claustrophobic studio apartment for a lot longer than she wanted. And while she had her cats for company, she missed being with someone. Andy hadn't exactly been around all that much but he'd been in close proximity when she lived above his pizzeria. And if she got lonely in the evenings, Katie trundled down the stairs to help out, enjoying the camaraderie of the teens who labored in his shop, and working alongside her man. But he wasn't her man any longer—and it had been her choice. Leaving him hadn't been a mistake.

It had been months, and she still wasn't at peace with being alone. She needed a distraction. Buying that little craftsman house would have been the perfect project.

And yet, she *did* have a project she could throw herself into: helping Margo set up the art gallery and choosing which of Chad's paintings to display and which to potentially sell.

As Chad's death had reminded her, no one knew how much time they might have on the planet. Squandering it seemed like a crime against nature.

She didn't like to think of herself as a criminal.

AFTER CHECKING in with Vance and making sure that the Alley was good to go for the day, a restless Katie walked over to the warehouse behind Victoria Square to see how things were progressing there. The newly installed, double plate-glass front doors were propped open, and she could hear the sounds of saws and hammering in the distance.

Katie found contractor Steve Harris standing in the building's atrium. The skylight had been boarded over years ago. While the makeshift artificial lighting was subpar, Harris stood over a makeshift table made of sawhorses and a full sheet of particle board, studying architectural plans. The man had to be in his mid-to-late sixties, but he was lean and still had a good amount of salt-and-pepper hair. He'd always been cheerful in his interactions with Katie, which was why she and the other partners had given him the contract to upgrade the warehouse and transform it into the retail and residential space they all dreamed of. No wonder Margo was attracted to the man.

"Hey, Steve, how's it going?"

"Katie! Good to see you. It's been a couple of weeks."

"Yeah, I should have made an appearance before now. Things have just been crazy," she fibbed.

"I spoke with Fred Cunningham," who'd been contracted to rent the spaces on the Annex, "and he's lined up another couple of businesses ready to stake out space here in the warehouse."

"Margo has dubbed it the Victoria Square Annex, and I'm inclined to adopt that moniker."

"She's a firecracker," the contractor said with a smile. Was the feeling between Steve and Margo mutual?

The older man quickly sobered. "I was sorry to hear about the trouble you all have been experiencing," Steve said sincerely.

"Trouble?" Katie asked warily.

"Yeah, the guy that died at Margo's party last week." The way he said *party* made Katie wonder if the contractor had been disappointed at not being invited to the soiree. Margo had admitted being attracted to the man. She must have had a reason for not inviting him to the party. Katie wondered why.

"I spoke with Fred yesterday, and he didn't say anything about potential renters for the Annex."

Steve look surprised. "Maybe he's waiting to get a more firm commitment before he mentioned it to you."

"Maybe," Katie acknowledged half-heartedly. She changed tacks. "So, how are things going?"

"Roughing the wiring is on track, and so is the plumbing in the spaces we've already blocked out for business and residential spaces. Are you going to wait to have potential renters specify their needs, or go ahead and put in the appropriate utilities and have them work around it?"

This was new territory for Katie.

"Can you give me some cost estimates so I can present them to the owners? Then we can vote on what we think might be best."

"We can duplicate what we're doing for Margo's loft on the other spaces on the third floor. Depending on how the space is allocated, you have the potential for five to six apartments. We need to figure that out in the next couple of weeks. Everyone needs a kitchen and a bathroom, and we need to lay out the plumbing and electrical for those areas. The rest of the space is open to interpretation."

Katie nodded.

"Draw up some plans, and I'll present them to the group."

"Great. When do you want them?"

"By next week? We only need a preliminary plan to make a decision. Can do?"

"You betcha," Steve said. "I've been doing this since way back when I was an apprentice and helped build one of the structures on the Square."

"When was that?" Katie asked.

"Hmm...let's see. I was about twenty. It was a little shop that sold ceramics."

Katie's eyes widened, and her gut tightened. "Tell me more."

Steve's gaze dipped, "I was just a young man—and pretty naive."

What was the man remembering? By his somber expression, it wasn't necessarily a good memory. Could Katie coax a truthful response from the man?"

Steve shrugged. "I was working for a guy named Gary Jordan. Great guy—a real great guy," Steve said, with the barest catch in his throat.

"I get the feeling something didn't go well with the job."

"I kind of thought he took a shine to the lady we were working with. They struck up a friendship, and as we worked on completing the building and adding the finishing touches, Gary would give me a few bucks to eat at the diner at the strip mall just up the road."

A diner had been a fixture in the village for decades before its current owner had purchased it.

"Why do you think he did that?" Katie asked, trying not to let her vivid imagination jump ahead of his narrative.

Steve shrugged. "She showed up to the site a few times with a picnic basket."

"Do you think your boss and Mrs. Preston were having an affair?" Katie asked, trying to sound as though such a thing might be as foreign to her as speaking Mandarin.

Steve shrugged. "Gary was married—and I thought happily so."

"But?" Katie asked.

"Nothing. We finished the job and went on to other things."

"How long did you work for Jordan?"

"About a year. He taught me a lot. And then I got hired by a big construction firm, and he took on another apprentice."

"Did you keep in contact?"

"That's the thing," Steve said. "A couple of months after I worked with Gary, he went missing. He was supposed to have gone fishing up in Lake Placid and never came home again. They figured he fell off a rental boat and drown. His body was never found."

Why did Katie's mind immediately think that it wasn't an accident but foul play that had been behind the contractor's disappearance?

"Had you been in contact with Mr. Jordan before his disappearance?" Katie asked.

Steve shook his head. "Not really. I fell in love, got married, and had a couple of kids. I didn't hear about what happened to Gary until a couple of years later."

"Lake Placid is quite a drive from here," Katie commented.

"Yeah, and it seemed kind of weird. I knew Gary liked to fish, but his family was surprised when he decided to take a trip up to the Adirondacks on his own on the spur of the moment."

This whole tale was sounding fishier and fisher by the minute.

"So you spoke to them after his disappearance?"

Steve nodded. "Years later, I ran into his daughter, Lisa. She told me about it."

"What did you think about that news?"

"Sad." And again, Steve looked away. "By then, I was divorced. Lisa and I kind of bonded over the loss." Steve's gaze again dipped to focus on the concrete floor. "We got married eight months later. We had three kids, and then Lisa was driving on the expressway, coming back from the mall in Victor, when some drunken asshole—in the middle of the day—was driving the wrong way on the expressway and hit her car head on."

"Oh, no," Katie lamented.

"Yeah. She was killed instantly," Steve said quietly. "But I got through it because of my kids—and my work. I'll never retire," he said bitterly.

Chad had also been killed in a car accident. Had Margo and Steve exchanged sad stories? If so, Katie didn't want to speak of her own loss and changed the subject.

"From what I can see, the work you and your team have done is exemplary."

"Thanks. We aim to please."

After that, Steve gave Katie a tour of just what his workers and subcontractors were doing to get the Victoria Square Annex ready for the formal unveiling later that year. Seeing how the retail and residential spaces were evolving was rather exciting. And while the loft apartments were intriguing, Katie didn't think she could live in that kind of space. Her thoughts circled back to the Inglenook in the Craftsman house Ray had made an offer on. How she longed to sit by a crackling fire with a glass of sherry and something good to read as the sun went down on a winter's evening. She could picture it in her mind as though she'd already experienced it. But then reality reared its ugly head.

Forcing a smile, Katie spoke. "Thanks for taking me around the building. I have a feeling this old warehouse could be just as successful—and a wonderful gathering place—as the Square itself."

"It never hurts to hear that kind of praise," Steve said, sounding pleased.

"Well, I'd better get back to work. I'll be back to check on the progress in a few days or a week from now."

"I don't usually encourage visits to an in-progress job-site," Steve admitted, "but feel free to drop by anytime."

"Thanks," Katie said with an inward frown. Shouldn't a client always be welcome when viewing a renovation in progress—just to ensure their vision was realized by the team hired to pull it off, or had he had a lot of pushy hangers on who keep the workers from doing their jobs?

Katie had planned on visiting Margo's gallery space, but then decided not to. She should have been in a better mood after speaking with Steve Harris, but there was something about their conversation that niggled in her brain. She would have to think about it, but there were other things to attend to that day, so she walked back to Artisans Alley with another couple of bricks of emotional weight on her shoulders, unsure what they were or how they might affect her.

Chapter Seventeen

The evenings were lengthening. In another eleven days, the unofficial start of the summer season would begin with Memorial Day weekend.

As the last one to depart for the day, Katie locked up Artisans Alley and left the building, walking with dread across the asphalt toward Tealicous and her studio apartment. She'd be glad to see her kitties and give them some quality time, but then she'd end up staring at the four walls that made up her home and try to distract herself enough not to go stark-raving mad. Now that she'd decided she no longer wanted to live there, she wanted out ASAP. Maybe she'd start looking at apartments on the weekend. No way did she want to live in a complex, so she decided she'd concentrate her search to duplexes and other houses that had been split into apartments. Of course, the fact that she had two cats would make the search that much more difficult, but she was ready to accept the reality. No way would she give up Mason and Della.

The cats descended as soon as Katie entered her extremely humble abode, eager for her attention and unhappy that they'd gone long hours without it. She knew their attitudes would soften as soon as she fed them and settled on the love seat to watch something on the tube. They were less forgiving if she went on the computer because then they'd jump up on her or insinuate themselves—either alone or collectively—in front of her monitor and try to interfere with her scrolling and clicking.

Katie opened her fridge and considered its contents, which weren't inspiring. The head of lettuce was oxidizing from lack of use. What else could she put in a salad—could she find the incentive to make one? She had a couple of withered carrots, some limp celery, and the remnants of a red onion puckering on its cut side. Her choices of dressing were limited, too. There might be a teaspoon in the bottle of balsamic vinaigrette and not much more in the bottle of lite ranch.

"You know, I might have to join you guys. Do you think Friskees fish paté would taste good on crackers?"

The cats didn't look up and kept scarfing up their dinner.

Of course, she could go downstairs and avail herself of whatever was left in the teashop's larder, but she hated to do so since she had no clue as to Brad's plans for the daily specials he concocted from the fridge and pantry contents.

It looked like it would be a bagel and cocoa once again. Katie hauled out the toaster and was about to take out the package of frozen everything bagels when a knock sounded on her door.

She hadn't heard footfalls on the steps. Who'd be calling on her?

Katie tip-toed over to the outside door and looked out the peephole, surprised to see Andy Rust standing outside her door, looking rather sheepish.

Without hesitation, Katie threw back the bolt and opened the door. "Andy, what are you doing here?"

Andy proffered a paper bag emblazoned with the Angelo's Pizzeria logo. "I brought you a peace offering."

Katie picked up the scent of something familiar—something she thought of as comfort food. A calzone as a peace offering?

"I didn't know we were warring," she said warily.

"No, but we haven't exactly been on the best of terms lately, either. I'd like that to change, Sunshine."

Katie bristled at his pet name for her. "Please don't call me that."

"Why not?"

Because she was no longer his sunshine. Katie considered the song. She'd always thought the sunshine referenced had cheated on the dejected lover. In this case, it was just the opposite. Katie considered slamming the door in his face, but she *was* hungry, and Andy made a mighty fine calzone. "Just because." Katie let him in, closing the door behind him.

Andy seemed to shrug off her reasoning. "Have you got any beer?"

"Sorry, just a bottle of white wine, but you're welcome to a glass." Whatever was on Andy's mind, he wouldn't have time to slug back more than that. That he'd left his pizza parlor at peak business hours to seek out her company had probably been a hardship for him.

Andy had seen the apartment before, but that was right after she'd moved in several months ago before she'd hung Chad's pansy painting and other pieces of art and finalized her kitchen set-up. He eyed the limited square footage.

"Are you sure you're happy living in such a cramped space?" he asked.

Katie forced a smile. "Happy as a pig in shit." Yeah, that phrase exactly captured her feelings.

Andy handed her the bag. "This is for you."

She figured it was.

"Thank you. Sit down," she said, gesturing toward the love seat. No way would she join him there. She'd snag the chair in front of the desk that served as her workstation and dinner location.

Katie poured two glasses of wine before plopping the still-hot calzone on a plate. She handed Andy a glass, grabbed a napkin and her glass and sat down, hoping to placate her stomach before it grumbled loud enough for Andy to hear. Meanwhile, the cats had retreated to the corner farthest from the human male intruder. They'd been affectionate with Andy in the past; that they no longer felt that way seemed telling.

"Salud," Andy said, raising his glass in a toast.

"To old friendships," Katie said. And she meant it. She remembered too many good times with Andy to throw it all away. And yet....

Katie took a bite of the calzone. It wasn't hot enough to burn her tongue, but the flavor bordered on ambrosia. She chewed the heavenly concoction, closing her eyes in ecstasy, before swallowing. "You make a damn fine product."

Andy shrugged. "I try to please. I've *always* tried to please you."

That had been apparent in the past, but a man who aimed to please his lady didn't step out on her, either.

Katie took another bite of the calzone, savoring the flavor. Swallowing, she asked, "How did you know I'd be scraping the bottom of the barrel when it came to supper tonight?"

"Because I know you inside and out."

He might have thought he did, but obviously, he'd thought wrong. His disloyal actions and her reaction to them proved her case. Even so, Katie decided not to refute his claim...just then.

She took another bite of the calzone, which didn't taste as good as before.

"I was thinking," Andy began, and took another sip of his wine.

"What?" Katie asked, her tone neutral.

"That maybe we should get back together."

"Oh yeah?" Katie said, an icy feeling crawling from her toes up her body.

"Yeah, we're adults. Things happen. We should be able to get past the uncomfortable moments we've experienced."

What uncomfortable moment was *he* willing to get past? That he'd been caught bedding someone other than Katie?

"What are you saying?" she asked, and took another bite of her calzone so as not to explode.

"Well, that I'm willing to take you back."

Katie's stomach turned. She swallowed the bite and stared at the mostly uneaten portion of calzone in her hand. "What did you say?" she asked quietly, raising her gaze.

Andy's expression was a mix of bashful triumph. Like a little kid caught with his hand in a cookie jar, he still expected a sweet delight. "That we should let bygones be bygones and get back together."

"No, that's *not* what you said. You said you'd be *willing* to take me back as though I'm some kind of damaged goods."

Andy's gaze soured.

Thoughts whirled through Katie's mind like a tornado's vortex. *He* had cheated on *her*. *He'd* been pleased with the idea he might have fathered a child with another woman during a one—or two or *more*—night stand. He'd been willing to throw away the time they'd shared because of a lie. And then he'd been a total jerk about the whole situation.

Get back together?

No. That wasn't going to happen.

With deliberate care, Katie returned the calzone to its paper sack, rose to her feet, and shoved it into Andy's hand. "Get out."

Andy frowned, confused. "What?"

"I said, get out. And don't ever come back."

Andy snorted out a breath, looking confused. "Maybe I should have phrased it differently."

"You sure could have—but even if you had, my reaction would have been the same."

Andy's confusion pivoted to anger. He placed his nearly empty glass on the floor, stood, and looked at Katie's spartan quarters and back to her. "Is this how you want to live for the rest of your life? An old cat lady squeezed into a closet?"

Better than being with you.

Katie studied the face of the man she'd come to love. But that love had faded with his infidelity. *Once a cheat, always a cheat.*

She didn't say the words aloud—that would only start another argument, and there was no point trying to convey the hurt and embarrassment Andy had caused her. He hadn't taken her words to heart before—and he wouldn't do so now.

Katie jerked a thumb in the direction of the door. "Please go."

Andy's cheeks flushed, his tone hardening. "You'll be sorry you blew me off. My cinnamon buns business is about to explode. I'm in the middle of executing a multi-million dollar franchise deal with a major corporation."

"Congratulations," Katie said, attempting to keep the sarcasm from her tone.

"It's a big *effin'* deal," Andy countered.

"Good for you," she said, straightening. And she meant it.

Andy's gaze hardened. "I'm moving up. I thought you'd be happy to share that success with me."

"I have my own successes."

"Do you know how many women would love to be with me?" he challenged.

"Well, don't count me as one of them," Katie said flippantly.

Mounting anger caused Andy's pupils to swell. "No, instead, you're stuck in this hole and up to your eyes and ears in debt. You've had to cow-tow to the likes of Nona Fiske over this stupid summer promo."

"I'm not cow-towing to *anybody*."

"Suuuurrre," Andy said, drawing out the word. His lip curled, and Katie waited for the next slur. "Even that *old man* Ray Davenport doesn't want you anymore."

Katie forced herself not to react. She just stared at Andy with pity. How had she ever thought she'd loved him?

Her lack of reaction seemed to infuriate him, and for a moment, Katie thought he might hit her. Instead, his fist clenched the grease-stained bag and crushed what was left of the calzone before he hurled it on the floor. Then, without another word, he stalked over to the door, threw it open, and slammed it shut behind him.

The cats went flying at the racket, knocking the glass over on the floor and spilling its contents, but there was nowhere for them to go, and they ended up cowering under the love seat. Katie strode to the door and threw the deadbolt. Then she grabbed some paper towels and crouched down to mop up the mess, thankful the glass hadn't broken. The sudden pounding in her head beat a tattoo. She took several deep breaths before she felt calm enough to address her cats. "I'm sorry, guys," she said softly, swallowing down a pang of regret. She collected their treat bowls, filled them with their favorite crunchy snack, and set them near them. The cats looked up at her warily.

"Never mind. You can eat when you're ready."

Katie's gaze turned toward the bag on the floor. She picked it up and walked the few steps to the trash bin. Tossing it inside, Katie bet she could find a few green leaves in that head of lettuce in her fridge.

Chapter Eighteen

K atie stayed up late that evening, putting on the feel-good movie *Pollyanna* for the third time. It was long at two hours and fourteen minutes, and by the time it ended, she finally felt sleepy enough to close her eyes and surrender to slumber. But she left the light on in her shower. Her conversation with Andy had left her feeling more than a little unsettled.

When she got up late the next morning, she fixed herself a cup of tea and wondered if she shouldn't talk about what had happened the evening before—not even with her closest friends. She'd made it plain to them that she and Andy were finished. His offer to reconcile and her refusal wasn't something they needed to know. And yet, keeping such a secret made her feel even less connected to those she knew, loved, and who accepted her just the way she was.

Brad had already arrived and was hard at work preparing the sweet treats for that day's Tealicious customers when Katie made her way down to the teashop's kitchen.

After taking out a tray of cream puff shells from the oven, Brad paused to speak to Katie. "That was a good idea to offer our guests cream puffs. Wait 'til you taste the filling I'm about to make."

"Can't wait," Katie said, but she hadn't been able to muster the joy Brad probably expected to hear, and he caught on immediately.

"Is everything okay?"

"Sure. Why wouldn't it be?"

Brad scowled but didn't comment. "What's on tap for today?"

"Just the usual," Katie answered and plodded over to the fridge to retrieve celery to chop for the salads.

"Uh-huh. Have you checked your messages this morning?" Brad asked.

After Andy's visit, Katie hadn't felt like communicating with the outside world and had turned off her phone. "No, why?"

"Nona Fiske has been sending out a load of messages instructing the merchants — and hangers-on like me — as to what she expects of them during the big summer promotion."

Katie frowned. "And what *does* she expect?"

"Apparently blind obedience," Brad remarked.

Although Katie had gone incommunicado, she'd still pocketed her cell phone before she'd left the apartment. Turning it back on, she saw a score of comment balloons littering her phone's main screen — the bulk of which were from Nona. As she scrolled through them, Katie's ire grew hotter and hotter. Nona had issued orders like an army general, expecting the troops to fall into line. While Katie was included in the group chat, it was obvious that Nona hadn't assigned her any duties. She had, however, included several Artisans Alley vendors with implicit instructions, telling them when and where to report on the big day.

Katie had no doubt that Nona was coordinating her battle plans from a whiteboard rather than a spreadsheet and

A Lethal Lake Effect

squelched the urge to storm the older woman's shop with a massive dry eraser in hand.

"What are you going to do about it?" Brad asked, as he strode to the fridge to grab the gallon jug of heavy cream he'd need to make the filling for the cream puffs.

"Do I need to do anything?" Katie asked.

"Yeah. Make sure Ms. Fiske knows that *you're* the head of the Merchants Association and that the operation should be funneled through *you*."

Katie shook her head. "Nope. This isn't my project. I can support it both from here and Artisans Alley, but this is Nona's show."

"From what I understand, she'd never undertaken a project like this before. What if it fails? It'll reflect badly on the Merchants Association."

Should Katie explain that she never wanted to take on the responsibility of leading the group? That she'd been suckered into it. That although she'd done her best for the association, if someone else wanted to step forward, she might just let them do it? While Nona certainly wouldn't be her first choice, and maybe it was hubris to think she was the only member of the group who'd shown herself to be a leader, but....

But....

Instead, Katie steered the conversation in another direction. "We need to come up with a menu for that day. Have you spoken to the Square's other food vendors?"

Brad shook his head. "I kinda thought maybe you should."

Of course, she was only juggling her duties at Tealicious, the sixty-plus vendors at the Alley and its day-to-day activities, coordinating with the contractor at the Victoria Square Annex while trying to figure out how to find a bigger home for her and her cats. Sure, she had all the time in the world to coordinate with the Square's other food vendors for a one-day event two

189

months away. And pigs regularly flew circuits around Victoria Square.

"I guess," she said, turning her attention back to the stalks of celery before her, suddenly feeling overwhelmed. She swallowed several times before picking up a knife to start chopping. She did so slowly, mechanically, desperately trying not to cry. And cry for what? Because her life was such a mess? It really wasn't. She was a successful businesswoman. She had two cats she loved dearly. Margo had become her staunch defender. She counted on Brad, Nick, Don, and Seth as friends. And...maybe Ray. These were people she could rely on. And yet...she didn't feel she could confide in them. No, she had taken on a lot of responsibility. She had to be strong because if she wasn't, everything around her would fall apart and dissolve into an abyss of darkness and despair, and so would she, and That. Just. Wouldn't. Do.

"Are you okay?" Brad asked, apparently aware of her distress.

"Oh, sure. I've just got a lot on my mind."

"Yeah."

Katie glanced in his direction. He didn't look at all concerned.

"If you ever need to talk, I'm willing to listen," he said mildly, continuing with his work.

Katie frowned. "Thanks." He had said the appropriate words, but was he really in her corner? It suddenly occurred to Katie that she *was* trapped in a corner. That she wasn't sure she could get out of it without some kind of support. She swallowed again and made her decision.

"If you want me to talk, then you need to really listen," she said, avoiding his gaze. "I'm not Wonder Woman. I've got a lot on my plate, and I *can't* do it all. Would you *please* talk to the other food merchants on the Square and come up with a menu for the promotion?"

Katie glanced askance at the shop's manager/chef to see him shrug. "Sure," he said.

Sure? He'd been ready to blow off the responsibility only moments before. Still, now that she'd spoken up, Brad *was* willing to take on that responsibility.

"Thank you."

Brad was quiet for a few moments before he spoke again. "From what I know about Nona Fiske, your troubles with her have just begun."

Katie shook her head. "They've been ongoing since the day I met her."

"And how do you deal with that?" Brad asked.

Katie let out a weary breath. "With difficulty."

THE FIRST TEXT message from one of the Victoria Square merchants arrived just before ten that morning from Sue Sweeney of Sweet Sue's Confectionery.

Nona says I can only sell salt water taffy during the promotion, as that was the most popular candy during the Pollyanna period.

Katie frowned before answering.

You have my permission to sell whatever you like, and if Nona gives you a hard time about it, just refer her to me.

Seconds later, Sue replied, *Thanks.*

Katie hadn't had time to pour herself a cup of coffee in the vendors' lounge before the next text hit her phone.

Do I really have to wear a period-appropriate costume during the summer promotion? asked Charlotte Booth. *It's like a sauna during August. And who's going to provide it? The Merchants Association? I certainly don't think I should have to pay for it.*

Katie took in a long, weary breath. *No, you shouldn't. Feel free to wear what makes you feel comfortable. Perhaps we can come up with some kind of uniform for the merchants, like a cap or an apron. What do you think about that?*

Charlotte's answer came within seconds. *I could live with that.*

It wasn't even lunchtime when the third text pinged Katie's phone, this time from Conrad Stratton of The Perfect Grape, the Square's wine store. *Nona says I can't participate in the summer promotion as wine is the devil's elixir. What the heck does that mean? The phrase is 'champagne is the devil's wine,' but that's beside the point. My business is being discriminated against.*

Katie resisted the temptation to bang her head against the steel file cabinets in her office. *Well, she's wrong. All the merchants are free to participate in the event. And if she gives you a hard time, tell her I said so.*

Katie knew that meant she would have to have a showdown with Nona. It wouldn't be the first time, but she wasn't about to let that horrible woman try to intimidate anyone on the Square.

It was almost two in the afternoon when Katie returned to Tealicious to snag a couple of leftover cucumber sandwich triangles and a scone for her lunch. She paid for that transgression by clearing tables and washing dishes, when she got yet another text, this time from Nick Farrell.

Nona says Don and I can't hire the Davenport sisters to hand out brochures during the summer promotion, insisting we have to do it ourselves. Why the hell?

Katie smacked her palm against her forehead and meditated for a few moments before answering. *She's wrong. Do as you please.*

Seconds later, Nick replied. *Thanks. And please tell Nona to leave us the hell alone.*

Katie texted back: *Will do.*

Unfortunately, Katie would now actually have to do so.

Chapter Nineteen

Katie had just arrived back at Artisans Alley when a text from Paula Mathews came in. *Nona says I can't participate in the summer promotion because I run a death shop. Apparently, she doesn't have the faintest idea about Victorian and Edwardian death rituals during the period she wants to reference for this event.*

Katie leaned back in her creaky old office chair and let her body go limp, feeling drained. She sat that way for at least half a minute, desperate to call on an inner strength she didn't think she could muster. But then, Katie shook herself. It was time to confront Nona.

It was hot for May as Katie walked across the tarmac to The Quiet Quilter. A couple of customers browsed the bolts of fabric when Katie entered. Nona didn't acknowledge her presence, she was so intent on glaring at the women inspecting the goods on offer, as though one of them might grab something, stuff it down her shirt, and flee the shop. With that kind of anxiety blanketing the store, it was a wonder Nona had any returning customers.

Katie inspected the display of colorful threads on offer,

waiting until the women made their purchases and left the store before she approached the cash desk to face Nona.

"Well, what are you doing here?" the sourpuss of an old lady asked Katie.

"Hello to you, too," Katie said mildly.

Nona glared at her as a couple of new customers entered the store.

"I've had several text messages today from Merchant Association members asking for clarification on what's expected of them during the *proposed* summer promotion."

"Proposed?" Nona asked, sounding confused as her gaze wandered to see what the women were inspecting. "It's a done deal," she said definitively.

"Not necessarily," Katie countered.

Nona's expression darkened. "Everyone seemed enthusiastic about it at our last meeting."

"That was before you started telling everyone what they could and couldn't do to participate."

"Well, I *am* in charge of the celebration."

"You're the *catalyst*, but you don't get to dictate what the merchants can sell or what they have to wear to participate."

"But we *have* to remain faithful to the theme!" Nona declared forcefully.

The women customers raised their heads at Nona's raised voice.

"Not really," Katie said quietly but firmly. "We can promote it as an old-fashioned get-together, but nothing's written in stone."

"Give me an for instance," Nona demanded.

"What do you know about Victorian and Edwardian death rituals?" Katie asked.

"You're talking about the Heaven's Gate shop? It's disgusting. Talking about dying and death. It's creepy. It'll turn people off."

"But we're *Victoria* Square. The death rituals that are accepted today are rooted in that era. Would you be surprised to learn that it was not only acceptable but expected, that a family took photographs of their dead—because in many instances, they were the only photographic evidence that the deceased person ever lived?"

Nona looked appalled. "That's disgusting," she reiterated.

"That's how things were in those days," Katie countered. "And it's not like Paula is flouting that kind of history. She promotes ways to remember those we've lost in a sympathetic manner."

Nona looked skeptical.

"And why should Sue Sweeney only offer taffy when all kinds of confections were available to patrons in the early nineteen hundreds? Besides, we're not a seaside town. It's more likely maple sugar candy would have been the most sought-after confection during that time period, especially in Vermont, where the novel was set. And why are you discouraging merchants like Conrad Stratton from participating in the promotion?"

"Because this is supposed to be a *family*-friendly gathering!"

At this outburst, the customers scurried for the exit.

Katie wasn't finished.

"You told the owners of Sassy Sally that they can't employ the Davenport sisters to hand out brochures. Why shouldn't we try to include younger people in the event?"

"Well, for one thing, it's not natural for two men to live together, and to expose their lifestyle to two young, impressionable girls is positively disgusting."

Katie's cheeks glowed. She took a deep breath before speaking, trying to control her anger. "Nick and Don are two of the kindest, most generous people I know. Sasha and Sadie Davenport will not only get to know and share information on the history of Sassy Sally's Bed and Breakfast, but they'll get public relations experience, which will be important in their chosen careers."

"They're children!" Nona spat.

"Whom *you* tried to exploit in the past. I hardly think you're interested in their well-being," Katie said firmly.

"Their father should be ashamed to even think of letting them speak to those—those perverts!"

Katie glowered. "I'm this close to not only shutting down this entire enterprise but booting you from the Merchants Association," she grated.

"For what?"

"For being a bigoted old biddy!"

Nona's eyes widened in umbrage. "What?"

"You heard me."

Nona glared at Katie, snorting breaths through her nose like an angry bull facing a toreador. "This time, Katie Bonner, you've gone too far. I'm going to contact the rest of the Merchants Association, tell them how you've insulted me, and ask that we vote to oust you as our leader."

"That's fine with me since I never wanted the position in the first place. But who do you propose to take my place?" Katie asked.

"I can think of one candidate with the time and dedication to do so."

"And who would that be?"

Nona stood just that much taller, jutting out her chin. "Me."

Katie let out a bark of laughter, which only seemed to further antagonize the old lady. "Nona, you've pissed off nearly everyone on the Square. Do you honestly think you have a chance of deposing me?"

Nona's lip curled. "We won't know until it's put to vote, will we?" she said derisively.

Katie stifled a laugh. "No, I guess we won't. Feel free to talk about it with the membership and we can discuss it at our next meeting."

"I will do just that," Nona said with conviction.

"Until then," Katie asserted, "I'm still in charge, and what I say goes. We'll go on the assumption that the gay nineties—or whatever else we decide to call it—promotion will go on. But you are not to dictate who participates and what they can do."

"But *I'm* in charge!" Nona practically screamed.

"No, you're not. As head of the Merchants Association, *I'm* in charge, and I say that all members are free to participate in any way they choose."

"You're deliberately undermining my authority," Nona accused.

"You don't have *any* authority," Katie countered. "The Merchants Association isn't a dictatorship."

"If you're the final authority, it most certainly is," Nona asserted.

Katie bit her lip to prevent her from saying anything disparaging. "We'll let the members decide that at next month's meeting."

"You'd better believe I'll challenge you on that," Nona threatened.

"Go right ahead," Katie said, and took a moment to consider how to diffuse the tense situation. "But until then, please keep in mind that every merchant on the Square deserves respect, and if you can't muster that, then just keep your opinions to yourself because nobody wants to hear them."

Nona's eyes widened in anger. "Are you threatening me?"

"No, just warning you that if you can't give respect, then you don't deserve it, either."

Nona stared at Katie, her cheeks glowing, looking like she was about to erupt. "Get out of my shop and never come back!"

"With pleasure," Katie said, turned her back to the old woman, and exited the store, knowing this wasn't the end of the discussion nor her troubles with Nona. As she stood on the asphalt outside the Square's quilt shop, Katie felt the need of encouragement. Wood U stood nearly exactly across the parking lot, but she didn't feel she could impose herself upon Ray. Then her gaze swung east and there sat Sassy Sally's B&B—what would have been hers had fate not taken a sharp left turn when her now-deceased husband had invested their life savings in Artisans Alley. For all Chad's good deeds and aspirations, he'd still betrayed her. Katie might have forgiven him had he lived, but that unresolved trauma still haunted her.

On impulse, she headed in the direction of Sassy Sally's, knowing she would find kindred spirits within Nick and Don, who she counted on as good friends, despite Nona's terrible opinion of the couple.

Katie could have just entered the bed and breakfast, but as always, she rang the bell and was surprised when Sasha Davenport greeted her.

"Oh. It's you," the teen said flatly.

"Is Nick or Don around?"

"Yeah, they're in the kitchen. I guess you want to come in, right?"

"That was my intention," Katie said mildly.

Sasha shrugged. "Follow me." As though Katie wouldn't have known the way.

Sure as shootin' there was no way Katie could vent about Nona or Andy with an audience.

"Hey, Katie—want some coffee?" Nick offered as she followed the younger Davenport sister into the room.

"Thanks, but not at this time of day."

"Wine?" Don offered and waggled his eyebrows.

Katie eyed the teenage girls. "It's a little early for that." But not that early, as the Davenport sisters were obviously out of school for the day.

"We're talking about the big summer celebration and how Sasha and I can help promote Sassy Sally's," Sadie said gravely.

"Yeah, we want to learn everything we can about the inn so we can talk knowledgeably about it to future customers," Sasha echoed.

"I think we might have the best ambassadors we could find for the job," Don said.

"We're going to research the Square and offer the information to all the merchants," Sadie said.

"For a price," Sasha echoed.

"Hush!" Sadie ordered. "Don't sound so darn crass."

They'd obviously taken Katie's idea to investigate Maxwell Preston and run with it.

"I think it's a good idea. What kind of price were you asking?" Katie asked.

"Maybe ten dollars," Sadie said.

Katie stifled a laugh and saw Nick and Don do the same. "Where will you get your information from?"

"The library has all kinds of old stuff; newspapers, pictures, microfiche. We might get hired by them this summer to help transfer some of that old-time stuff to computers. We're still negotiating," Sasha said.

At this rate, Katie had no doubt the sisters would be millionaires before they hit their twenties. They were hard-working and motivated for success.

"Well, I'd certainly be interested in anything you can dig up about Artisans Alley. I was told it was an old applesauce warehouse, but I don't know much more. Would you be willing to research that for me?"

"In a heartbeat," Sadie said. Sasha didn't look as enthusiastic about the invitation.

"Great. But I think you might want to rethink your pricing for that information."

"Is it too much?" Sadie asked.

"Maybe not enough," Katie stated.

The sisters shared a glance, dollar signs lighting up their eyes.

"We'll have to talk about it," Sadie said reasonably. "But first, we need to do some research. If the theme of the summer extravaganza concerns the past, we've got our work cut out for us."

"You've got most of the summer to figure it out," Nick pointed out.

"Not really," Sasha said, "we've got other items on our agenda."

Again, Katie had to stifle a grin. The girl sounded so focused. "Well, I hope you young ladies will take a little time out for yourselves this summer. You deserve to have some fun."

"Fun?" Sadie asked, looking bewildered. "What could be more fun than this?"

"Yeah," Sasha echoed. "We've been talking about a Power-Point presentation we can give about the inn when the big weekend comes around."

"Won't one of you need to help your Dad in the shop?" Katie asked.

"We're going to split our time. But for now, we're on a gathering mission. We're going to make this happen," Sadie said, her tone grave.

"We're talking about offering our signature cookies and lemonade to potential guests," Nick mentioned.

"Brad will be contacting all the Square's food vendors to coordinate the menus so they won't be competing."

"We've got a lot to plan," Sadie agreed. "But for now, our focus will be on learning about all the buildings on the Square, including the people who built them and their history. Maybe we could even write a book about it," she said, her eyes widening as though this was a brand-new concept.

"You think so?" Sasha asked.

"It might be something you could do in conjunction with the Merchants Association," Katie agreed.

Suddenly, the girls looked absolutely thrilled, their gazes meeting, looking like they were stifling screams of joy.

Sadie swallowed a couple of times, and when she spoke, Katie could tell she was trying to mask the excitement she felt. "Yeah, I guess we could do that."

"That sounds terrific," Don said. "I think we should celebrate. What would you like, girls? Some cookies and iced or hot tea?"

"Hot," Sadie said.

"Iced," Sasha declared.

"We can have both," Nick said, and turned to fill the electric kettle that sat on the counter.

For the next hour, the five of them brainstormed while Sadie took notes and nibbled on homemade oatmeal cookies, and it seemed the girls temporarily forgot to view Katie as an enemy, for which she was grateful. She'd always enjoyed being with the sisters and despaired at their rejection of her. But now that their father was dating another, perhaps they might not see her as threatening their future. And for that, Katie was grateful.

Now, if she could only feel that good about herself.

Chapter Twenty

It was near closing by the time Katie made it back to Artisans Alley. She helped by staffing the second cash desk, processing the last-of-the-day shoppers before she cleaned out the tills and squirreled away the day's receipts in one of the file cabinets in her office. She'd take the cash to the bank the next day.

As Katie was locking the door for the night, her phone pinged. She pulled it out and saw it was a message from Margo.

If you're not doing anything for dinner, why not come out to the lake?

It was a little late for such an invitation, but Margo probably figured — and rightly so — that Katie had no other offers and would readily accept, which she did.

Be there in fifteen minutes, Katie texted back, gave her cats a snack, and jumped into her car to drive the two miles or so to Margo's rented lake house.

Katie knocked on the front door and heard Margo call, "It's open."

Katie entered and found her dead husband's mother in the kitchen, stirring a pot of marinara sauce, which smelled heavenly.

"Homemade?" Katie asked hopefully.

"Alas, no. But it came from a very expensive jar, so I hope we'll enjoy it."

Katie saw a salad bowl and a plate of sliced Italian bread waiting on the kitchen counter.

"Would you like a glass of wine?" Margo asked.

"After the day I've had, I'd welcome it."

"Oh, dear. Tell mama Margo all," she said, the word 'mama' causing Katie to inwardly cringe.

After pouring the wine and clinking glasses, Margo gave Katie a once-over. "You look like someone stole your lollipop. What's happened?"

Katie's head dipped. "Andy came by to see me last evening."

Margo's eyes widened. "And?" Was she hoping to hear of a reconciliation, or would she be pleased to know that Katie had once and for all called it quits with the pizza man?

"He said he was willing to forgive me."

Margo's expression darkened. "What for?"

"Breaking up, I guess."

Margo pursed her lips, refraining from commenting…at least, for a long moment. "And then?"

"I threw him out of my apartment."

Margo's lips curled upward. Was she happy that Katie had taken a stand against a misogynist pig or that Katie rejected Andy in favor of the memory of Margo's son?

"I'm sorry," Margo said at last.

"Because?" Katie ventured.

"Because you deserve so much more than that," Margo said with sincerity.

"That's a very generous view," Katie commented.

"I'm serious. Chad's gone, but you're young enough that you deserve to find happiness with someone else."

"And what about you?" Katie asked.

A hint of a smile touched Margo's lips. "Steve and I are going to have dinner next week."

"Next week? Why so far in the future?" Katie asked.

"I think neither of us wanted to look too desperate."

"Are you desperate?" Katie asked.

Margo shook her head. "It's just a game. A little flirting wouldn't hurt until we get to know each other better."

"Dinner is a good place to start," Katie agreed.

Margo nodded. "How do you feel about cutting ties with Andy?"

Katie let out a breath. "Relieved. But I admit it'll be hard to see him around the Square. And I'll have to go back to eating frozen pizza for the rest of my life."

"Surely not *that* long," Margo said.

Katie shrugged.

"Well, I'm sorry. I like Andy. I thought the two of you were good together...until he proved that wasn't true."

"Thank you for that. I thought we were good together, too. It's my fault since I introduced him to Erikka Wiley. I thought I could trust him. In the long run, and hurtful as it was, him showing his true colors was a gift."

"Thatta girl," Margo encouraged. "What else is going on?"

Katie related all the petty grievances of the day.

"Sounds like Nona Fiske needs a good kick in the butt," Margo commented.

"I'll say," Katie agreed.

"But I'm intrigued by the possibility of the Davenport girls putting together an historical booklet on Victoria Square. As part of my job at the big PR firm in New York, I often oversaw the layout of like-minded projects. I'd love to volunteer my services to the girls."

Katie brightened. "They absolutely love you, and I think they'd be thrilled to work with you on the project."

"I'll call Ray in the morning to see if the girls and I can get together to discuss the project." Margo looked thoughtful. "I wonder if we can find some vintage photos of the Square and the old home that's now Sassy Sally's."

Katie looked doubtful.

"You know, I've been in touch with a local artist who does line drawings," Margo remarked. "He'd like his work to be included in my gallery. If we can't get permission to use actual photographs, I'm sure he could be commissioned to make artistic renderings of the original buildings on the Square."

Katie looked doubtful. "This would be a shoestring operation. The girls couldn't afford to—"

"Nonsense. If I can get Chris to sign onto the project, he could allow us to use his art and sell numbered prints of it, too. It would be a win-win situation."

Margo sounded so sure of herself. Katie wanted to believe in the possibility because it would benefit many people and bring some much-needed attention to the Square. But then her rational mind kicked into gear.

"We're talking two high-schoolers putting together a collection of essays."

"Those girls are *smart*. And, sadly, a great portion of the current population doesn't read beyond the eighth grade level—if that. And anyway, isn't that what a thesaurus was invented for?"

Katie couldn't help but smile. "If they aren't aware, I'm sure you'll teach them about it."

"Of course. But mark my words, those girls could be the next Martha Stewart."

"Yes, but Martha is one person—we're talking two souls here."

Margo waved a hand in dismissal. "There's not only safety in numbers, but smarts. And the Davenport girls have that in spades."

Katie nodded, sipping her wine as Margo doled out angel

hair pasta into shallow bowls and ladled out sauce and meatballs.

Grabbing their bowls, the women retreated to the table, where they slathered garlic butter onto the bread slices and portioned out salad before starting their meals.

"This situation with Nona concerns me," Margo said, twirling pasta onto her fork.

"I wish I could say she was all bark and no bite, but I've seen how cruel she can be."

"Would you fight to keep her from running the Merchants Association?" Margo asked.

"I don't think I'd have to. Most of the merchants can't stand her. She's been objectionable to every one of them at one time or another. For what it's worth, I think I'm stuck with the job."

Margo raised an eyebrow. "Really?"

Katie shrugged. "So far, nobody else has stepped up to take my place. They're fine with someone else running the organization."

Margo nodded, taking a sip of her wine. It was more than a minute before she spoke again. "What would you think if I threw my hat in the ring?"

Katie's eyes widened. "Really?"

"As I'm opening a gallery on the Square, I've recently become a member of the Merchants Association. Is there any time restriction in the bylaws that says you have to be a long-standing member to take on the position?"

"No. In fact, I hadn't even officially inherited full control of Artisans Alley before they made me the head of the association."

Margo smiled. "Then there you go. I'm nowhere near perfect, but I bet I'm a better person to take on the task than Nona."

"And you're acquainted with most of the merchants. If it came to an election, I'm sure you'd win."

"Well, then, maybe we'll just have to put it to a test," Margo said with a sly grin.

"Nona intends to challenge my leadership at the next meeting," Katie said.

"Then she won't see me coming at her like a crossfire hurricane," Margo said sweetly, with just a hint of the acerbic woman Katie had first known but now respected. Despite the thought, Katie frowned. "I really would like to lighten the load on my shoulders."

"I know, darling girl, and since I moved to McKinlay Mill, I feel like I can take on the world."

"Really?"

Margo nodded, taking another sip of her wine. "My spirit was dying in New York. I'd conquered every professional mountain I could climb, and at my age, nobody gave a damn about me professionally. But here I've got a second chance to succeed at projects that have real meaning for me."

"I'm glad you feel that way." That gave Katie the opening to discuss the subject of Chad's paintings.

"I know you've been speaking to Steve Harris about finalizing the plans for your gallery."

"Just think, I could be open for the fall season."

"Speaking of which, I want you to look at a painting at Artisans Alley. A couple of my vendors consider themselves fine-art painters. One of them has just completed a gorgeous still life."

Margo raised an eyebrow. "Sounds interesting. How about I drop by in the next day or so to have a look?"

Katie nodded, hesitating before she broached what could be a sore subject. "We should also talk about what we want to keep or sell of Chad's paintings."

Margo's mouth quivered. This was obviously going to be a delicate negotiation. "I'm of two minds," she said diplomatically. "I only own one of his paintings." It was of a young woman standing in the wheat field that currently hung in the rental home's living room. "I know the rest belong to you. Are you in a hurry to dispose of them?"

"Dispose? Not at all. But Chad painted them with the thought they'd sell and be enjoyed by others."

Margo nodded, her gaze dipping to her bowl of pasta.

"There are forty-seven paintings stored at Artisans Alley. I thought we should each pick out our five favorites—in addition to the one you already own—and see if the world at large would be interested in the rest."

Margo nodded sadly. She pursed her lips, took another sip of wine, and seemed to weigh what she wanted to say before speaking. "I've got a friend in New York who I'd like to evaluate the paintings. I wouldn't want him to know who painted them. I'm sure we could obscure the signature via Photoshop, right?"

Katie nodded.

"Perhaps I'm just a doting mother who thought her child could do no wrong, but I think Chad's paintings might be worth a lot more in a bigger market. We could still display them here in my gallery, but if I could get a respected art critic to evaluate them, they might find a broader, more lucrative audience."

Katie knew that Margo didn't give a damn about the money the paintings might bring. What she wanted was a legacy for her son—the proof of his talent as an artist—and to find an audience for his work.

Katie gave Margo what she hoped was a sweet smile. "I think that's a wonderful idea. But the painting's first showing would have to be in your gallery."

"Oh, that's a given," Margo said, raising her glass. She smiled, but then it faded. "I'm sorry I doubted you."

"What?" Katie asked.

"I didn't think you and Chad were a good fit. To be honest, I didn't think *anyone* was good enough for him." She let out a sigh. "I know he was selfish in what he did to cut short your dreams, but I also think he believed Artisans Alley might have a bright future, and under your leadership, it's flourished. I'm only sorry he died before he could see his dreams fulfilled."

"So am I," Katie remarked. "So am I."

Chapter Twenty-One

Wednesday dawned like most others, but for the first time in a while, and after spending quality time with Margo the evening before, Katie felt like a bit of the weight had been lifted off her shoulders. Brad was in a great mood, singing and dancing around the Tealicious kitchen. Katie joined in, and the sound of their laughter made her spirits rise even higher. For some unknown reason, Katie felt like things were taking a turn for the better. Maybe on this day, Carol Rigby would come up with the answer to who killed Maxwell Preston. Maybe Margo would agree that Bonnie's painting was as good as Katie thought it was. Maybe the sun would go around the moon.

With the salads, scones, and rolls made for the day, Katie left Tealicious literally with a song in her heart. That song was "Stayin' Alive" by the BeeGees, which had been playing on Brad's phone's oldies playlist as she left Tealicious. It had a great, strident beat that propelled her forward on her counter-clockwise power walk around the Square. As she approached Wood U, Ray opened the door and beckoned her to join him. Like her, his smile conveyed his mood: upbeat.

"I've got everything bagels from Tanner's. Come and join me

for breakfast," he said.

"Gladly," Katie answered, having fed her cats but neglected to feed herself that morning.

Belle lay in her bed as Katie and Ray entered the inner sanctum, but her tail thumped with pleasure as the humans doctored their coffees and spread cream cheese over their bagel halves.

"To what do I owe the pleasure of this awesome breakfast?" Katie asked, taking a bite of bagel. Tanner's had done a superb job of encrusting the top of the bagel with seeds, onion bits, and garlic. The taste was pure heaven.

Ray cocked an eye in her direction. "Why not celebrate the joy of being alive?"

Katie nodded. "You're right. The weather's fine; I decided I'd try my best to avoid interacting with Nona until the next Merchants Association meeting, and I get to share breakfast with a good friend."

Ray smiled. "I'm glad you feel that way. I've got a special reason for feeling happy myself."

Katie grinned. "So, spill it!"

"We got the house!" Ray crowed, a wide grin splitting his face.

For a moment, Katie just stared at him in shock, feeling like she'd been punched in the gut, and then her eyes filled with tears.

"Hey, what's wrong?" Ray asked, sounding confused.

Katie shook her head, blinking rapidly. "I'm so happy for you and the girls," she managed, despite the urge to choke. "I know they've been wanting this for a long time."

"Yeah," Ray said, yet all the joy had leached from his voice. "You weren't seriously interested in the house, were you?"

Katie shook her head. Not after she knew that he and his children wanted it. "Nope. It would have been a cute project, but there are other houses out there, and I'm sure I'll find the perfect one ... eventually."

Ray looked uncomfortable. "I'm sure the girls would love your input once we take possession and start to decorate."

Katie snorted a chagrined laugh. "Not on your life. Sadie and Sasha can't stand the sight of me."

"Oh, that's not true," Ray said, although not convincingly.

Katie shrugged. "That's okay. I don't live for universal acceptance." And she certainly didn't need two teenage divas' approval to value her worth. She swallowed before speaking again. "Have you got a closing date?"

"The end of August—right before the girls go back to school. It doesn't give them much time to put their stamp on the place, but then I'm certainly not in a hurry to make drastic changes." He rubbed his fingers together, indicating money might be a problem.

Katie nodded. It took all of her control to form the next question. "So, what does Carol think about the house?"

Ray frowned. "Uh, well, I haven't yet had a chance to tell her about it."

"Well, I'm sure she'll be thrilled for you and the girls."

"Maybe," Ray said, not sounding at all certain.

They sat in awkward silence before Ray broke the quiet. "I'm sure once we're settled the girls will want to throw a house-warming party. If we do, will you come?"

"You bet," Katie said, not sure she was telling the truth. She'd lost out on owning the Webster Mansion, and now she'd lost the little Craftsman bungalow, too. How much more loss was she supposed to endure before she found her forever home?

The irony of that statement hadn't eluded her. Forever homes were associated with pets—like her cats Mason and Della. She'd only remembered one home where she felt safe and secure—under the roof of the little Cape Cod home owned by her great aunt Lizzie. Since her aunt's passing, Katie had lived in a succession of apartments. She longed for a real home of her own. A place where she could lie awake on summer nights to hear the pitter-patter of rain on the roof. To hear the howl of the wind during a winter storm knowing that she and her cats were safe, warm, and secure. A place where she could have both veggie and flower gardens to feed her belly and her soul. Was that really too much to ask of life?

Forcing a smile, Katie spoke once again. "I'm so happy for you guys. Really, I am."

"Will you continue your house search?" Ray asked.

"It's not a priority," Katie lied. She couldn't wait to ditch the apartment over Tealicious, but she wasn't about to trade one bad experience for another.

"I hope you find what you're looking for," Ray said kindly.

"Like I said, right now I'm just looking—for the fun of it," she amended and braved a smile. From the look in Ray's gaze, he didn't believe a word she said. That was up to him.

Katie took the last bite of her bagel before dusting off her hands. "I need to get going. Keep me in the loop about the house. I can't wait to see what the girls come up with."

"Yeah, I will," Ray said without enthusiasm. Katie caught Ray's gaze and gave him a big smile—one she knew didn't extend to her eyes. "If you'd care to, keep me informed. And I wish you and your family the best and that you'll be happy in your new home."

"Thanks," Ray said. Was there just a tinge of regret in his voice?

Katie wasn't sure she wanted to know.

"We'll talk again soon," Katie said.

"Yeah. I'll look forward to it," Ray said.

"See ya!" Katie said cheerfully as she left Wood U, but as she crossed the tarmac toward Artisans Alley, and although she held her head up high, Katie couldn't stop the tears from flowing. She'd lost the house of her dreams.

There were other houses out there that could fill the void when it came to square footage, but the thought that no matter where she went, Katie would only have the company of her cats in the deepest, darkest, stormiest nights of her life in the here and now and in the shadow-filled unknown future filled her with dread.

Upon arriving back at Artisans Alley, Katie poured herself a cup of coffee, leaving a quarter in the cup to pay for the privilege, and returned to her office. She quietly closed the door, set her coffee mug on the desk's blotter, hunkered down in her chair and gave in to silent sobs, not sure exactly what she was crying for. Chad, her breakup with Andy, or the loss of the house filled with potential that she'd hoped would become her home.

After a minute or so, she grabbed a tissue from the box on her desk, blew her nose, wiped away her tears, and turned toward her computer.

She had work to do.

~

GOING over the Alley's accounts was mind-numbing, which was just what Katie needed. After a couple of hours, a rap on her door caused her to look up from her computer screen. Katie sighed, hoping another problem wasn't about to be dumped in her lap. "Come in."

The door opened. "Have you got a minute?" Bonnie Wozniak asked.

"Sure. What's up?"

Bonnie looked about ready to burst with excitement. "I just had lunch with your Mom—"

Katie did her best not to wince at the noun, realizing it was later than she thought. "And?"

"She loves my still life and wants to include it in her first show this fall. She thinks it could be worth thousands."

"Thousands?" Katie asked, emphasizing the S at the end of the word.

"Well, at least *a* thousand. I've never sold a painting for more than a hundred bucks. We talked about other subjects I might want to cover."

Katie suffered another inward cringe. "You realize that all art critics' opinions are subjective and that she might have different ideas when it comes to the final selection of paintings for the exhibit."

Bonnie's smile faded a bit. "Margo did mention that. But she loved the one painting. I hope I can entice her to show more of my work. This could be a real boon to my career."

As far as Katie knew, until then Bonnie had been just a hobbyist. But—whatever!

"I'm so pleased for you. Just keep doing your best, and you'll find an audience," Katie said encouragingly. "And, I urge you to explore what else you're capable of. And if that takes you out of Artisans Alley, you definitely need to go for it."

Bonnie's expression was a mix of awe and confusion. And Katie had a feeling that once Margo opened her gallery, Artisans Alley would have another open booth. The thought pleased her as it meant that she'd helped one of her vendors move up in the greater art world.

"I never thought of it that way before," Bonnie said.

"Taking bold steps can be scary but rewarding. I can't wait to see your next painting," Katie said.

"I feel inspired to go home and start a new one right away. But I think I'll take a day or so to think about what I might do. Maybe make a few sketches."

"That sounds like a great plan," Katie said.

Bonnie nodded, said good-bye, and pulled the door until it was almost closed, giving Katie back her privacy.

The stars seemed to be aligning for Bonnie. Maybe someday soon, Katie's stars would move back into alignment, too.

Chapter Twenty-Two

Tealicious had closed an hour earlier, and Artisans Alley had also emptied for the day. Katie was finishing off the last of her admin duties when her phone pinged; a text from Margo.

Darling girl, are you free for dinner?

Was she ever!

See you in ten or fifteen minutes, Katie replied.

The wine's on ice.

Katie smiled, shut down her computer, grabbed her sweater, and headed for her car.

Minutes later, Margo greeted Katie at the door of her rental home with a glass of chardonnay. "You made it in record time. Come in, and we'll sit and look at the lake."

"Sounds like heaven," Katie commented, and accepted the glass.

It was too chilly to sit outside that evening, so Margo placed the room's upholstered chairs in front of the floor-to-ceiling windows overlooking the water and the women took their seats. Twilight was still a couple of hours away as they sipped their wine, gazing at the horizon. Canada lay forty miles to the north.

"I could get used to this," Katie said, settling deeper into her chair, feeling pent-up tension leave her body.

"I've got plenty of room," Margo quipped, raising her brows in what looked like hope.

Yes, Margo did. Katie thought about the offer. It would sure get her out of the shoebox where she currently lived. But….

Margo studied her daughter-in-law's face and laughed. "You don't have to say it. I wouldn't want to move home either—not after being out on my own for over a decade."

Margo and Katie had never shared a home and likely never would.

Katie didn't voice the thought.

"I'm going to miss this place when I move into my loft," Margo said with a sigh.

Some might not feel as comfortable knowing a murder had been committed within their sight line. Katie didn't voice that thought. "Are you sorry you committed yourself?" she asked.

Margo shook her head. "Not at all."

They looked out on the blue water in front of the home. Unlike the last time she'd arrived for dinner, no heavenly aroma wafted from the kitchen. "What's on the menu tonight?" Katie asked.

"I hope you don't mind not having a home-cooked meal, but Brad sent me home with an assortment of cold cuts and cheeses."

"Better to use them than waste them," Katie agreed.

"And I picked up a loaf of French bread at Tanner's. Have I told you my secret vice is mayonnaise?" Margo was as slim as a willow branch.

"I won't say a word," Katie promised. "How're things going at the gallery?"

A smile crept onto the older woman's lips. "Steve and his team are doing an amazing job. Most of the stud walls are up, and they should be starting drywall next week. I've started planning my first show."

"Speaking of paintings, I had a visit from Bonnie Wozniak this afternoon. She was excited about your asking to show her still life."

"I'm excited to be showing it," Margo remarked.

"But what if she can't come up with anything as good?" Katie asked.

Margo sighed. "I've thought of that. I understand she had something to prove with that painting."

"That's what I mean. What if she can't replicate that kind of passion?"

Margo looked thoughtful. "All art is subjective. I like the piece, and I think others will, too. I can encourage her to do more, but I did warn her not to churn out pieces of the same ilk in hopes of cashing in on past success."

"In those words?" Katie asked.

"Of course not. If nothing else, my career in public relations taught me to couch bad news with a positive spin."

Katie nodded. "And what did you think of Wanda's watercolors?"

Margo frowned. "They were adequate. Nothing wrong with them, but nothing particularly special, either."

That was too bad. Katie was particularly fond of watercolors and found Wanda's to be charming, but acknowledged she was no art critic.

"Bonnie said I must be very proud of my daughter," Margo said casually.

Katie wasn't sure how to react or what to say.

"I told her I was," Margo said.

Tears filled Katie's eyes. She swallowed before commenting. "It's been a long time since I was anyone's daughter."

Margo smiled, reaching out to clasp Katie's hand. "And isn't it lucky that we were able to finally connect?"

Katie returned the squeeze. "Yes. Yes, it was."

The women were silent for long moments before Margo moved on to another subject. "I hired Janice Grayson, the Square's photographer, to take pictures of the paintings."

Katie had not renewed the lease of the previous inhabitant of that retail spot for non-payment of rent. It wasn't long after that another photographer rented the space.

"If nothing else," Margo continued, "we should have a photographic record of everything Chad created. You know, in case we might want to put out a definitive book on the collection."

Margo always thought big. She was banking on Chad's paintings to bring in big bucks. If they did, that was to Katie's benefit. She'd made substantial inroads to paying off her debt. If the paintings brought in enough, she might even offer to buy off her partners on the Square properties.

But all that was wishful thinking at that point.

"Chad didn't sell a lot of paintings, but I know of a couple of the buyers, and it's a long shot, but it's possible I could track down some of them through the Alley's computer system and hopefully convince them to lend the paintings for your show."

"That's fantastic!" Margo exclaimed, but then her smile faded. "Janice has already returned the paintings to the store-room in Artisans Alley. I saw the proofs. She's going to give me two copies of each. She'll Photoshop out the signatures on one set so I can send them to my friend in New York and ask for his honest opinion."

"What if he doesn't appreciate them as much as you and I do?" Katie asked.

Margo frowned. "Then I just have to face the fact that he's an idiot."

Katie blinked. But again, she saw the twinkle in Margo's gaze, and they both laughed. However, seconds later, Margo sobered. "If the world at large doesn't appreciate Chad's work, at least the two of us do."

Katie nodded and sipped her wine. The women stared at the rippling water beyond the breakwall, lost in their thoughts, quiet to forestall their emotions from becoming maudlin.

Finally, Margo cleared her throat. "Anything new on the Square?"

Katie sighed. "Not so much *on* the Square but with one of the merchants."

Margo raised an eyebrow.

Katie bit her lip before continuing. "Ray and the girls got that charming little bungalow we visited on Sunday."

Margo frowned. "You don't exactly seem happy for them. I didn't know you'd fallen in love with the place."

"I'd be lying if I said I didn't."

"I'm so sorry," Margo said sincerely.

"But if anyone was going to get it, I'm glad it was the Davenport family."

Margo nodded. Noticing their glasses were empty, she got up and brought the bottle over to refill them.

"Speaking of the Davenports, have you spoken to the girls about their proposed book?" Katie asked.

"Those girls are sharp as tacks. They've already uncovered a treasure trove of information."

Hmm. They hadn't yet given Katie a report on what they'd found out about Maxwell Preston. She'd have to remind them of it.

"So, what are some of the Square's secrets?" Katie asked.

Margo settled back, that twinkle reappearing in her eyes, ready to dish. "It seems the owners of the Webster Mansion, which is now Sassy Sally's B&B, came upon hard times. The family owned hundreds of acres outside the village and made their fortune based on apple production. They built the apple-sauce factory that's now Artisans Alley."

"Why on earth did they build it so close to their home?" Katie asked.

Margo shrugged. "Who knows? To be close to the end product? That said, it's a bit of a hike from the house to the Alley."

Yes. It took a minute or two to traverse what was now a sea of asphalt between the buildings.

"But applesauce wasn't their only product. They also had a cider mill and sold apples in bulk."

"Where did the girls find all this information?" Katie asked.

"They've been pouring over old microfilm and microfiche files of old newspaper reports, both at the McKinlay Mill Public Library and online sources via the Rochester city library system. They've also been talking to someone at the local historical society. They've asked for and been given permission to use some of their archival photographs. I'm telling you, this booklet we're producing could be a *real* boon for the Square, the village, and the girls."

"What do you think of their writing skills?"

Here, Margo looked a little less enthused. "Right now, their manuscript reads like a tenth-grade essay with no formatting to delineate chapters. But they seem willing to learn. My job is to encourage them as I correct them. They've mentioned they want to write a series of books on interior design. This is their first test."

"Maybe you should have been a teacher, like Chad," Katie suggested.

"I'm sorry I tried to discourage him from the teaching profession. From what I've heard, he was good at it."

"Yeah," Katie agreed. "He loved his students. Since he passed, more than a few of them have come into the Alley to tell me so."

Margo nodded sadly. But then she shook herself. "Much as I'd like to live in the past, we have to be present in the here and now."

Katie raised an eyebrow, pleased to hear that. "What else is in the manuscript?" she asked.

Margo's expression darkened. "They've also come up with a lot of information on the Webster family. Apparently, a relative left a stack of papers and memorabilia to the historical society."

The couple who'd owned the inn before Nick and Don had also found boxes of paperwork. Did the new owners still have them? She'd have to ask. "Sounds encouraging."

Margo wrinkled her nose. "Maybe not. Some of the diary entries record the brutality leveled against their workers."

Katie's hand tightened around the stemmed glass she held.

"The girls did some research on the Square's current inhabitants, too," Margo added.

"And?" Katie inquired.

"It's not all lollipops and roses," Margo said quietly.

Katie wasn't sure she wanted to hear stories disparaging the people she'd come to know as colleagues and friends. The whole idea of a booklet chronicling the history of the Square was beginning to seem like a bad idea.

"Do you think it's wise to continue with the project?"

"I do. Trying to erase history doesn't change the fact that it happened. And reporting the facts doesn't have to be salacious, either. Don't worry; it won't be a slam piece on the Square. We want to promote it *and* its history."

Katie would have to take Margo's word on that. Salacious gossip? Was it about Preston and Charlotte Booth—or that Conrad Stratton had an affair with a married woman? These days, such peccadillos were commonplace, but they weren't the kind of information Charlotte or Conrad would want repeated.

"Can I read the next version?"

"I don't see why not. In fact, we may want input from other sources, such as some of the village's seniors for personal accounts."

Katie nodded, and her stomach growled. It had been many

hours since she'd shared breakfast with Ray. "I'm getting hungry. How about you?"

Margo got up from her seat, and Katie followed her into the kitchen. Her priority just then was sustenance. And maybe—just maybe—both women could slather their bread with an extra helping of mayonnaise.

Just because.

Chapter Twenty-Three

For Katie, mornings had taken on a boring routine. After her evening with Margo, she certainly had a lot to think about during her stint in the Tealicious kitchen with Brad. That said, she was definitely in a rut. What made each day different was the people she met on her morning walk. On that day she headed east and passed Nick and Don walking their dog, Ru, going west. She saw Ann Tanner through the big glass window of Tanner's Cafe and Bakery and waved, and as she approached Wood U, Ray Davenport popped out of his shop. He had to have been waiting for her because his workroom was in the back of the building.

"Katie wanna cuppa coffee?" he called, smiling, parroting a parrot.

"I wouldn't say no," she replied, and strode up the steps to the porch outside his shop. Ray held the door open, and Katie entered. She followed him deeper into the building to the back room, where the aroma of fresh brewed coffee filled the air and a happy Belle welcomed her with a wagging tail. A Tanner's bakery box sat next to the coffeemaker.

"Can I offer you a glazed donut?"

Katie wasn't a big doughnut fan but wasn't opposed to the confection on offer, either.

"Thanks," she said as Ray presented her with the doughnut on a pretty cocktail napkin depicting seashells on a sandy beach. "This is nice," she commented.

"Sasha is big on thrifting unopened napkin packages. Her stash is getting pretty big, so she brought a few packets to the shop."

As a dedicated thrifter herself, Katie couldn't fault the girl.

"So," Ray said, handing Katie a mug of coffee with just enough coffee creamer to turn the dark concoction from black to the right shade of tan, "what's new with you?"

Katie took a bite of her doughnut and chewed, savoring the puffy dough and excellent glaze, before answering. "I spoke with Phoebe Preston the other day."

"And?" Ray asked, leaning against his scared workbench and taking a sip from a chipped Disney World mug, no doubt a souvenir from a trip to the Magic Kingdom.

"What she told me has me kind of puzzled."

"In what way?" Ray asked.

"According to her father's will, Phoebe isn't able to make any substantial improvements to the property."

"What a stupid proviso. Doesn't that make you suspicious? What's the reasoning?"

"Apparently, Mr. Preston wanted to preserve the building as a shine to his deceased wife."

"That's just ridiculous," Ray repeated.

Katie nodded. She took another bite of her doughnut, chewed, and swallowed before taking another sip of coffee and voicing what was on her mind. "So, Phoebe isn't allowed to mess with the site, but what would happen if someone else did a little digging?" Katie mused, sounding oh-so innocent.

"Literally or metaphorically?" Ray asked.

"Uh, literally," Katie said casually.

"First off, it would be trespassing," Ray pointed out.

"And how much jail time would that entail?"

"None. But one could be fined by the municipality for non-permitted work. And—the property owner could also sue. And why would you want to dig—figuratively and literally—around the Preston property?"

Katie took her time before answering, taking another bite of doughnut, enjoying it, and then another swallow of coffee. "You just said his edict for no improvements sounded suspicious." She repeated what Steve Harris told her three days before. "It seems awfully funny that Linda Preston's supposed lover disappeared and was never heard from again. What if, in a fit of passionate rage, Maxwell killed the guy and buried him under the property he owned on the Square, which is why he wouldn't want his daughter to disturb the area?"

"That's a pretty big if," Ray commented dryly.

Katie eyed him sourly. "Surely you had leaps of faith and/or logic that you pushed to investigate when you were a sheriff's detective."

"Yeesss," he said drawing out the word with apparent reluctance.

"Did it—or them—ever pan out?"

Ray hesitated before answering. "Sometimes."

"How many times?" Katie pushed.

"We're not talking about the past—we're talking about the here and now," Ray asserted.

"Isn't *all* your experience relevant?" Katie pushed.

Ray's gaze narrowed. He looked like a dad about to reprimand a recalcitrant kid—but she wasn't a kid. She might be almost a generation younger than him, but she also saw herself as an equal, and wasn't about to be treated otherwise.

Ray said nothing.

Katie shrugged. "Anyway, in order for the big red X to be removed from the building, the rotten planks would have to be replaced. I don't see why I can't do a little digging to see what I come up with."

"And what if someone sees you?" Ray asked.

"The only people on the Square after hours are Nick and Don, and I don't think they're about to turn me in to the cops — especially if I warn them about what I'm going to do."

"And make them accessories to the crime?"

Katie frowned. "Really?"

Ray nodded.

"Is it *really* a crime to dig on private property?"

"We've already established it would be trespassing," Ray said gravely.

So they had.

"And what's the point? If you did find the bones in the dirt, what would that establish? That a recently deceased man was responsible for killing someone decades ago?"

"What about giving closure to the missing guy's family? Don't you think that's worth something?"

"And what if you find nothing?" Ray demanded.

"Then I've built up a sweat and burned a few calories."

Ray rolled his eyes, looking heavenward as though seeking strength. When he looked back at her, he shook his head, perturbed. "Katie Bonner, you try my patience."

"Then, at least I have your attention." Katie's eyes widened in shock at her own words. *Had* she been seeking to draw his attention?

Ray scrutinized her face. Was he thinking the same thing? He took in a breath and focused his attention on the floor. "Well, I guess if you're determined to poke around *where you should not*," he said pointedly, "it's none of my business."

"No, I guess not," Katie said, feeling disappointed. She'd hoped he might be in for an adventure. But he was too schooled in the law to see it her way. She could understand that. And now that she'd confided her plans to him, should he be called to testify against her, she knew his code of ethics would compel him to do so.

"This is all hypothetical," Katie said offhandedly, as though she had no intention of actually doing the deed—which she knew he didn't believe for one moment.

Ray cleared his throat. "With that line of reasoning, what, if anything, would the death of Preston's wife's lover have to do with Maxwell Preston's murder so many years later?"

It was a good question.

"I'm not sure. Maybe nothing. But if it could give Gary Jordan's family some form of closure, wouldn't it be worth it?"

"That's a pretty big if," Ray remarked. "More likely, you're just going to stir up a big pot of nothing."

"The better to burn off those calories I consume from eating buttered bagels and hot chocolate for my dinners."

Ray's expression morphed from annoyance to concern. "Wait, is that all you have for your dinner?"

Katie sighed. "I live alone. I'm not going to cook a roast just for myself. My cats don't even want human food leftovers. They prefer kitty tofu from a can."

"But you're such a wonderful cook. Why wouldn't you do it for yourself?"

"You've never eaten my food. How would you know how good a cook I am?" she countered.

"I know you make great stuff for Tealicious. And you owe me a home-cooked meal. You promised it last year and never came through."

So she had.

"Sadly, these days, I can't do much more than microwave a dinner for myself in my tiny studio apartment or consume Tealicious leftovers. I can't entertain anyone for more than a cup of tea and a cookie or a scone."

"Is that why you're looking at houses?" Ray asked.

"In part." Katie sighed. "In order for me to buy a home, I'm going to have to divest myself of at least one of the projects I'm tied to on Victoria Square."

"That's too bad," Ray said, genuinely sounding sorry. "I know how much it's meant to you to spearhead those projects. Which one will you give up first?"

"The building on the Square. The warehouse annex is far too interesting to abandon quite yet, but if I have to, I would."

"You could take a partner for Artisans Alley," Ray suggested.

Katie shook her head. "I've got too much invested in that place—financially and emotionally to just throw it all away. And for now, I'm keeping my share of Tealicious, too. I couldn't part with it—that is, unless Margo wants us to be rid of it."

"And why would she?"

"She wouldn't because so far it's been a goldmine. We pay Brad market value for his talents, and we still make enough profit to make keeping it worthwhile."

"I'm sure Sophie will be glad to hear that."

Katie's expression darkened. "By the way, have you spoken to her about our previous conversation?"

Ray looked guilty. "Uh, not as yet."

"When will you tell her?"

"Soon. Soon," Ray repeated, but then he averted his gaze so he wouldn't have to look Katie in the eye.

Katie glowered at him. "It had better be before she starts working for us. Otherwise, it'll be a terrible shock to her if Brad or I have to pull rank and lay down the law. You did agree that mooning over Brad had to stop and that hearing that should come from you," Katie pointed out.

Ray nodded guiltily. "I know. It's just hard to break bad news to someone you love."

"Better to hear it from you than to be embarrassed by Brad telling her off. That could be emotionally crippling." Katie paused. "Both Brad and Sophie are gifted pastry chefs. He could teach her a lot in a commercial setting that she won't get during her culinary school classes, that is, if she could pay strict attention."

"You make a great point," Ray admitted. He looked chagrined. "Okay. I'll call her tonight and give her the bad news."

"You can soften the blow by telling her that this kind of hero worship happens all the time and that it's nothing to be embarrassed about."

"So, how many times did it happen to you?"

Katie wondered how honest she should be, but then, if she was passing off the dirty work to Ray, she figured she ought to come clean. "Three times. But I never once let on—never embarrassed myself."

"Lucky you," Ray muttered.

"No, I grew up as the ward of a Scot. She taught me to keep my feelings in check. Or at least not to flaunt them."

"She did a good job," Ray muttered.

Katie wasn't about to be baited into that discussion.

"Meanwhile, your two other little entrepreneurs are doing quite well. Margo tells me they've dug up all kinds of dirt on the history of the Square for their booklet."

"Maybe a little too much," Ray agreed. "I've talked with them about what is and isn't appropriate sharing. And, anyway, Margo is going to edit the booklet. She's assured me nothing included in it will be cause for a lawsuit."

Katie nodded and realized they were running out of topics. It was time to turn Ray loose. "Well, thank you for the coffee and doughnut and for taking time to answer my questions."

"Even if you didn't like the answers?" he asked.

She sighed. "Yes. It doesn't hurt to listen to a second opinion."

"As long as one *does* listen," he said pointedly.

"What are you insinuating?" Katie asked, frowning.

Ray shrugged. "Nothing. Nothing at all."

Yeah. Right.

Chapter Twenty-Four

The lights from the lamps that ringed Victoria Square cast stark shadows. Katie waited until Angelo's Pizzeria closed and Andy's truck left the lot before she ventured out of her apartment above Tealicious. She snagged the shovel she'd bought that afternoon and started walking close to the other buildings on the Square. There shouldn't be anyone else around, and she was thankful that the Merchants Association had voted down the proposal to install cameras. The idea came up at least once a year, and the next time one of the businesses was broken into, she was sure it would get voted in. After all, she had been the latest member to propose the investment.

Katie stopped outside the abandoned building that had belonged to Linda Preston, studying the rotting wooden deck that sat before the abandoned store's entrance. It should be pretty easy to pry up the deteriorated wood, although it would be evident to Phoebe that someone had tampered with the deck the next time she arrived on the Square. But then, if Katie found what she thought she might, Maxwell's secret might be the top story on the following evening's six o'clock news.

Katie had just stuck the tip of the shovel against the seam

between two boards when a voice behind her called loudly, "Hey!"

Cringing, Katie whirled to face Ray Davenport.

"What are you doing here at this time of night?" she demanded.

"I might ask you the same question," he said harshly.

Katie glowered at him. "You know darn well why I'm here."

"You think you're going to dig up Gary Jordan's long-lost remains."

"Yes!" she said defiantly.

"You're trespassing."

"Only if I find nothing."

"And if you find something?" Ray almost yelled.

"Then it'll prove a crime *was* committed, *and* I get to give a family closure."

"And destroy Maxwell Preston's reputation," he retorted.

"If he murdered the man, why would that matter?" Katie countered.

"But what if it *wasn't* Maxwell who did the deed?" Ray asked.

"What?"

"You heard me. What if it was Maxwell's wife who killed her lover? And why would he *or* she bury the guy under the porch?"

"I made a few calls this afternoon. According to town records, this porch was put in about the same time Jordan disappeared. Someone could have buried the body here, and the builders could have just built the deck over the dirt."

"All very convenient."

Katie's expression remained sour. "I'm going to pull up a couple of boards. Unless you intend to call the sheriff's office on me, you can either go home to your nice warm bed or give me a hand."

"And be an accessory?" Ray asked, aghast.

"As you mentioned, if you don't report me, you're an accessory by default, right?"

Ray's expression tightened into anger. "Damn you, Katie Bonner."

"Now, are you going to just stand there, or are you going to help me?"

Ray lowered and shook his head like a bull about to charge. "Why I put up with—"

"You don't put up with me at all," Katie countered.

"No, I *don't*. I—" But then Ray shut up, looking like he might explode.

Katie turned and lifted the shovel once again, placing the tip between the boards and using it like a crowbar to try to lift the splintering wood. Try as she might, she wasn't successful at prying up the board. She shifted position several times, but the rusty nails weren't budging under her efforts.

"Oh, give it to me!" Ray groused, snatching the shovel from Katie's hands.

Ray was at least twenty years older than Katie, but he was stronger than her and soon lifted the first board, grabbing it around the middle and pulling it off the studs that had held it in place for decades, the rusty nails shrieking in protest as they were yanked from the wood.

"Will you be quiet!" Katie hissed.

"Tell that to the nails," Ray retorted.

He yanked up another two boards before there was enough room to comfortably start digging. "Where do you want to put the dirt?" he asked.

Katie blanched. "Uh…I guess I hadn't thought that far ahead. Couldn't we just put it on the deck itself, and then if we find nothing, kinda brush it back into the hole?"

"You really haven't thought this whole thing through, have you?"

"Well, crime's just not my thing," she said defensively.

Ray glowered at her for a long moment before he thrust the shovel back in her direction.

"You want me to dig?" Katie asked, aghast.

"Wasn't that why you came out here tonight?"

With reluctance, Katie nodded. She mounted the deck and looked into the darkened space that Ray had uncovered. She thrust the shovel into the dirt, hit the top hard with her right foot, and pulled up a satisfying load of dirt, dumping it on the boards in front of the crumbling building.

Shovel after shovelful of dirt bore no sign of a body having been buried in the space, but Katie dug on. She was breathing hard by the time she'd made a trench some four feet long, a foot wide, and six inches deep, and was sweating like she'd been in a sauna with nothing to show for her efforts.

"Had enough?" Ray asked.

"No," she said, glaring at him. "Whatever is left of the body has to be buried deeper."

"Likely so," Ray agreed, yet he seemed content to let her do the digging. Was that so he could make a citizens arrest if she found nothing, or was he more worried about the effects of that kind of labor on his cardiovascular system? She dug a little slower at that thought. The last thing she wanted was to be responsible for Ray having a heart attack and dying on her.

She stopped digging for a moment, swallowing. Dying on *her*? What was she thinking?

"Did you talk to Sophie?" Katie asked as she thrust another shovelful of dirt onto the deck.

"Yeah."

From the somber tone of his voice, Katie deduced that the discussion hadn't gone well.

"And?" she asked as she dumped more dirt onto the pile.

"The poor girl was mortified."

Katie continued to dig. "But is it enough to keep her from working for us this summer?" That wasn't what Katie wanted.

She liked Sophie and wanted to not only encourage her talent but have bragging rights when the young woman broke out as a superstar baker, which Katie was sure Sophie would.

"Sophie's feeling a bit raw right now, but I think she'll pull it together before she comes home for the summer. She realizes what an opportunity she has to learn from a master baker."

"Good," Katie said, feeling much better about the situation. "Sophie will find her special someone someday. People usually do."

"And have you?" Ray asked bluntly.

Katie sighed, lifting yet another shovelful of earth. "I thought I had. Twice. I was wrong."

"Does that mean you're giving up on love?"

Katie thrust the shovel into the earth once more. "I'm sure not actively looking for it. Why would I after my disastrous past?"

Ray shrugged. "You never know what the future holds."

Katie lifted another shovelful of dirt. "Work, work, and more work."

"There must be something that keeps you going besides that."

Katie added more dirt to the pile. "My cats. Apparently, I'm destined to be an old cat lady. If that's my fate, I'll just have to accept it."

Ray shook his head. "That's a pretty cynical view from someone so young."

It probably was, but Katie's back was starting to show the strain from digging. The whole idea of looking for Gary Jordan's earthly remains now seemed like a wild goose chase.

She stomped on the top of the shovel, sending it deep into the crusty earth, yanked up the dirt, and deposited it onto the growing pile.

"Hold it!" Ray called out.

Katie straightened up, grateful for even a brief rest. Ray

took out his phone, switched on its flashlight, and ran the beam of bright light over the pile. Then he bent down and retrieved a dirty piece of wood about six or seven inches in length.

"Tree root?" Katie asked.

Ray turned, his face deathly pale in the glare of the Square's lampposts, and turned the object over and over in his hand. "Nah. I'd say it's part of a femur."

CAROL RIGBY WAS NOT PLEASED to be dragged out of bed. And when she found out why, she was absolutely furious.

"Do you know how many laws you've broken?" she accused Katie.

"No, but I'll bet you do," Katie muttered.

"What was that?" Carol demanded.

"No, ma'am, but I'm sure you'll tell me."

Carol glared at Katie. "Now, what brought you out In. The. Dead. Of. Night?" she enunciated, "to look for the earthly remains of — who did you say?"

"Gary Jordan. At least, I *think* that's who it is."

Carol turned her wrath on Ray. "And what in heaven's name were you doing out here with *her*?"

"Trying to keep this young woman out of trouble," Ray said blithely.

Carol glowered at him. "And apparently, you didn't stop her."

"Look," Katie began reasonably, "isn't the possibility of solving a cold murder case worth a little leeway here?"

"That's up to the district attorney to decide," Carol decreed.

Uh-oh! Katie knew the first item on the morning's agenda was to call her pseudo-big brother and ask him for the name of a criminal attorney. Although...maybe he would be up to defending her himself. She sure hoped so. At least that way, she'd get the friends-and-family discount for his services.

A sheriff's office technical officer held the piece of bone in gloved hands.

"Is that *all* you found?" Carol demanded.

"Well, Ray said we should let the forensic team finish the job," Katie said.

Again, Carol turned a jaundiced eye on Ray, who shrugged helplessly. "We'll speak about this later," she said. It sounded like a threat.

"Well, now that the techs are here to finish the digging," Katie said, waving a hand toward the host of officers swaddled in hazmat suits, "can I go home?"

Carol's gaze narrowed so much that Katie was reminded of a cobra ready to strike.

"Wouldn't we *all* love to go home to our warm beds?" Carol shrilled. She was definitely not a happy camper. She let out an exasperated breath. "Yes, go. Get out of here. But you'd better be available in the morning to make a statement."

Katie held back from saluting the sheriff's detective, feeling it might just cause the woman to detonate. The last thing the tech team needed was to be covered in the detective's blood and guts, not to mention the bony remnants of what was probably Gary Jordan remains.

"Thank you," Katie said genially. She glanced in Ray's direction, but his expression was as dark as a thundercloud. Perhaps they'd exchange thoughts the next morning. Perhaps.

"Um, can I have my shovel?" Katie said.

Carol stalked up to what was left of the deck, forcefully yanked the shovel from its resting place against the building, and thrust it at Katie. "Good night, Ms. Bonner."

Katie forced a smile. "And to you, Detective Rigby."

Shovel in hand, Katie headed back toward Tealicious and her apartment above it. Unfortunately, she couldn't see what was happening on the Square, as her apartment's only window was the skylight in the building's roof. But it was late, and Katie had a busy day ahead of her. Still, as she lay down in her bed, her cats settling around her, she couldn't help but wonder what this latest development might have to do with Maxwell Preston's death. Had he been killed for killing another? If so, why had someone waited so long to take revenge? Or what if Ray had been right, and it was Linda Preston who'd killed her lover and buried him in front of her store? If that were the case, she would have had to have been better at digging than Katie. Or, impossible as it might seem, what if the entire area in and around Victoria Square had been an ancient burial ground? It might be teeming with bones.

With that myriad of thoughts, Katie finally drifted off into sleep. But upon waking the next morning, she had far more questions than answers about what she'd found the night before.

Chapter Twenty-Five

B rad must have been working in the kitchen below Katie's apartment for at least an hour before she finally awoke from her slumber. She threw on a pair of yoga pants and a T-shirt, shoved her feet into her sneakers, and trundled down the stairs to the Tealicious kitchen.

"Everything okay?" Brad asked, scrutinizing Katie's eyes, which she suspected might be a little bit bloodshot.

"Sure. What's the special of the day going to be?"

Brad checked on the commercial mixer with its bread hook industriously kneading dough for the Parker House rolls he made several times a week. "I thought we ought to feature shortcake. Strawberries are at peak right now—at least in some part of the country—and I got a fantastic delivery this morning. Look at those beauties," he said, and pointed toward a dishcloth where at least a hundred berries were drying after being washed.

"They're one of the most beautiful fruits on the planet," Katie agreed, thinking how cooked shrimp and sliced kiwi came in as close seconds. Yet she knew they weren't local. Those berries would come in about a month. She didn't want to consider how large a carbon footprint these out-of-towners possessed. It was up to Brad to set a reasonable price for the dish, yet make a profit. He was good at that. Katie lamented the day he would leave Tealicious to start his own restaurant.

But what if she and Margo brought in Brad as a partner? Or what if she sold him her share in the business? That would keep him on Victoria Square—and at Tealicious. As Katie chopped celery for the protein salads, she pondered the repercussions. She was overextended here on the Square. If she sold her shares of the buildings that housed The Flower Child and Tealicious, she could afford to buy a house without a crippling mortgage. But what would Margo think about that scenario? She'd only bought into Tealicious to please Katie. And, of course, she was willing to co-sign a loan for any home Katie wanted to buy. Margo was far more generous than Katie deserved or wanted. What she wanted was to earn her home and on her own terms. It was the Scot in her that yearned to be independent as well as self-sufficient.

Katie caught sight of Brad staring at her.

"What?" she asked.

He shook his head, averting his gaze, turned off the mixer, and began rolling the dough into balls to make the rolls. "I was just wondering if you'd thought more about moving out of the apartment."

"Yeah, I have. But I don't know where I'd go. I don't want to end up back in one of the village's apartment complexes—"

"Tell me about it," Brad grumbled.

"And I'm not likely to because I've got two cats, but there aren't a lot of other rental options around here. And I'm so overextended I don't think I can swing a mortgage."

"Sounds like a Catch-22."

"Yeah," Katie agreed. "How long have you got left on the lease to your apartment?"

"I'm doing month-to-month right now," Brad admitted. "But

I absolutely hate the place I'm stuck in. I swear, nothing in the complex except for the kitchen and laundry room appliances has been updated since the nineteen seventies."

Katie could identify with that. Before she'd moved into the apartment above Angelo's Pizzeria, she'd been stuck in the same apartment gulag.

Then, just for the heck of it, she decided to ask Brad the question that had so recently laid heavy on her mind. "I know you're saving up to open your own place — "

Brad raised a hand, presumably to protest, but Katie waved her own as though to erase his words. "But what would you think about buying a share — or the entirety — of Tealicious and making McKinlay Mill your home for the foreseeable future?"

Brad stared at her for long seconds, but then a smile quirked his lips. "I *hadn't* given it any real thought. Now that you mention it, it *might* be something I'd consider, but I'm not sure I'd want to keep it a tea shop."

Although Katie wasn't pleased to hear he'd change the nature of the business, her heart skipped a beat. Much as she loved Tealicious and the opportunity it gave her to at least experience part of the dream she'd held for opening the English Ivy Inn and holding tea parties for guests, it now seemed much more critical to have a comfortable place to land when her workday was through. A place she could decorate with each season. A place where her cats had more than a couple of hundred square feet to call their home.

Was she selfish to want more?

EVIDENCE of the early morning activities in front of what Katie had come to think of as the Preston edifice was starkly apparent. Nothing remained of the porch in front of the building, with the lumber it had consisted of being stacked beside the structure, and the front of the building was wreathed in yellow crime tape. Katie was determined to put her suspicions out of her thoughts and instead counted her steps along with her pedometer. She was lucky to get in more than twenty thousand steps on her daily walks, which was good as she too often indulged in the luscious Tealicious leftovers. Better to eat them than throw them out, she told herself. That's right. She was keeping methane-producing scraps out of the waste stream. Yeah, that's what she told herself.

On her second circuit around the Square, Katie noticed that Nona Fiske's car was now parked by the side of The Quiet Quilter. Ha! If ever a business had been misnamed! Nona was not only vocal, but loud when it came to people and events that displeased her. Katie had no clue how the older woman had stayed in business for so long.

Averting her gaze, Katie headed toward Tanner's Cafe and Bakery when she heard her name being called.

"Katie!" came the thin, shrill voice.

Katie stopped in her tracks, waiting for Nona to catch up to her.

"Yes, Nona," Katie said with no inflection. She wanted to speak to Nona like she wanted to sprout a third ear.

"I pulled my car into the lot and what do I see but a load of crime tape on the building next to mine!" Nona shrieked. "What in God's name has happened on the Square now?"

Katie wasn't about to spill the tea on what she knew, or at least not tell *all* that she knew.

"Apparently the police were here digging in front of the Preston building."

"What were they looking for?"

Katie shrugged.

Nona's eyes narrowed. "Besides those gay guys at the inn," she practically spat, "you're the only other person who lives on the Square. Surely you saw what was going on."

And instigated it, too, Katie thought, but she wasn't about to tell Nona that. "I saw a lot of lights from the police cars," she remarked. That was a one hundred percent true statement.

"Didn't you think to leave your apartment to investigate?"

"Uh. . ." And here Katie didn't feel she could lie. "I did speak to Detective Rigby of the Sheriff's Office. She was accompanied by a tech team."

"And?" Nona demanded.

"Apparently they were tipped off that there might be a body buried under the building's porch."

Non looked horrified. "Did they find one?"

"Well, what remained of one." Katie struck what she hoped was a thoughtful pose. "There are all kinds of rural cemeteries around here. In the olden days, people would bury their dead on their own property. Maybe that's what happened here." And maybe the moon was made of green cheese and pigs flew.

Nona looked skeptical. "Well, I don't like it."

"It is what it is," Katie said quietly. "Perhaps the local news channel will have an update. Have you thought to look?"

"Of course not! I've only been on the Square about five minutes. I would have thought you, of all people, would have been up-to-date on such things!" she said tartly.

"Me of all people?" Katie inquired.

"Yes. You seemed to have your fingers in every pie on the Square."

Katie was in no mood to get into it with Nona. "I need to finish my laps before I start my workday at Artisans Alley."

"Sure, sure, blow me off," Nona said, and without another word she retreated to her store, grumbling all the way.

Katie exhaled an exasperated breath before continuing with her power walk. But as she approached Sassy Sally's Bed & Breakfast, the door opened and Nick poked his head out. "Katie, come on in and have breakfast with us."

Knowing how good a cook Nick was—and his partner

wasn't all that shabby, either—Katie gladly interrupted her walk to join her friends.

Once she was seated at the counter in the inn's kitchen, with a steaming cup of coffee in front of her, Katie had her pick of two different kinds of warm sweet rolls. Feeling reckless, she chose one of each, using the polished silver tongs to plop them on the plate Don provided for her.

"Okay, spill it," Nick said.

"Spill what?" Katie asked innocently.

"We saw all the cop lights flashing on the Square last night," he said.

"What were you doing up so late?"

"Nature called," Don said succinctly.

Katie sighed and used the fork provided to cut away a part of the sticky bun before her, grateful it wasn't a cinnamon bun. Thanks to Andy's latest visit, she'd gone off them. "I may have been looking for buried—" And here she stopped, for no way could someone's bones be considered treasure. "Evidence," she finished.

"And?" Nick prodded.

"Ray showed up. What I thought might be a tree root, he deemed to be part of a femur."

"That's a leg bone, right?" Nick asked, looking rather disconcerted.

Katie nodded and tapped her left thigh.

"And then?" Don asked.

Katie cut a piece of the other roll, forked it up, and tasted it. Ahh, its lovely orange-flavored tasted like ambrosia. It about melted her heart it was so good. "Well, I have a couple of theories," she said.

Both Nick and Don leaned in to listen.

She told them about the possibility it *could* be a contractor who Maxwell Preston *may have* suspected to be his wife's lover. Or maybe Linda Preston killed her lover in a fit of rage, spite or

—for making a lousy cup of coffee—who knew? And then she mentioned the conversation she'd shared with Nona Fiske and her displeasure at not being kept in the loop.

"There's no pleasing that woman," Don said, turning aside to top up his coffee mug. "Believe me, I've made it my life's work *not* to please her."

"Don!" Nick chided him.

Don merely shrugged.

"This is all very interesting," Nick said, and took a bite of his orange-infused bun, "but what has it got to do with Maxwell Preston's death?"

Katie toyed with her fork. "Nothing, I guess. But it's a mystery that may or may not be solved. The contractor, Gary Jordan, had children, or at least has living grandchildren." She didn't mention Steve Harris's connection to the case. "I'm sure they could test their DNA and compare it to the bones that were found."

"Yeah, and that could take a year or more. That's the way these things work." What Don said was true.

"What's been worrying us," Nick said, his voice not much louder than a whisper, "is that it had to be someone at Margo's party who killed the old man."

So, that fact hadn't been lost on others.

"It wasn't either of us," Don piped up. "We'd never even met the man before the party, and I doubt we exchanged more than a hello—if that—with him before we left that evening."

"We pretty much stuck together like we were glued," Nick agreed. "And we spent a lot of the party talking to Margo and Moonbeam."

Don nodded in agreement. "We're friendly with the other merchants on the Square, but I wouldn't say we were friends with any other than to offer their products to our guests. That's just good business sense to showcase local wares. Many's the guest who's asked about the jams and jellies, soap, or wine we serve, and we cheerfully plug the other merchants," Nick said.

"And we're pretty damn sure most—if not all of them—don't suggest guests stay with us," Don added.

"To be fair," Nick said pointedly, "I'm not sure that kind of recommendation would be asked for when someone wants to buy a box of chocolates or a hand-crafted wooden jewelry box."

No, it probably wouldn't.

Katie polished off the last of the decadent orange bun, savoring the sharp citrus that contrasted with the sweetness of the icing. "I'm glad you're such enthusiastic cheerleaders of the other Square merchants. Thanks."

"We like to think of ourselves as the Association's merchants of good neighbors."

"And we haven't killed anyone yet," Don joked.

Katie and Nick turned sour glances in his direction.

"It was a joke," Don said defensively.

"You can't joke when we're probably suspects in old man Preston's death," Nick cautioned.

Don turned to face Katie. "Are we?"

Katie shrugged. "Maybe...but probably not. Has Detective Rigby harassed you?"

Nick shook his head. "Just that one visit, but she wasn't at all friendly."

Don scowled and shoved the last of his bun into his mouth, chewing savagely.

Katie polished off her sticky bun and coffee and stood. "I need to get to work. But first, I'll need to do another couple of circuits around the Square to work off the calories from those amazing buns. Are you sure I can't entice you to share that orange sweet roll recipe with me to tempt my Tealicious customers?" she asked hopefully.

"Not a snowball's chance in hell," Don quipped. "We've got

to have at least one to-die-for enticement on our breakfast menu."

Meanwhile, Maxwell Preston had never had the opportunity to imbibe one of those fantastic buns.

It made Katie sad. But then...she was beginning to think that perhaps Preston, who may have been a murderer, might not deserve such sympathy.

Chapter Twenty-Six

After leaving Sassy Sally's, Katie did another two circuits around the Square and its annex, and as she made her final pass, she watched as Ray parked his junky old car behind his shop. He exited the vehicle, retrieving a leashed Belle from the back seat.

"Hello!" she called.

Ray looked up. "Hello, yourself. Want to join me in a cup of coffee?"

"Is there room for both of us?" Katie asked, employing a dad joke that was probably older than Ray.

"You tell me," Ray said. He waited as she threaded her way down the embankment to join him behind his shop.

"To tell you the truth, I'm coffee-saturated, but I wouldn't say no to a little conversation."

"Speaking is one of my best attributes," Ray said.

Considering the antics that occurred early that morning, Ray seemed pretty cheerful. Had all been forgiven? Katie stood behind him as Ray unlocked his shop. He swung open the door and gestured for her to enter before him. The shop was rather dark, and Katie moved to her left, letting Ray step in beside her to flick on the workshop's light switches. Katie inhaled the scent of wood chips and waxes, finding the aromas enticing and wishing she had some kind of artistic ability. Arts and crafts just weren't one of her gifts, and she wondered what her sainted Aunt Lizzie might have contributed had she had the opportunity to have a booth in Artisans Alley.

"Are you sure you don't want a cup of coffee?" Ray asked, removing the leash from Belle's collar.

Katie shook her head. "I had my morning usual and then stopped in to Sassy Sally's for another couple of cups with Nick and Don. I expect my bladder to explode in an hour or so."

Ray laughed. It suddenly struck Katie how joyful a sound it was. It made her smile.

"I'm sorry I don't have anything decadent to offer you. Just some ginger snaps the girls picked up at the dollar store. They just discovered them and think they're the coolest thing on the planet, not knowing they've been around for generations."

Katie laughed. "May they make many more such happy discoveries."

Ray nodded. "I hope you don't mind waiting while I make a fresh pot of coffee. The girls emptied the pot at home before they went to school. Is it healthy for teenagers to take in that much caffeine so early in the day?"

Katie shrugged. "Better than some other things they might want to try."

Ray nodded.

Katie sat on one of the workshop stools, scratching behind Belle's ears, watching as Ray puttered around until the brewing cycle finished. He poured himself a cup and grabbed a couple of cookies from the opened bag. "Now, what's going on?" he asked.

Although it might bring up a sore subject, Katie told him about her encounter with Nona. He nodded, sipping his coffee and nibbling on a ginger snap.

"Have you heard from Carol?"

"Not yet, but she had plenty to say after you left the old ceramic shop." How had he known what the shop's business was? Had he read the information his daughters had dug up?

"I guess I'm not her favorite person," Katie said dryly.

"You've got that right."

"Anything else?" Katie asked, wondering if Ray's mood was about to make a rapid change.

He scowled. "I don't think we need to go into that."

Katie nodded. "I suppose we've both got to give statements to the sheriff's office."

Ray nodded. "I'll probably go after the girls get out of school."

Katie wondered if she could blow it off for a day or so. She really didn't have it in her to take off from work when she had so much responsibility weighing on her.

"So, what do you think about the girls writing a book?" Katie asked.

Ray's expression darkened. "They've dug up much more dirt than anything I could have anticipated."

"So I gathered. Margo still thinks it could be whipped into a positive PR piece."

"I think so, too."

Had the girls mentioned they were working for Katie to look up dirt—no, not dirt, information—on Maxwell Preston? If so, he didn't say it. She'd text Sadie as soon as she got back to Artisans Alley to find out the status of that work.

AFTER LEAVING WOOD U, Katie realized she still had more than half an hour to kill before Artisans Alley opened. She decided to make one more power walk circuit around the

Square. But when she approached The Quiet Quilter, Nona again pounced on her like a tick on a dog.

"I've got a bone to pick with you, Katie Bonner!"

Katie sighed. Was there ever a time when Nona *didn't* have a complaint against her?

"And that is?" Katie asked with a sigh.

"I understand that some of your Artisan Alley vendors who aspire to participate in the extravaganza *aren't* offering time-appropriate crafts."

"For example?" Katie asked.

"One of your *vendors*," she said the last word as though it was an expletive, "will be offering *machine*-embroidered pillow slips, potholders, and anything else she can monogram."

Katie folded her arms across her chest. "So?"

Nona's eyes bulged. "Well, I believe that anything offered for sale *on* the Square *during* the event *should* be time-appropriate."

"Does that mean you won't offer machine-pieced or quilted coverings?" Katie asked.

Nona seemed to hesitate. "I have no problem with Rhonda Simpson, as all her work is handmade—" and also that Margo had brokered a peace deal so that Rhonda's cross stitch pieces coordinated with some of Nona's quilts and patterns, "—but the woman who does machine embroidery does it with a computer-driven sewing machine!" she cried, outraged.

And how did Nona know that?

"Are all the quilts you sell hand-sewn?" Katie asked.

Nona stood a little straighter, her lips pursing. "I don't understand what you're getting at."

"Well, if we apply your standards, anything you offer for sale would have to be totally handmade as well." Except *Pollyanna* was published in 1913, and the sewing machine was invented in 1830 by Elias Howe, so Nona would be in the clear for using a machine to sew. Katie allowed herself a smug smile. All those years of watching *Jeopardy* sure paid off.

Nona's expression soured.

"You don't produce the fabrics used in your quilts, do you?" Katie pressed.

"Of course not. And neither did the woman of that age. They made quilts, and some made clothing, out of feed sacks."

"And are your quilts made of vintage fabrics?"

"Don't be stupid. A lot of old cottons rot because of the unstable dies used. But all that's beside the point,"

"Is it?" Katie asked, letting her ire color her words.

"The Square's Dickens Festival is based on history," Nona continued.

"Well, not really. *A Christmas Carol* is a work of fiction. And although the merchants and Artisans Alley vendors dress up in period-appropriate costumes, no one expects them to reenact the horrors of that age, either." Nona just stared at her. "Nona, we live in the twenty-first century. I don't think people expect the things they buy at a craft fair to be totally made from scratch."

"And why wouldn't they?" Nona demanded.

"Because—" But then Katie didn't have a ready explanation of why. "Just because." It sounded lame, even to Katie, but she wasn't going to let Nona's reasoning cut anyone out of participating in the promotion.

"I think you need to concentrate on your own business and let the others on the Square tend to theirs," Katie said.

"But that's not what I want," Nona said with pique, and Katie was surprised the woman hadn't stamped her foot, as well.

"You don't get to call the shots," Katie asserted.

"And you do?" Nona demanded.

"Yes, as the head of the Merchants Association, I do. And

I'm not about to cut anybody off who wants to participate in the promotion—whether you approve of them or not."

"Well, we'll just see about that!" Nona said, turned on her heel, and marched back to her shop. The door slammed behind her.

Katie's stomach did a little flip-flop. Too much coffee. Or did she have a sour stomach from too much Nona?

Chapter Twenty-Seven

K atie took a very quick shower, changed, and headed toward Artisans Alley, hoping she wouldn't run into any other distractions before she started her workday.

As Katie crossed the Square, a flash of bright orange caught her attention. A big sign hung in the plate glass window of Angelo's Pizzeria that hadn't been there even half an hour before.

UNDER NEW MANAGEMENT
SAME GREAT PIZZA!

Andy must not have been kidding when he said he was moving on with his cinnamon bun business.

Katie stared at the sign for long seconds, then looked around for Andy's truck, but it wasn't in the lot, which it should have been at that time of day.

Under new management. Did that mean he'd sold the business, or had he just found someone to take care of the pizzeria?

Katie stood in the parking lot for long seconds, trying to decide how she felt about Andy leaving Victoria Square. He'd been a part of her life since the first week she'd taken over managing Artisans Alley. Together, they'd weathered all kinds of storms, although the last one had literally blown them apart.

New management.

Katie continued on her way to the Alley, but instead of coming in through the front door, she decided to walk around to the south side of the building, entering through the back door and into the vendors' lounge, thankful she didn't bump into any of the regulars before entering her office.

Sitting at her desk, she wondered what she should do next. She did and *didn't* want to know what Andy was up to. After all that she'd been through, she shouldn't care what he did. She'd let Andy know that they were through. That she never wanted to see him again. But was that true? He'd more or less told her that he was her last chance at love. But that couldn't be true. She hadn't even hit middle age. If he couldn't have what he wanted—a sycophantic girlfriend—then he wanted to degrade her so she felt worthless. Yeah, her self-esteem had hit a low, but she had no intention of letting the man have that much power over her.

Still, she reached for the old-fashioned Rolodex on her desk, flipped through to Fred Cunningham's card, picked up the phone's receiver on her desk, and punched in the number."

"Katie Bonner," Fred called after answering on the second ring. "What's up?"

"Hey, Fred. I was just wondering what you knew about the new management at Angelo's Pizzeria."

"I guess as of today, it's no secret that the business has been sold."

Sold. Andy would be gone. Gone from the Square. Gone from Katie's life.

Gone.

She no longer wanted Andy in her life, so why did the news seem so ... so final?

"Yeah, Andy contacted me a couple of months ago. He didn't want to devalue the business by making it common knowledge that he wanted to sell, so I put out some feelers and found a couple who were interested in buying the business."

"And now it's a done deal," Katie said, desperately trying to keep her tone neutral and wondering why it seemed so important to do so.

"Yeah. A fellow and his wife are taking over."

What would happen with the wayward, at-risk kids Andy had hired? Would the new owner take over that responsibility? It was one of the traits that had first attracted Katie to Andy. He'd been an at-risk kid; he'd made mistakes, but he'd been taken under someone's wing and straightened himself out. That he was willing to do so for other kids had endeared him to her. Would he do the same with his new cinnamon bun franchises? She hoped so. Andy wasn't a totally messed up human being. He cared for the kids he helped. She admired that quality in him. That he couldn't be monogamous was another matter.

"I'm glad the Davenport family finally found the house of their dreams," Fred said conversationally. "They've been looking for a long time. Why, I must have shown those girls at least sixty or seventy houses."

"The girls?"

"Mostly." He laughed. "Those young ladies want to put their stamp on something that needs a lot of cosmetic changes, but not too much DIY, although Ray told me they've been taking industrial arts courses in school so they could do a lot of the work themselves. I guess they're pretty good at it."

Katie hadn't known that.

"The youngest one concentrated on electrical and plumbing, and the older one on construction. I'd say that's pretty smart, considering they want to be interior designers. If they don't do the work themselves, they'll never get stiffed by a shady contractor."

"Yeah, they're smart girls," Katie agreed.

Fred seemed to sense something was amiss in Katie's tone. "You didn't fall in love with that house, did you?"

"Yeah, I guess I kinda did," Katie admitted.

"I can keep my eye out for something similar if you like."

"Practically speaking, I'm not in a position to take on any more real estate."

"You do have your finger in a lot of pies on Victoria Square," Fred agreed.

Was he channeling Nona Fiske?

Katie waited a long moment before asking her next question. "I suppose Andy's selling his home up on Main Street, too."

"Yep. I'm hosting an open house on Sunday from one to three."

So, Andy was cutting all ties with Victoria Square. Maybe that was a good thing. Katie didn't want to run into him at the grocery or liquor stores, either.

And yet … she felt sad. Sad for the way things had ended. She'd loved Andy. That he'd not only let success go to his head, but he seemed to be drinking some kind of toxic testosterone elixir as well.

Katie brightened her tone. "Well, thanks for the information, Fred. And thanks for speaking with Phoebe Preston. I know she appreciated it."

"My pleasure," Fred said.

"I'll be in touch when I'm ready to start looking for houses again," Katie promised.

"Sure thing. See ya."

Katie said good-bye and hung up the phone, feeling suddenly—terribly—alone.

Well, Andy was a thing of the past, and although Katie didn't regret her decision to end her relationship with him, the wound was still pretty fresh. What she needed was a distraction. Then she remembered what she'd wanted to accomplish upon entering the Alley. Was it too early in the school day to text Sadie Davenport? Maybe. She knew some schools confiscated phones to avoid distractions during classes, but then decided to go ahead and text her. Sadie would eventually see the message.

Anything to report on Maxwell Preston?

It wasn't more than a minute later when Katie received a reply.

Sure. I'll email it to you. Give me an address. And here's our Venmo address.

Katie frowned. Those little Davenport entrepreneurs might be slow on delivery, but they didn't waste time asking for their fee, which Katie dutifully paid.

Minutes later, Katie checked her email, and found the email from Davenport Designs already in her inbox. Before she could read it, Margo swooped into her office, exuding almost palpable excitement.

"What have you got to tell me?" Katie asked, filled with anticipation.

"I heard from my friend, the art critic, in Manhattan!"

"And?" Katie prompted.

Margo looked absolutely gleeful. "He loved Chad's paintings. He said they were reminiscent of Georgia O'Keefe's work."

Katie let out a breath. "Wow—that's quite the compliment."

"That's not the best thing. He showed them to a friend who'd like to borrow them for an exhibit in his Soho gallery."

Katie knew that to be in Manhattan—not London. But still —Soho!

"What do you say?" Margo asked with trepidation.

"That I'm thrilled and would *love* for us to go to New York for the show's opening."

Margo beamed. "I was hoping you'd say that." But then her

joy faded just a bit. "I wonder what else Chad might have painted if…."

If a vengeful woman hadn't killed him?

Yeah, Katie wondered, too.

She shook herself. "When would this guy schedule the showing?"

"Not for a year, at least. And if we sold any of the paintings, it would have to be under the proviso that they would be available to be shown at the New York gallery."

"I'm not an art world aficionado, but that could only enhance the value of the paintings, right?"

Margo nodded, her eyes sparkling with pride.

"I'm so happy I could dance on air," Margo said, and did a little jig in Katie's doorway, making her laugh.

"If there was room, I'd join you," she said and grinned.

Margo did a final twirl and collapsed against the doorjamb. "We should celebrate. What should we do?"

"Champagne seems an appropriate way."

"I wonder if Conrad stocks Dom Perignon at The Perfect Grape."

"I bet he does."

"I could host a dinner party for our closest friends."

Katie tried not to cringe. Margo's last party had ended in disaster.

"Who'd be on the guest list?"

"Nick and Don, Brad, of course, Steve Harris—it would be a safe setting to get to know him better—and maybe Seth. He's been such a recluse since Jamie's death. I worry about him."

Seth and Jamie had been engaged to be married before Jamie's untimely demise.

"Sounds good," Katie said, noting the lack of female attendees. And another notable exception, which Margo seemed to pick up on. "I'd invite Ray, but then he'd want to bring that disagreeable woman."

"She's a pill, all right," Katie remarked and told Margo about the events that had happened in the wee hours of the night.

Margo shook her head ruefully. "Why a smart, strong man like Ray wastes his time with a woman like that is beyond me. She wants to lead him around by the nose—and he lets her!"

Katie shrugged. "She must have some appeal," although Katie couldn't fathom what that might be—and didn't want to speculate. "When would you schedule the party?"

Margo shrugged. "There's no real hurry. Maybe next weekend. I'll put out some feelers—maybe a save-the-date text chain to see if everyone's available. I'll figure it out," she said confidently. Then she grinned, practically bursting with pride. How sad it was that the celebrant—Chad, of whom all the fuss was being made—had to miss out on the excitement—and the acclaim.

"Are you busy on Sunday?" Katie asked.

"No, why?"

"I thought it might be nice to go to the cemetery and plant some flowers on Chad's grave. We could go to one of the nurseries in Greece and pick them out together."

"I'm not much of a gardener, but I'd love to."

"Great. Then let's plan on it."

Margo nodded, her eyes a little dewy. She sniffed. "I love you, darling girl."

Katie, too, was suddenly overcome with a wave of affection. She stood, and the women embraced.

The sound of someone clearing his throat broke them apart. "Am I interrupting anything?" Vance asked.

Margo wiped a hand across her damp eyes. "Just a little mother-daughter moment," she explained.

Vance raised an eyebrow but didn't comment.

"I'd better get going. Lots to do," Margo said.

"We'll talk again soon," Katie said before adding the moniker "mom."

Margo's grin was positively radiant. "You bet." And with that, Margo left the area.

Vance moved to take Margo's place in Katie's doorway, his gaze focused on his shoes. "Mom?"

"Lots of daughters-in-law call their husband's mother Mom."

Vance seemed about to say something before thinking better of it. "Uh, that they do."

It was Katie's turn to clear her throat. "What was it you wanted to see me about?"

"The toilet in the bathroom by the photography studio has a crack in it. It might be a good idea to replace it before we get a leak. The last thing we need is for it to drip onto the dance studio's wooden floor and ruin it."

"Good idea. Will you take care of it?"

"Of course. That's why you pay me the big bucks," Vance said, grinning.

Maybe it was time to give Vance a raise, too, for noticing such things. She'd make that happen before his next paycheck —and mention it as she handed him the envelope.

"Anything else."

"Yeah, I've got a few concerns. Care to take a walk with me around the Alley?"

"Sure," Katie said, pulling her office door closed and following him. She'd read the file Sadie Davenport sent later. After all, it wasn't likely to contain any bombshells of information.

Right?

~

THE REST of Katie's day was nonstop, and it wasn't until the Alley was about to shut down for the day that she remembered to print out the file Sadie Davenport had sent that morning, intending to read it with a glass of wine that evening. Why not? She didn't have anything better to do.

After letting herself into Tealicious, Katie scrounged the fridge for something for her supper. Oops! She'd been so busy that day, she'd forgotten to eat lunch and was now famished. Brad always left items for her pickings in a specific spot in the main fridge. It wasn't always the healthiest of foods, but that night she hit the jackpot with a big bowl of tossed greens and a container of tuna salad to go with it. Heaven. Maybe Brad deserved a raise, too!

Katie trudged up the building's inner staircase to her studio apartment, placed her dinner in the fridge, and then attended to the cats, who were attention starved, giving them lots of pets and a bowl of treats before she poured herself a generous glass of wine and settled into the love seat with the pages Sadie had sent her, ready to be bored.

Instead of a narrative, Sadie had assembled the information the girls had discovered in bullet points. Katie read through them.

Preston was hired by the Main Street Apothecary after graduating from the University of Rochester School of Pharmacology and Physiology.

Preston was elevated to head pharmacologist five years after being hired. Two years later, he'd taken over as owner. How he'd accomplished that wasn't explained. Who had backed him? Had he taken out loans? Had he inherited a fortune to buy such an establishment outright?

Within the pages were several screen shots of articles that had run in to the local Penny Saver and another from the Rochester Democrat & Chronicle, telling the rags-to-riches tale of one Maxwell Preston.

The girls had found Linda Preston's obituary, which included a black-and-white photo of the grave site filled with wilting flowers. (And where had they found that?)

But then the tale took a more sinister turn.

Some ten years before, Preston had been charged with Medicare fraud, submitting claims for non-existent patients. The suit had been dismissed on a technicality, but the report supposed that Preston had made millions from his deceit. Was that the estate Phoebe hoped to inherit? Did she know where the money came from?

So, Preston was a cheat, a dirty old man, and hid his own or his dead wife's involvement with the probable death of Gary Jordan. With the deaths of all three, it wasn't likely a final conclusion could be established for Jordan's death. Katie hadn't seen everything that had been discovered in the dirt under the Preston's store deck, but she supposed, like Preston, the remains of whoever had been buried in that shallow grave could have suffered a fractured skull. Whether that had killed him or if he'd died from premature burial, there was no way to know.

Still, nothing the Davenport girls had uncovered seemed to connect Preston's death with that of his wife or the skeletal remains found buried on his property.

Something big was missing from the Preston death equation.

On impulse, Katie got up, snagged a yellow pad of paper from her desk and started jotting down the names of all the guests who'd attended Margo's housewarming party.

Of course, the Tealicious team was there: Margo, Katie, and Brad, but also Ann Tanner, Sue Sweeny, Charlotte Booth, Ray Davenport and his date, Carol Rigby, Moonbeam Carruthers, Nick and Don from Sassy Sally's, Conrad and Gilda Ringwald-Stratton, Paula Mathews, and Nona Fiske.

It wasn't likely a stranger had hung around the home's grounds to bonk Maxwell on the head with a blunt instrument, sending him into the drink. Random acts of violence like that just didn't happen in the sticks.

Charlotte and Maxwell had been romantically linked and she hadn't been forthcoming when it came to the status of her relationship with Preston at the time of his death. Then again, Katie and Andy had been known as a couple for a couple of years, but she assumed everyone knew of their breakup. She hadn't bonked him on the head and killed him after they parted and she hoped Charlotte hadn't done so, either.

The only other person on the Square who had a beef with the man was Nona Fiske, and for the most mundane of reasons. She didn't like the fact that his shabby building stood next to hers. But surely that wasn't reason enough to murder a man.

And yet . . .

Katie had never met a person as petty as Nona. She'd harassed the former owners of Tealicious, when it was known as Afternoon Tea, infringing on the parking at the side of the shop, putting up signs saying that the space between them was only available for her shop, and threatening to tow anyone who infringed upon that area.

On more than one occasion, Nona had spread vicious gossip about people on the Square. Nona had even shielded her nephew, who'd tried to run down and kill Katie!

Good grief! How much more incriminating evidence did one need to point the finger at the old woman? And yet ... Katie knew that legally she couldn't prove anything she might accuse Nona of doing.

Katie mulled over what she knew—or thought she knew. What she needed was a second opinion. Should she talk to Seth...or Ray? Seth had dealt with Nona on only one or two occasions when it came to signing the contracts to buy into the property on Victoria Square and the annex behind the Square. He hadn't seen her unpleasant side. And, oh! She meant to have consulted him about digging around and finding skeletal remains.

On the other hand, Ray had been present during at least one of Nona's meltdowns and had dealt with the woman on more than one occasion. Like Katie, Ray knew Nona had more than one screw loose.

But no, not even Nona was cruel enough to kill someone because their property was an eyesore and spider haven.

Could she?

That an arrest hadn't been made wasn't material at this point. Sometimes it took years before investigators came up with enough evidence to indict a suspect. But in the eyes of the law, Charlotte *had* to be the chief suspect in Preston's death.

Feeling frustrated, Katie set the pages and pad aside, ate her dinner, and, feeling a troubling sense of disquiet, again cued up to watch *Pollyanna*.

The movie played as background noise, but Katie kept ruminating over the events of the past week or so. If Nona was Preston's killer, how would Katie ever prove it?

Pollyanna's Glad Game seemed so innocent. But despite the film's uplifting ending, Katie still felt unsettled. Nona was her chief suspect, but she had no proof to give Detective Rigby, who seemed disinclined to believe anything Katie had to say anyway.

Katie decided to sleep on her suspicions, but slumber didn't come quickly, and when it did her dreams were filled with menacing shadows and disquieting images that kept her from peaceful rest.

Chapter Twenty-Eight

The following morning, Katie arrived in the Tealicious kitchen soon after Brad. He looked up from piping chocolate frosting onto a 10-inch cake and scrutinized her face. "Everything okay?"

"Why wouldn't it be?" Katie asked, despite again feeling the weight of her suspicions spoiling her mood.

Brad shrugged. "You look a little...." But he didn't finish the sentence.

Disheveled? Poorly? Depressed? Those words were apt descriptors for how Katie felt. She barely scraped a brush through her hair before winding a tie through it to make a ponytail. No makeup. Dressed in yoga pants and one of her rattier T-shirts, yeah—perhaps disheveled was the right word. "Why spiff up before I shower and get ready for the work day?"

"You don't consider what you do here work?" Brad asked.

"Yes, it's work, but it's only you who sees me."

"And I'm not worth spiffing up for?"

He wasn't going to take her to dinner or offer her a ring. He wanted her to move out of her apartment so that he could move in. No, she had no plans to spiff up for him.

"If you don't want my help—" she began.

"Oh, no," he quickly backpedaled, "I want and appreciate everything you do for setup."

Of course he did, because she was cheap—unpaid—labor, and there wasn't money in the budget to hire anyone else to give a hand in the kitchen. Well, at that moment. It wouldn't be long before Sophie Davenport was paid to take over Katie's duties— or at least most of them. Katie would still help out, and that usually meant mopping the floors and cleaning the restrooms— not her favorite jobs.

"It's just that ... I think I may have figured out who killed Maxwell Preston."

Brad's eyes widened. "And when are you going to call Detective Rigby?"

"I don't know. I should probably run my suspicions by Ray before I say a word to the detective. For all I know, she may have already come to the same conclusion."

"Then why hasn't she made an arrest?" Brad asked.

Katie shrugged. *Probably to spite me*, she thought.

Her cell phone pinged. She stopped what she was doing and pulled the phone from her pocket. It was a text message from Vance.

Did you know Nona's telling our vendors they can't set up booths in the back parking lot? She says we need every space for the public to park. But you own part of the lot, right?

Yes, she did.

I'll handle Nona, Katie replied, her blood beginning to boil.

We should discuss the whole idea of who gets to have a booth outside. Maybe do a lottery?

Exactly what Katie had suggested at the vendor meeting. Hadn't he been listening? *We'll talk later.*

Katie was rewarded with a string of thumbs-up emojis.

"Anything wrong?" Brad asked.

Katie shook her head. "Just more edicts on high from Nona Fiske."

Brad let out an exasperated breath. "I've enjoyed speaking with every merchant on the Square—except for her. What is her problem?"

She's a crank. She's a bigot. She's a murderer, Katie thought.

"She's a pain in my butt," she answered and went back to her task.

Brad went back to decorating his cake. "I'm glad she's your problem and not mine."

"Really?" Katie asked acidly.

Brad seemed to realize the mistake he'd just made. "No, sorry. I'm sorry *you* have to deal with her at all. In every organization, there's always one big pain in the ass. Nona is the one for the Merchants Association."

He had that right. But it wasn't in Katie's nature to say such things publicly.

"I'll speak to her this morning. This power trip she's on has got to stop."

"And you're the one to do that," Brad said cheerfully.

Cheerful? That wasn't at all how Katie felt. With every power move Nona tried to pull, the more Katie was convinced of her potential for violence. If it hadn't been directed toward Maxwell Preston, it might well be aimed toward one of the Square's merchants or the Artisan Alley's vendors. It had to stop. And it had to stop that day.

Now, if only Katie had a plan to make that happen.

As Katie told Brad, she had no plans to win a beauty contest when she set out on her daily walk around Victoria Square and its surroundings. She was on her third circuit when she saw that Nona had arrived at her store. There was no way she would confront Nona about her suspicions before she had a chance to speak to Ray and seek his counsel. But it seemed that she wouldn't get that opportunity, for when she approached The Quiet Quilter, Nona burst from her shop's entrance as though shot from a cannon.

"Katie Bonner!" she shrieked.

Katie stopped dead in her tracks, her fists clenching. "Yes?" she answered tartly, turning to face a pale and drawn Nona.

"I can't deal with that poor excuse of a manager you've got working for you at Artisans Alley," Nona declared.

"And why's that?" Katie asked. Everything about the woman before her grated on her nerves, from her severe hairstyle to the lack of any attempt to look attractive to the outside world. She was dressed in a cotton shift that looked like it had been thrifted in the 1930s. A yellow sewing tape measure hung around her neck.

"He thinks you *own* the parking lot behind Artisans Alley and intends to set up tents for your vendors."

"Well, if you look at the site map associated with the Alley, you'd see that's true. Only half the lot is designated as a municipal parking area."

Nona's eyes widened with indignation. "I beg your pardon."

Katie felt reckless enough to answer, "I don't think you do."

Nona started. "I don't what?"

"Beg my pardon," Katie retorted.

Nona's jaw dropped in fury. "What are you implying?"

"That you might want to rethink your role in the summer promotion."

"What?" Nona demanded.

"You came up with a great idea, but that's it. What have you done to make it come to fruition except alienate the people who could help make this operation a profitable exercise?"

"I've done *all* the work," Nona shrilled.

"I told you what needed to happen to make it a success. What have you done?"

Nona pursed her lips. "None of your business."

"Oh, but it is. Especially if you want me to release the funds for paid promotion."

"Why do we need that? I've spoken to the people who print the local Penny Saver."

"And how large is their reach?" Katie countered.

"I don't know. I don't care."

"Well, you should. Otherwise, we're just whistling in the wind. We need to entice the people outside McKinlay Mill to visit the Square."

Nana didn't look convinced.

"Do you know how many people live in the village?"

"A couple thousand," Nona answered.

"Yes, and our neighboring town to the east has over a hundred *thousand* inhabitants. And thousands more beyond that. How will they find out about our celebration if all you've decided to do is connect to only our village?"

Nona's brow furrowed. "Well, isn't that *your* responsibility?"

"Oh, no. You said *you* wanted to be in charge of the whole operation. It's up to you to figure these things out."

Nona glared at Katie. "You've set me up for failure," she accused.

Katie shook her head. "You've sealed your own fate."

"You don't know what you're talking about."

"I do. And I know," Katie said, glaring at the woman before her.

"Know what?" Nona bluffed.

"About what you did at Margo's party two weeks ago."

Nona's lips tightened into a thin line. "You don't know anything."

"Oh, yes, I do."

Nona's expression changed from umbrage to outrage, her eyes widening so that they bulged.

Out of the corner of her eye, Katie saw Sasha Davenport walking the family dog in front of Tanner's Cafe and Bakery, her gaze fixed on her cell phone. She instinctively turned south, heading straight for The Quiet Quilter. No way did Katie want to continue this conversation with a child in such close proximity.

"We'll finish this discussion later," Katie said, backing away from Nona.

"No, we won't. We'll finish it now! Just what is it you think you know?" Nona demanded.

Katie turned to get away from the shrew, but Nona grabbed the tape measure from around her neck, threw it around Katie's head, and yanked her forward. "Answer me!"

"Did you kill Maxwell Preston?" Katie managed as Nona quickly knotted the tape measure and pulled it taut.

"Of course I killed him!" Nona shrilled. "He devalued *my* property by not taking care of his own!"

"Nona!" Katie protested, yanking at the tape as she took a step back, a jolt of fear shooting through her.

"You don't understand," the older woman said, her pupils widening with fury. "I've been dealing with this horrible man and his refusal to act for more than a decade. I confronted the idiot at Margo's party, and he said he had no intention of fixing up the property. And then he taunted me. He *taunted* me!" Nona wailed. "He said I was an old busybody. He cast other aspersions on me and laughed. That awful man *laughed* at me!" Nona practically screamed.

And that was enough to kill Preston?

Perhaps to a mind as warped as Nona's, it was.

Katie pulled at the tape, which only increased the pressure on her windpipe.

Katie heard loud barking and turned her head enough to see

that Sasha had her phone outstretched—recording the altercation while trying to keep the dog from escaping her grasp.

Katie sank to the ground, her knees smashing into the asphalt as Nona screamed, "Die, bitch, die!"

"Lily, no!" Sasha screamed as Katie's vision began to darken.

The barking grew to a savage pitch, and suddenly, the pull on the tape measure was gone, causing Katie to fall back. The barking turned to a menacing growl, and then it was Nona screaming. Katie fell back on her butt, her vision returning to see a mass of multi-colored fur wrestling with a body—Nona—biting and snapping, its muzzle scarlet with the old woman's blood.

"Sasha! Katie!" hollered a familiar voice, and suddenly Ray was there, grabbing the dog by the collar and hauling it off a still-screaming Nona. "Call nine-one-one," Ray hollered, trying to control the dog lunging for its prey.

Katie managed to loosen the tape measure from around her throat, coughing and sputtering, trying to catch her breath.

Sasha approached, looking scared, still on the phone, presumably talking to a dispatcher.

Nona's screams had morphed into agonized sobs.

"What in God's name is going on?" Ray demanded.

"Nona," Katie managed, "she killed Maxwell Preston."

The dog still pulled on the leash, eager to return to the attack, but Ray held it it back.

"Lily!"

Suddenly, Moonbeam Carruthers sprinted across the Square. "Oh my goodness! Is she hurt?"

"She attacked Nona," Ray said, relinquishing the dog to Moonbeam.

"Lily? I thought that was Belle," Katie said hoarsely.

"Sasha's been walking her for me weekday afternoons and twice on weekends," Moonbeam explained.

It was apparently just another service the entrepreneurial Davenport sisters were prepared to offer.

"Nona tried to choke me," Katie explained, struggling to her feet and brandishing the tape measure as proof.

Lily had calmed down and jumped up at Katie, offering her doggy kisses. "She must have seen what was happening and leaped into protection mode."

"I tried to hold her back," Sasha cried, sounding panicked, as though she might be blamed for the dog attacking, "but I couldn't hold onto the leash because I was filming."

"Filming what?" Ray demanded.

Sasha jerked a thumb at Nona, whose sobs had downgraded to soggy moans as she rocked in pain.

"Sasha—go get the first aid kit from the shop."

Sasha took off at a sprint as Ray's training snapped into gear and he turned to assess the damage the dog had caused the old woman, whipping off his shirt to try to staunch the blood.

Suddenly, the sound of sirens cut the air, and within half a minute, the local fire department rescue squad and a police car pulled into the parking lot, just as Sasha arrived with the no-longer needed first-aid kit.

Katie looked toward Ray, the old woman, and the pooling blood on the tarmac, suddenly feeling woozy.

"Whoa!" Moonbeam called, and grabbed Katie before she could fall. "Let's sit you down," she said encouragingly.

No sooner was Katie on the ground than Lily crawled into her lap, her warm body giving comfort—and making her shirt a bloody mess. Nona's blood.

"Are you okay?" Moonbeam asked, concerned.

Katie sighed. "Is it too early for a good stiff drink?"

Chapter Twenty-Nine

The EMTs gave Katie a once-over, but after the initial shock wore off, she felt just fine and declined a trip to the closest hospital to be checked out.

Sasha volunteered to man the counter at The Flower Child while Moonbeam gave Lily a much-needed bath in her florist slop sink. Ray left Sadie in charge of Wood U, and walked Katie back to her apartment above Tealicious. He sat her on the love seat, and the cats immediately surrounded her, sensing something was off-kilter.

"I called Margo. She should be here at any minute," Ray said.

"Thanks. Did you call Carol?"

"No, but that's the next thing on my list of things to do. I assume you confronted Nona," Ray said with disapproval.

"I started to, but then I saw Sasha approaching, and my first inclination was to get the heck away from Nona. I didn't want Sasha to get in the middle of an altercation with that horrible woman."

Ray shook his head, and Katie could almost feel the waves of anger radiating from him. "She could have killed you!"

"Who knew a tape measure could be so lethal," Katie quipped, but Ray was not amused.

"How could you do something so, so—"

"Stupid?" Katie supplied.

"Unwise," he amended.

Katie shrugged. "Nona has always gotten under my skin, but I guess now she'll likely be off my back for good."

"Sasha got most of the confrontation on video. Damn. She'll be called as a witness for the prosecution if or when this thing goes to trial."

"That girl—young woman," Katie amended, "is made of tough stuff. All your girls are."

Ray nodded. "Like their mother."

"Like you," Katie countered.

"Maybe a little bit of me, too. They sure didn't get their looks from me, thank God."

"God had nothing to do with it," Katie muttered.

Ray merely shrugged. "What will you do now?"

"Margo is going to insist on taking care of me, and she can't do it here, so I'll probably spend the night with her at the lake house."

"I could feed the cats in the morning—if you want," Ray offered. "That way, you wouldn't have to rush home."

"I'd appreciate that."

Home. Katie looked around the tiny room. This was no home, but she wouldn't mention her feelings about it to Ray. She rubbed her forehead, feeling heartsick. "Tell me something that gets my mind off what happened on the Square."

Ray pulled up Katie's office chair and sat down. "Well, Sophie's coming home next week. She's excited to intern with you and Brad for the summer."

"And we're square about her not mooning over Brad?" Katie asked.

"Yeah," Ray said, sounding just a little embarrassed. "Now

that she's had a few days to think about it, she seems to be okay with it. She realizes it's a terrific professional credit she can use when searching for her perfect job."

Katie sure hoped so.

"And there's another thing," Ray said, not meeting Katie's gaze.

"Yeah?" she asked.

Again, Ray looked embarrassed. "Carol and I broke up."

Katie schooled her features and nodded. What was she supposed to say? Hallelujah, while helium balloons rose toward the heavens and colorful confetti fell like rain?

"I suppose your girls are happy about it," Katie said neutrally.

"Ecstatic," Ray deadpanned.

"And how do you feel about it?"

Ray let out a breath. "To tell you the truth, relieved. Carol has a lot of good qualities, but jealousy isn't one of them."

"Who was she jealous of?" Katie asked, confused.

Ray hesitated before answering. "You."

Katie nearly choked. "Me? Whatever for?"

"Because..." Ray swallowed a couple of times. "Because she knew I was attracted to you."

As Margo had told her two weeks before.

"Don't be silly," Katie protested, averting her gaze so she didn't have to look into Ray's dark eyes.

"Yeah. It *was* silly. Imagine the two of us as a couple. Me an old coot, and you a sexy young thing."

Katie's brow wrinkled. She was currently dressed in jeans and an old ratty sweatshirt. She wasn't clad in the slinky, sequined, form-fitting dress she'd worn when she'd accompanied Ray to the poker club six months before. She hadn't donned lipstick, eyeshadow, or mascara. And her nails hadn't seen a lick of polish for months. Who in the world would even think of her as sexy?

Ray?

Katie gulped.

"And what do you think about her rationale?" she asked.

Ray swallowed. "That she's a hundred percent right."

Sudden terror rushed through Katie's veins. She was frightened because she didn't know how she felt about what he'd said —and that she didn't want to admit she was attracted to him. Because ... because of their age difference. Because his daughters didn't like her. Because Andy had betrayed her and she wasn't sure she could trust her heart to another, at least not so soon. Maybe not ever.

"That was pretty hard for me to admit," Ray said, sounding sheepish, his tone begging her for a reaction.

"I'm extremely fond of you, too," Katie admitted.

Ray's head dipped, and when he spoke, he sounded defeated. "But not in *that* way."

Katie took a deep breath and let out a heavy sigh before answering. "That's where you're wrong."

Ray did a double take. "What?"

"I said you're wrong. I *am* attracted to you. I'm attracted to your sense of responsibility—even though you were once an absolute jackass, and I blame alcohol on that occasion," she said, referring to their undercover sting at the poker club. "But I'm pretty sure that'll never happen again." She took another fortifying breath. "I think you're one of—if not *the*—most kindest and decent man I've ever met."

Ray offered a tender smile. "But?"

"But your children hate me."

Ray leveled a perturbed glance in Katie's direction. "They don't *hate* you."

"It sure ain't love they aim in my direction," Katie remarked.

Ray frowned, his gaze dipping once again. "They miss their mother. It's only been a few years."

Almost four years, but there was no timeline for grief. "I

know," Katie said sympathetically. "And I know from experience that it takes a long, long time to get over the death of a parent." She'd had to get over the death of *two* parents and at a much younger age than the Davenport sisters. Maybe she'd never gotten over it.

Ray looked dejected. "So where does this leave us?"

Katie shrugged. "I honestly don't know."

"Could we at least…date?" he asked sheepishly.

Katie frowned. "Date how?"

"Well, for starters, just spend some time together."

Katie nodded. "Starting slow is probably the best way. I already consider you a friend, but I'd like to get to know you better."

"You mean like having coffee or lunch dates or something?"

"That would be hard when you've got a shop to run."

"And you've got two businesses to take care of, plus everything else on your plate."

"That's true," Katie agreed. "And I absolutely *have* to find somewhere else to live. With only a skylight, I feel like I'm living in a submarine. This little studio apartment makes me feel claustrophobic. Brad has expressed interest in taking it over, so now I just have to find somewhere else to live, but it has to be close to the Square. I need to keep my finger on the pulse of the place."

Ray offered a sly grin. "I understand the apartment over Angelo's pizzeria might be available for rent in the not-too-distant future."

Katie gave him a crooked smile. "Is that so?"

Ray nodded. Katie had enjoyed living in that little apartment. Little—but more than double the size of the studio apartment over Tealicious. "Well, I guess I'll have to look into that," she said, smiling, still unwilling to admit to Ray how much she'd wanted to buy the house he and his girls were going to occupy by the end of the summer.

"So, what are *we* going to do?" Ray asked, sounding somewhat defeated.

"You mean about dating?"

"Yeah."

Katie thought about it. "Maybe we could go bowling. Or maybe I could bring you lunch over at Wood U."

"And maybe sometimes I could invite you to lunch or dinner?"

"Before you do any of that, you need to talk to your girls."

Ray shook his head. "No. They can have their opinions about you, but I can't let them be in control of my life."

Katie shook her head. "But you live with them every day."

"Yeah, and in a few years they'll all fly the coop and leave their old man alone. Sophie will probably find a job in another —bigger—city. Sadie and Sasha are hellbent on becoming interior designers and opening their own business. And then what am I supposed to do? Live the rest of my life alone?"

Katie's gaze dipped as depression settled over her like a heavy cloak, the events of the past hour suddenly catching up with her. She'd welcome Margo taking her to the lake house and spoiling her for a day or so before she had to gather the courage to return to real life.

"I've got a lot to process. And after breaking up with Carol, so have you. So, friends first?"

Ray shrugged. "I'm okay with that."

Katie gave him a wan smile, hoping he understood where she was coming from.

Ray reached out a hand, and Katie accepted it.

"I wish we had some champagne to toast to it," Ray said.

"I'm so tired, I'd fall asleep after the first sip."

"Then we'll keep that thought on the back burner for a while.'

The sound of hurried footsteps pattered on the stairs. "Darling girl!" Margo called.

Ray got up to open the door for her.

Margo swooped into the room, rushing toward Katie with open arms. "Are you okay?" she asked, worriedly, gathering her in a hug.

A rush of gratitude coursed through Katie. "Thanks for coming, Mom."

Epilogue

As it happened, Andy never got around to renting the apartment over the pizzeria before selling the property. So, when Katie broached the subject of leasing the space with the new owners, they were happy to discuss it. They wanted more than Andy had asked, but after checking around, Katie found it wasn't an unreasonable sum and signed a one-year lease. She might and might not try to find a house in the interim. And she'd been able to move in on the first of July, with Brad taking possession of the digs above Tealicious on the same day.

Mason and Della were at first wary but soon seemed to realize they'd returned to the home they'd known before. Since Katie had left the apartment immaculate when she'd left, all it needed was a quick dust and vacuum to be move-in ready. Nick and Don volunteered to help her move her furniture and bric-a-brac that had been in storage, and within a day, Katie had the place looking as though she'd never left it. It felt like home.

Although Maxwell Preston's killer had been unmasked, there wasn't enough evidence to show whether it was Preston or his wife who killed Gary Jordan decades before. The man had indeed died of a skull fracture. Had Preston buried him under the porch and had Linda helped him? They'd never know. But Seth was sure a judge would rule the proviso that no work be done on the building—or have it razed—could be dispensed with as it was made to cover up a crime. So, one way or another, it was likely a new business would occupy the space. Jordan's remains were buried next to his daughter, giving Steve Harris and his children closure at last.

After being treated for her injuries, Nona was arrested for the murder of Maxwell Preston and remanded to the Monroe County Detention Center to await trial. On the same day, Margo took over managing the arrangements for the Square's big summer promotion, and did a superb job. Her organizational skills rivaled Katie's, and she had a knack for soothing ruffled feathers. Within weeks, Katie planned on stepping down as the head of the Victoria Square Merchants Association and had no qualms about nominating Margo to take her place. She had a feeling Margo might be the best thing to ever happen to the Association.

But despite the change for good in Katie's life and their resolve, time spent with Ray wasn't easy to come by.

The third Saturday in August started murky, with the humidity as oppressive as a wet cloak. As the morning lengthened and the merchants on Victoria Square began to roll out their sidewalk displays for the Dog Days of Summer Extravaganza, as it was being heralded, a crisp wind blew from Canada across Lake Ontario, whisking away the humidity, leaving a sunny but comfortable temperature. Not too hot, and not too cool. Just perfect. All but one of the buildings on the Square was decked out in red, white, and blue bunting, looking like a 4th of July spectacle.

The 8-by-16-foot vinyl sign the Davenport sisters designed had versatility in mind. Instead of touting just the present celebration, it could easily be modified for different dates and seasons. It was great for Artisans Alley; not so great for the sign maker who might've hoped for multiple commissions throughout the year.

Brad and the other food vendors on the Square had coordinated their offerings, incorporating some of their neighbors' wares in their recipes, like candy or jams. Brad offered slices of ice-cold watermelon, lemonade, thumbprint cookies, and slabs of red velvet and chocolate cake, more or less like those offered in the movie the promotion was based on. Tanner's Cafe and Bakery covered the more modern-day combo of hot dogs, soda, and individual-sized bags of chips, along with their monster chocolate chip cookies, and, of course, their bakery was full of other delectables.

The rest of the merchants were just as well represented. Katie hadn't seen the parking lot as full since the last holiday season. Despite all the grief Nona had put the Square and its member merchants through, she *had* come up with a great promotional idea—one Katie thought could be an annual celebration. It was too bad Nona would never be a part of it. But then, Phoebe Preston was in negotiation to buy The Quiet Quilter. Having a new, more stable presence on the Square would be good for everyone.

Brad and Sophie, as well as a couple of the waitresses, had everything under control in front of Tealicious, and Vance had taken charge of the Artisans Alley vendors. Everything on those fronts seemed to be moving along smoothly. Still, Katie kept traveling around the Square to see if anyone needed a hand. Nick Ferrell ended up sitting with Sasha Davenport outside Sassy Sally's, making a great team. After major prepping, the girl knew almost as much about the old Victorian Home as Nick did. Meanwhile, her sister, Sadie, helped keep things moving at her father's shop. Katie hadn't made a point to visit Wood U...yet.

The first edition of *Life On Victoria Square* by Sadie and Sasha

Davenport, edited by Margo Bonner, was available for sale in front of Sassy Sally's Bed & Breakfast. The hundred-copy print run had sold out early in the afternoon, but Sasha promised a reprint before the snow fell. Katie told the young woman she would be happy to feature the book at Artisans Alley, which she hoped would win her a few brownie points with her staunchest Davenport critic.

Instead of being scarred by the events back in May, Sasha seemed eager to tell her portion of the story in court. She was always ready for a new adventure.

Todd and Tonya Malloy, the new owners of Angelo's Pizzeria, had not only kept the shop's name the same—as had Andy—but had kept on nearly all the staff, as well.

Finally, as the celebration was winding down, Katie worked up the courage to visit Wood U. Sadie manned the sale items displayed on the porch outside her father's shop.

"How's it going?" Katie asked.

"Really well," the young lady said excitedly, indicating all the blank spots on the tables and shelves that were nestled against the building. "Dad's going to have to go into overdrive to restock the shop for the holidays."

"That's great," Katie said, giving the girl a wide smile.

"Excuse me," said a woman, holding a carved Santa. "Can I pay for this here?"

"You sure can," Sadie said, and Katie stepped away, letting the teen take care of her customer. She didn't think Sadie noticed when she entered Wood U.

Ray sat behind the counter, working on yet another carving. Despite the whirlwind of people on the Square, his shop was devoid of customers.

"Hey, there," Katie said.

Ray looked up and smiled. "Hey there, yourself."

"Sadie seems to think you might be in trouble restocking."

"And isn't that a great problem to have?" Ray asked, his grin widening.

Katie nodded.

"So, are you excited about the closing?" she asked, referring to the Craftsman house.

Ray set down his carving knife. "You bet. The girls are ecstatic. They all want to come with me when I sign the papers on Wednesday. You *will* give Sophie time off to attend, won't you?"

"Of course. I'm happy to cover for her at Tealicious. I'm sad that she'll be heading back to school in just a couple of weeks. She's been such an asset to the tea shop this summer."

That said, if Brad decided to jump ship and open his own place, Tealicious might present the perfect opportunity for Sophie to gain experience running a small restaurant before she, too, looked to ply her skills in a much bigger market.

"So, when's the big moving day?" Katie asked.

"Next Saturday. That gives Sadie and Sasha time to paint their room, which is apparently a hideous shade of green and, therefore, unlivable. I have a feeling we'll exist in a world of white primer until they decide how they want to put their stamp on the rest of the place."

Katie bit her lip to keep from laughing, then cleared her throat. "Are you all packed?"

"Nearly. I travel pretty lightly. I don't have nearly as much stuff as the girls."

"Would you like some help on moving day?" Katie asked.

"I'd love it," Ray said rather emphatically, but then his happy demeanor quickly faded. "I've hired Vance, his son, and a couple of your other vendors with pickups to do the deed. I think we're good."

What he wasn't saying was that Sadie and Sasha didn't want her there. Well, they were still kids processing their grief. They might one day come around and again consider Katie a friend.

Or not.

"Once we're settled, maybe I could invite you over for dinner. Nothing fancy, but I grill a mean burger!"

"Sure," Katie agreed, knowing a formal invitation wouldn't be extended any time soon.

"In the meantime, we've both got Monday off. Maybe we could do something for lunch," Ray suggested.

"Won't you need to use that time packing the rest of the house?"

Ray waved a dismissive hand. "Apparently, I'm not trustworthy when it comes to handling delicate objects."

Katie nodded. "I've got nothing penciled in on my calendar. The weather is supposed to be nice. Maybe we could go on a picnic."

"That sounds good. How about we hit Hamlin Beach State Park, stake out a table and—?"

"You could grill a couple of mean burgers, and I could bring potato salad and dessert."

"I'd like that," Ray said sincerely. "I'd like that a lot."

Katie's smile was tentative. "So would I."

Ray reached out a hand to clasp Katie's. "It won't always be like this."

"You promise?"

He seemed to think about it for a long moment. "Sorry. I can't," he said sadly. "Sasha still has two more years of high school to get through. Until then…." His words hung in the air as heavily as the humidity had done earlier in the day.

"Well, then I guess we'll just have to take it day-by-day," Katie said reasonably.

"And you don't mind?" Ray asked.

Katie frowned. "I sure as hell do."

"But?" Ray asked, uncertainty coloring his tone.

Katie shrugged. "Luckily, I'm a busy woman. I'll find things to do. All I need to know is that you're in my corner."

"You bet I am."

"Then we're agreed. We're going to continue to take this slow."

"Slow doesn't mean a standstill," Ray opined.

No, it didn't.

Ray walked around the counter and pulled her close. "So what are *we* supposed to do?"

Katie looked up into his dark eyes. "Well, for starters, we could kiss."

Ray gave her a crooked smile, placed a hand on her chin, tilted her head upward, and placed a gentle kiss on her lips.

She kissed him again.

And again.

And again.

Margo's Cocktail Party Recipes

Margo's Shrimp Puffs
Ingredients
2 large eggs, separated
¾ cup milk
1 tablespoon olive oil
1 cup all-purpose flour
1½ teaspoons baking powder
1½ teaspoons onion powder
1 teaspoon salt
½ teaspoon black pepper
3 cups cooked white rice
1 pound small uncooked shrimp, peeled, deveined, and chopped
¼ cup minced fresh parsley or 2 tablespoons dried parsley
½ teaspoon hot pepper sauce
Oil for frying

In a large bowl, beat together the egg yolks, milk and oil.
Combine the flour, baking powder, onion powder, salt, and
pepper. Stir in the rice, shrimp, parsley, and hot pepper sauce.
In a mixing bowl, beat the egg whites until soft peaks form.

289

Fold into the shrimp mixture. In a large skillet or deep fryer, heat the oil to 350°F (180°C). Drop the batter by tablespoons into the hot oil. Fry the puffs, a few at a time, for 90 seconds on each side or until golden brown. Drain on paper towels. Serve warm.

Yield: about 3 dozen

Curried Chicken Balls

Ingredients
8 ounces cream cheese, softened
¼ cup mango (or other) chutney
3 teaspoons curry powder
2 cups chopped cooked chicken (breast or thighs)
⅔ cup chopped cashews
¼ cup chopped green onions

In a large bowl, beat the cream cheese with an electric mixer until creamy. Add the chutney and curry powder and mix well. Stir in the chicken, cashews, and green onions until well mixed. Form the mix into 1-inch balls. Chill for at least 2 hours before serving.

Yield: 48 balls

Buffalo (Hot!) Deviled Eggs

Ingredients
4 large hard-boiled eggs
3 tablespoons mayonnaise
2 teaspoons butter, softened
4 teaspoons hot sauce (think Tabasco/Frank's etc.)
1 teaspoon of yellow mustard
1 tablespoon chives, chopped
smoked paprika to garnish

Halve the cooked eggs lengthwise and scoop the yolk into a bowl. Mash the yolks with the mayonnaise, butter, hot sauce, mustard, and chives. Pipe or spoon the mixture into the egg halves.

Yield: 8 egg halves

Stuffed Mushrooms
Ingredients
1 pound bulk pork sausage (or hot or sweet Italian bulk sausage)
¼ cup finely chopped onion
1 or 2 garlic cloves, minced
1 package (8 ounces) cream cheese
¼ cup grated Parmesan cheese
⅓ cup seasoned bread crumbs
2 teaspoons dried basil
1½ teaspoons dried parsley flakes
30 large fresh mushrooms (about 1½ pounds), stems removed
3 tablespoons butter, melted

Preheat the oven to 400°F (200°C, Gas Mark 6). In a large skillet, cook the sausage, onion, and garlic over medium heat, breaking up the sausage into crumbles, until meat is no longer pink and the onion is tender, 6-8 minutes; drain. Add the cream cheese and Parmesan cheese; cook and stir until melted. Stir in the bread crumbs, basil, and parsley.

Meanwhile, place the mushroom caps in a greased 15x10x1-in. baking pan. Brush with melted butter. Spoon the sausage mixture into the mushroom caps. Bake, uncovered, until mushrooms are tender, 12-15 minutes.

Yield: 30 mushrooms

Brad's Sesame Seed Cookies

Ingredients

1¼ cup butter

2 cups packed dark brown sugar

1 large egg

1 teaspoon vanilla extract

1 cup all-purpose flour

½ teaspoon baking powder

¼ teaspoon salt

1 cup sesame seeds, toasted

Preheat the oven to 350°F (180°C, Gas Mark 4). In a mixing bowl, cream the butter and brown sugar; add the egg and vanilla. Combine the rest of the ingredients; add to the creamed mixture. Drop by teaspoons, 2-inches apart, onto a greased baking sheet. Bake for 7-9 minutes or until golden brown. Cool in the pan for a minute before removing them to a wire rack to completely cool.

Yield: Approximately 9 dozen

About the Author

The immensely popular Booktown Mystery series is what put Lorraine Bartlett's pen name Lorna Barrett on the New York Times Bestseller list, but it's her talent—whether writing as Lorna, or L.L. Bartlett, or Lorraine Bartlett—that keeps her in the hearts of her readers. This multi-published, Agatha-nominated author pens the exciting Jeff Resnick Mysteries as well as the acclaimed Victoria Square Mystery series, the Tales of Telenia adventure-fantasy saga, and now the Lotus Bay Mysteries, and has many short stories and novellas to her name(s). Check out the descriptions and links to all her works, and sign up for her emailed newsletter here: https://www. lorrainebartlett.com

If you enjoyed *A Lethal Lake Effect*, please help spread the word by reviewing it on your favorite online review site. Thank you!

Connect with Lorraine Bartlett on Social Media

Also by Lorraine Bartlett

Writing as Lorraine Bartlett

THE LOTUS BAY MYSTERIES

Panty Raid (A Tori Cannon-Kathy Grant mini mystery)

With Baited Breath

Christmas At Swans Nest

A Reel Catch

The Best From Swans Nest (A Lotus Bay Cookbook)

THE VICTORIA SQUARE MYSTERIES

A Crafty Killing

The Walled Flower

One Hot Murder

Dead, Bath and Beyond (with Laurie Cass)

Yule Be Dead (with Gayle Leeson)

Murder Ink (with Gayle Leeson)

A Murderous Misconception (with Gayle Leeson)

Dead Man's Hand (with Gayle Leeson)

A Lethal Lake Effect

LIFE ON VICTORIA SQUARE

Carving Out A Path

A Basket Full of Bargains

The Broken Teacup

It's Tutu Much

The Reluctant Bride

Tea'd Off

Life On Victoria Square Vol. 1

A Look Back

Tea For You (free download in most countries)

Davenport Designs

A Ruff Week

Recipes To Die For: A Victoria Square Cookbook

TALES FROM BLYTHE COVE MANOR

A Dream Weekend

A Final Gift

An Unexpected Visitor

Grape Expectations

Foul Weather Friends

Mystical Blythe Cove Manor

Blythe Cove Seasons (free download in most countries)

TALES OF TELENIA

(adventure-fantasy)

STRANDED

JOURNEY

TREACHERY

SHORT WOMEN'S FICTION

Love & Murder: A Bargain-Priced Collection of Short Stories

Happy Holidays? (A Collection of Christmas Stories)

An Unconditional Love

Love Heals

Blue Christmas

Prisoner of Love

We're So Sorry, Uncle Albert

Sabina Reigns (a novel)

WRITING AS L.L. BARTLETT

THE JEFF RESNICK MYSTERIES

Murder On The Mind

Dead In Red

Room At The Inn

Cheated By Death

Bound By Suggestion

Dark Waters

Shattered Spirits

Shadow Man

JEFF RESNICK'S PERSONAL FILES

Evolution: Jeff Resnick's Backstory

A Jeff Resnick Six Pack

When The Spirit Moves You

Bah! Humbug

Cold Case

Spooked!

Crybaby

Eyewitness

A Part of the Pattern

Abused: A Daughter's Story

Off Script

Writing as Lorna Barrett

Made in United States
North Haven, CT
30 June 2024

54242412R10167